Praise for the Colorado Wine Mysteries

"*Killer Chardonnay* offers a wonderful blend of suspense and humor. You'll raise your glass to Parker Valentine, the charming sleuth at the center of this twisty and satisfying mystery. A most delightful debut!"

—Cynthia Kuhn, author of the Agatha Award–winning Lila Maclean Academic Mysteries

"Parker Valentine . . . will steal your heart and pair it with a smooth mystery in this sparkling debut. A wine rack full of suspects won't stop the determined sleuth and vintner from bottling up a killer and saving her dream. *Killer Chardonnay* has legs!"

—Leslie Budewitz, Agatha Award–winning author of the Spice Shop Mysteries

"*Killer Chardonnay* is an engaging mystery filled with wine knowledge, romance, and a gutsy protagonist. Kate Lansing is a delightful new voice in the mystery genre, and I can't wait to read the next one in this series."

—Nadine Nettmann, author of the Anthony, Agatha, Lefty, and Mary Higgins Clark award–nominated Sommelier Mystery series

"Lansing's brisk style and her heroine's efficient approach make her debut a treat." —*Kirkus Reviews*

"Lansing takes you on a thrilling mystery ride with red herrings th vine barrel for the k sh Fiction

"A solid start to an enjoyable series, especially if you are a fan of the foodie vibe created in this story or a lover of winery mysteries!"
—The Genre Minx

"Likeable characters, engrossing mystery, and excellent storytelling make *Killer Chardonnay* a killer cozy series debut."
—The Book Decoder

"I absolutely loved this book; the setting of Boulder, Colorado, could not be more perfect . . . I enjoyed the storyline, the side romances, with clues and red herrings thrown in that kept me guessing."
—Cindy's Book Stacks

"Kate Lansing is a fantastically descriptive writer combining the delicacies of winemaking with the delectable nature of wonderful food [and] a mystery that will keep your mind working."
—Coffee Books Life

Titles by Kate Lansing

Killer Chardonnay
A Pairing to Die For
Mulled to Death

Mulled to Death

Kate Lansing

BERKLEY PRIME CRIME
Published by Berkley
An imprint of Penguin Random House LLC
penguinrandomhouse.com

ISBN: 9780593100226

First Edition: October 2021

Printed in the United States of America
1 3 5 7 9 10 8 6 4 2

Book design by Alison Cnockaert

To John, my valentine now and forever

Chapter One

Snowflakes settle on the mirror outside my passenger-side window. Normally I would marvel at their unblemished sparkle or muse over their uniqueness. Now I glare at the offensive flakes as if I could melt them with the sheer force of my concentration. Of course, they don't melt and snow continues to accumulate, each flake chipping away at my patience.

I-70, the gateway to the mountains, is a glorified parking lot. And an icy one at that, thanks to this ill-timed storm. A sheer rocky cliff looms above us while the Colorado River surges below, and all around us: cars. Sedans, SUVs, trucks, and even semis—none have moved more than an inch in at least five minutes and I'm beginning to panic.

I must let out an audible groan because Reid reaches

across the console for my hand, never taking his eyes off the road. "Don't worry, Parks, we'll get there."

The nickname Reid has taken to calling me rolls off his tongue. Parks, short for Parker, which is ironically what he may as well do with his jeep.

I study his profile: the scruff covering his chin, mussed sandy-blond hair, soft flannel shirt rolled to his elbows, head subtly bobbing to the beat of the indie band playing over the speakers.

I give his hand an appreciative squeeze, my fingertips grazing the calluses he's garnered from expertly wielding a chef's knife. Reid owns the hottest farm-to-table restaurant in Boulder, which he left in the charge of his capable sous chefs so we could fly the coop.

"It's not the getting there I'm worried about," I say. "It's the *when*."

My brother's voice carries from the backseat, where he and my best friend, Sage, are engrossed in a game of rock-paper-scissors with a neighboring minivan. "Remind us again why you scheduled a work meeting when we're supposed to be relaxing."

Liam's forte is relaxing, even when he should be focusing on his freelance photography or doting upon the goddess he happens to be dating, aka Sage.

"No, go paper this time," Sage interjects, sensing their adversary's proclivity for choosing rock. Her strawberry-blond hair is pinned back with one of her trademark nerd-canon barrettes, this one a lightsaber pin.

"Because this could be huge for Vino Valentine," I explain, tugging on the beaded necklace around my neck. "I can't pass up the opportunity."

Despite a couple snafus in the form of dead bodies,

I've somehow managed to establish my business as a premier winery in Boulder. In large part thanks to a rave review from a popular food-and-wine blogger and a fruitful fall harvest.

It was harder to leave my shop than I care to admit. But between a new assistant and continued support from my mom, it's in good hands.

Because this weekend is important. For me and Reid, for Sage and Liam, and also for Vino Valentine. The deal I'm hoping to secure would mean not only expanding geographically, but also in product. That is, if we ever make it to Silver Creek.

I'm due to pitch my Snowy Day Syrah and accompanying mulling spices to the wine director of the famous ski resort in T-minus thirty minutes, but I don't see how I'll make it in time.

We pass the exit for Loveland Pass, one of the many competing ski resorts lining the interstate. If only that were our final destination, but alas, my contact—and in—is at the Silver Creek Lodge. I throw myself back in the passenger seat. Here I thought I would just have to contend with nerves for the meeting, not missing it altogether.

"It's gonna go great," Reid says, the embodiment of supportive boyfriend. He takes his foot off the brake and we move infinitesimally forward.

My heart soars for a moment before plummeting to somewhere around my navel when we come to an abrupt stop again.

"Who knew Valentine's Day was such a popular travel holiday?" Sage asks.

"It makes sense," Reid starts, his thumb tracing small

circles on my hand. "What's more romantic than a secluded mountain getaway?"

Oh, right. It's Valentine's weekend, a holiday revered by some, dreaded by others, and barely tolerated by me.

It hasn't always been this way. Growing up with the surname of Valentine predisposed me to the purported day of love. Especially because of my late aunt Laura.

She made a huge deal out of the holiday, combining rituals from around the world until it became something uniquely Laura. She'd throw a big bash every year and invite all the women in her life, a sort of Galentine's Day extravaganza before Leslie Knope made it a capital *T* Thing. Laura would decorate her place with crepe paper and silk in shades of pink and red, hang handcrafted letters full of love and empowerment from the branches of her indoor hibiscus tree, and serve sweets aplenty from chocolate to marzipan.

But that all ended after she died.

Even though it's been over two years, I still can't bring myself to celebrate the holiday without her. Which is why, when Reid suggested we forgo gifts in lieu of this trip, I readily agreed, hoping getting out of town would help me get out of my head. Escape my painful memories. Not that Reid knows the full extent of my emotional baggage. In the few short months we've been together, my complex feelings toward Valentine's Day haven't come up. At least that's what I keep telling myself.

I rest my hand on the back of Reid's neck, fiddling with the collar of his flannel shirt.

"Dude, if you insist on talking about your relationship with *my sister*, can you at least get us by a different car? This kid is driving me crazy," Liam says, exasperated as he loses once again in their game. "It's like he's telepathic."

"Professor X in the flesh," Sage mutters.

And this convo right here is exactly why my brother and best friend are so well suited for each other. I can't help the smile that spreads across my face, even as my stomach churns at the thought of missing my meeting. Which is basically an inevitability at this point.

But it's just a meeting, right? What's the worst that can happen?

My brain immediately supplies the answer. That the wine director takes my no-show as an insult and promptly alerts her contacts—potential clients—and I'm blacklisted. The wine world is small, after all.

My throat constricts and I struggle to swallow. If there's one thing I hate more than good wine going to waste, it's being late.

Laughter bubbles out of me, an uncharacteristic cackle that has Reid shooting me a concerned look.

I blame stress. Bowing my head between my knees, I take a deep yoga breath. On my exhale, cars begin to move and we crawl forward, up and up toward the Eisenhower Tunnel.

"Ah, we had him that time," Sage says as we leave their rock-paper-scissor foe behind. Catching my eye when I turn to glare at her, she adds, "I mean, yay, we're moving!"

We pick up speed as we enter the tunnel, the passageway through the vast mountain a reprieve from the storm.

"Hold your breath the whole way through, your wish will come true." Liam says the words that were our parents' mantra whenever we drove through this mile-long tunnel growing up. It dawns on me now that they were probably just looking for a moment of peace and quiet.

"You first, bro," I challenge, knowing full well the impossibility of accomplishing such a feat.

By some miracle, we make it through the Eisenhower Tunnel without stopping and exit the congested interstate onto a winding road that will take us the rest of the way. The storm calms and soon the full moon is visible, pale straw against a dusk-blue sky.

I'm bouncing in my seat by the time we descend into Silver Creek. The resort is nestled in a valley surrounded by majestic, snowcapped peaks. Spotlights shine on its famed runs, lighting the way for those braving the slopes at night. Skiers and snowboarders are mere specks from this distance, and the pine trees lining the mountainside look like legs of jammy cab dribbling down the side of a glass.

Lights twinkle in the picturesque surrounding village, composed of pedestrian streets and quaint shops. Even from afar, I can tell it's bustling with tourists tromping back from the mountain in their snow gear, perusing shops, or tucking in for happy hour at one of the many inviting venues.

The Silver Creek Lodge is impressive. It features a rustic log exterior and sleek floor-to-ceiling windows that boast a view to die for and all the luxuries the modern traveler could desire. While we're oohing and aahing, Reid turns in to the main entrance.

It happens fast. So fast I barely register the streak of silver coming toward us.

A flashy BMW cuts Reid off midturn, fishtailing on the icy asphalt. Reid slams on the brakes and cranks the steering wheel. We avoid a collision, but only by driving headfirst into a snowbank.

It's funny how when you're consumed with worry about one thing, life blindsides you with something else entirely.

My heart is hammering as I take a mental inventory. Breathing? Check. Body intact? Check. Mental capacities? Disputable.

I twist in my seat to check on my companions. Reid's hands are gripping the steering wheel with white knuckles, his chest heaving. In the backseat, Liam yanks at his seat belt and Sage straightens, holding a hand to her temple, dazed.

"Everyone in one piece?" I ask.

"Think so," Reid says, appraising us and then our surroundings.

We're shaken—as evidenced by the expletives pouring from Liam's mouth—but otherwise unharmed.

As for the BMW, it continues as if nothing amiss occurred, coming to an ungraceful stop near the main lobby. Seriously, where's a cop car when you need one?

Reid shakes his head and slowly shifts his jeep into reverse. It's only because it's four-wheel drive that he's able to maneuver us out of the mound of snow with an uneven lurch, one tire spinning in the air with a high-pitched *vroom* before finding purchase on the road. After cautiously glancing in either direction, Reid turns into the resort.

The second he parks, I'm out of my seat and ready to give the driver of the BMW a few choice words. Because not only was that abhorrent driving, it was dangerous. It was purely thanks to Reid's quick reaction that we're okay.

A man gets out of the BMW. Medium height and build, and a gray coat that almost matches his car. With slicked-back hair and a pointy chin, he gives off a weaselly vibe. But what strikes me is the entitlement he exudes, striding toward the hotel as if he were blissfully unaware of the rest of the world.

I clench my jaw and make to take a step forward, but Reid intercepts me, holding both hands up. "Parks, let it go," he says, his voice a well of calm. "It's not worth it."

"But that ass—"

He grips my shoulders, his grapevine-green eyes searching mine. "We're all okay. That's what matters." His breath swirls between us as he continues, "You need to focus on your meeting."

I slouch in resignation. Reid's right. Besides, the driver of the BMW is already long gone. He stalked into the resort while Reid was talking sense into me.

I lift my chin, raising one eyebrow at Reid. "I thought you'd be seething."

Since I first met him last year, Reid has proven to be the stereotypical bad boy—impulsive, fearless, and irrevocably attractive. I mean, this is the man who once almost got into a fight with frat dudebrahs because they trash-talked his friend; the man who spent a stint in jail last fall (for a crime he didn't commit, mind you).

He shrugs, opening the trunk of his jeep, where our suitcases and snow gear are piled up. "Sure, I could get angry. Or I could get a run in before the slopes close." Reid runs a hand through his hair, gazing longingly at the mountainous backdrop.

Chairlifts whisk a dwindling crowd of skiers and snowboarders up the mountain, while a gondola runs parallel for those interested in taking in the views without the sport. Excitement courses through me at strapping on my skis and facing down the mountain, but that will have to wait until morning. On the upside, delayed gratification is like a good cabernet sauvignon, the waiting enriching the experience.

I wrap my arms around Reid and kiss his stubbly cheek. "Have fun. Be safe."

He spins me around and pulls me into a deeper kiss, his hands resting on my waist. His lips smile against mine before they soften, moving purposely and divinely in a way that leaves me swooning. He pulls away too soon, tucking a stray lock of hair behind my ear.

Reid says with a wink, "Good luck with the wine director."

"Who?" I ask, momentarily stupefied.

Then I remember where I'm supposed to be, and how long ago I was expected. Leaping into action, I adjust my fleece and gratefully take the box Reid hands me. It contains bottles of my Snowy Day Syrah and tiny mesh packets of mulling spices. Aromas of cinnamon, cloves, and citrusy orange wash over me, not nearly as comforting as they usually are.

Liam and Sage appear, polishing off a bag of trail mix.

"Have fun *working*, sis," Liam says, grabbing his skis. Tall and gangly and exuding a carefree demeanor, it sometimes seems like the only things Liam and I have in common are our matching raven hair and blue-gray eyes.

"Have fun eating snow." My jibe falls flat because we

both know that, despite his many other shortcomings, my brother is a decent enough skier that he'll do no such thing.

"Ignore him," my friend says, giving me a quick hug. "Go be awesome."

I nod and book it for the lobby entrance as fast as my boot-clad feet can carry me.

The resort comprises the main building, bookended by two soaring towers. Multiple stories of posh relaxation are at my fingertips. Strands of icicle lights adorn the awning, twinkling among fresh-fallen snow, and the Lincoln Log exterior smells of damp pine.

The entrance is marked by an intimidating wooden door embellished with wrought iron. My mouth goes dry and a pit opens in my stomach, a sense of foreboding prickling like tannins through my body.

I maneuver the box I'm carrying so the bulk of it leans against the crook of my elbow as I reach for the handle. I'm about to get my knee involved when a helpful concierge comes to my rescue.

"Thank you," I say, breathless.

Laughter, chatter, and warmth waft from inside. Still, I step over the threshold with trepidation, my nerves choosing this moment to turn on me. Maybe it's been too long since I challenged myself. Maybe it's a fear of failure. Or maybe it's unresolved anxiety after almost being hit, of being taken out of this world in the same way as my aunt.

Aunt Laura was the bravest person I knew before she was unceremoniously hit by a drunk driver one night on her way home. She was kind, supportive, and one of those people who lived life to the fullest. What would she think of me now? Unable to face the holiday she once revered, a mess of anxiety at the prospect of a simple pitch meeting.

She wouldn't fault me, which somehow hurts worse.

Come on, Parker, you can do this.

After one more deep breath, I force myself to stand up straight and march through the lobby with my chin held high.

Chapter Two

A cat greets me in the reception area. That's right, a cat.

It's sitting atop the trunk of a tree fashioned into a desk. A long-haired beauty with white hair tinged with smoky gray, pale-gold eyes, and a navy-blue collar with a bell attached. The cat twitches its tail at me before hopping down with a jingle and trotting to a velvet cushion beneath an embellished table and a painting of elk grazing in a meadow.

The cat's absence puts me face-to-face with a sullen woman I hadn't even noticed before. She's perched behind the desk, staring at a computer monitor, clicking the mouse.

"Is that your cat?" I ask.

"No, it's the resort cat," she answers without even looking away from her screen. Her dirty-blond hair is pulled into a low ponytail and her blazer is at least one size too big, the shoulder pads slightly askew. I would pinpoint her as a few years my senior, but that could be overestimated because of her frown.

"What's its name?"

The woman finally deems my presence worth acknowledging, perhaps realizing she might be dealing with a paid guest. She gives me a wan smile and when her eyes meet mine, I'm struck by the dark smudges beneath them.

"Madeline," she says, brushing a strand of limp hair away from her face.

"Hi, Madeline," I coo to the kitty, who emanates a purr before nuzzling her head into her plush cushion for a nap.

"Can I assist you with something?"

"I, uh, have a meeting with the wine director. My name is Parker—Parker Valentine." I set the box down and hold out my hand.

She sniffs, eyeing me skeptically before taking it. Her handshake is loose and uncertain, a complete contrast to her decisive tone as she responds, "You're late."

I'm tempted to ask for her manager when I notice HOTEL MANAGER listed on her name tag, right over the name PAISLEY MOORE.

"Hit a little traffic."

"There's always traffic."

If anyone needs a glass of wine, it's this chick. I'm tempted to offer her a bottle of Snowy Day Syrah so she can kick back and relax with Madeline, which sounds mighty fine right now, to be honest, but I need the bottles to impress the wine director.

"Right," I say, keeping my voice polite as I seamlessly shift into entrepreneur mode. "But you see, Paisley, this was more than usual. Honestly, our ETA was two hours ago." Really, I deserve a medal for not booking it to the ladies' room.

Paisley chews on the inside of her cheek, considering.

"Please, you won't be sorry." I pat the box at my feet for good measure. This tête-à-tête certainly isn't helping my frayed nerves.

She turns abruptly and makes her way out from behind the desk. "Fine. This way. I'll see if Akira still has time."

Relief floods through me as I pick up the box and catch up with Paisley. It's not hard, since she doesn't seem accustomed to walking in her heels, her ankles wobbling every few paces. I pretend not to notice.

The lobby is all comfort and class. Overhead is a grand chandelier constructed out of antlers, and underfoot, attractive rugs line the hardwood floors, providing traction against tracked-in snow and ice.

The centerpiece of the room is a large dual-sided fireplace, surrounded by comfortable armchairs and couches, where guests mill about, relaxing after a long day of hitting the slopes. In an adjoining room, billiard tables and flat-screen TVs provide additional entertainment. Through sliding glass doors that lead to a wraparound deck, I catch a glimpse of the large ice-skating rink and the mountains behind.

I wonder if Reid—and Liam and Sage, for that matter—have made it there yet, or if they're still getting settled in.

I refocus on the present and practically have to run to catch up to Paisley.

Not one for awkward silences, I ask, "So, how long have you worked here?"

Paisley tugs at the lapels of her blazer, which does little to help the fit, her posture prim. "Nearly ten years now."

My eyebrows shoot into my bangs, surprised to hear she's worked here for so long, especially considering her lacking enthusiasm for customer service. Her job must come with stellar perks. "Do you get free ski passes?"

She throws me a withering glare. "Yes, but don't assume that will extend to you."

"I wasn't— That's not what I was getting at," I stammer as we enter a dining room. It's empty save for us, the hour being too early for dinner, but from the savory aromas wafting from the kitchen, meal prep is well under way.

Tables bedecked in linens the color of butter gleam with pristine plates, flatware, and stemware, and log pillars scattered throughout the space give a sense of privacy. The dimmed lighting and centerpieces—flickering tea lights and vases of red roses—ooze atmosphere and romance.

While the upscale decor is nothing like the eclectic Valentine's mishmash Aunt Laura used to tout, it still makes me think of her. Like a punch of sadness straight to the gut. I force myself to swallow the sudden surge of emotions.

"Wait here," Paisley says. "I'll track down Akira."

"Actually, can I borrow a burner to warm the wine?"

Paisley looks me up and down—from my Uggs to my slim navy slacks to my maroon fleece—as if I'd uttered an offensive slur. It's clear I've blown any chance of gaining her approval. Not that I had much of a chance to begin with.

I continue, "If Akira isn't available, I'll totally understand and leave the mulled wine for the staff to enjoy."

Finally, with a click of her tongue she gestures toward an archway off to my right. "Kitchen's through there."

Then Paisley leaves me alone, panicked, bewildered, and completely stressed.

This is a dumpster fire.

The resort manager hates me, I may not even be able to meet with the wine director, and my mulled wine isn't ready yet. Which means I need to get moving. Pronto.

I head toward the kitchen, ready to take the turn of events in stride, but loud voices behind one of the pillars give me pause.

"I thought we had a deal," a man hisses.

With my feet still rooted in place, I peek around the pillar. The man from the parking lot is pointing a finger at a woman I recognize on sight: Annmarie Bauer. Olympic gold medalist in Alpine skiing—downhill, super G, *and* giant slalom—back in 2008, and owner of the Silver Creek Ski Resort and this very hotel.

She's sleek in a perfectly tailored, midnight-blue pantsuit with ruby suede pumps, her long blond hair draped down her back. There's a slight tan line around her eyes from goggles, a smattering of freckles prominent on her cheeks. Her arms are crossed over her chest, her lips are pursed, and she's giving a glare I'd hate to be on the receiving end of.

"You should know better than that, Hudson. We had a conversation," she calmly informs the man, studying her fingernails. "Nothing was ever signed."

Inwardly, I rejoice to hear the jerk—Hudson—who almost crashed into us so thoroughly reprimanded.

"You owe me." His tone turns threatening and his pointy chin juts out as he adds, "Don't think I've forgotten."

Annmarie remains firm, replying coolly, "I owe you nothing."

"This isn't over."

Hudson pivots on his boots and stalks straight toward me. I try to blend in, which is impossible, given I'm a slightly frantic woman holding a box of wine in the middle of an empty dining room. And yet, his eyes glaze over me as if I'm not even here. I would be insulted if I weren't so relieved.

After he's gone, I turn back toward the kitchen, sidling around the pillar. Annmarie has her back to me. She squares her shoulders and marches confidently in the opposite direction.

I try to shake off what I just witnessed—shake off everything that's transpired in the last hour. I'm not nearly as successful as Taylor Swift.

The kitchen is immaculate. I would expect nothing less from an establishment of this caliber. Stainless-steel appliances that sparkle, even with the food being prepped on every surface. Line cooks and sous chefs dart about, following the orders of a guy stalking by the stovetop, critiquing a steaming soup.

He has tawny skin and black hair that's fashionably faded on the sides and curly on top, a faint smattering of stubble across his chin. A bronze cross dangles from one ear and a simple gold chain adorns his neck. The Silver Creek emblem is embroidered on his chef's coat, the sleeves of which are rolled up his forearms. He must be the executive chef.

I clear my throat awkwardly, eyeing a saucepan I

would literally kill to use. Okay, maybe not *literally*, but you get the gist. I want that saucepan; I want it bad.

His eyes cut to me, curious and commanding. "You lost?"

"No," I say with a nervous chuckle. "Paisley said I could use a burner."

His face remains stoic, even as he barks directions over one shoulder to a sous chef.

I continue, shifting my weight from one foot to the other, "For my mulled wine, you see. I have a meeting with Akira." Well, *hopefully* I have a meeting.

At Akira's name, he flashes me a cheeky smile. "I'm just giving you a hard time, though if you went through Paisley, you've probably been through enough." He tosses a hand towel over his shoulder. "I'm Cash."

"Parker," I say.

I set the box down and shrug out of my fleece coat, thankful I wore my nicest cashmere cardigan and floral blouse. I can use all the extra confidence I can get. I remove a bottle of wine and an opener, proceeding to wield the corkscrew like a master swordsman.

"Do you always have a wine opener on you?" he asks, clearly amused.

"Hazard of the trade." The *pop* of the cork is followed by an intense aroma of cherries, currents, and vanilla.

"Fair enough." Cash nods in approval, snags a saucepan from a hook, and places it on a burner. "If anyone gives you a hard time, tell them to come talk to me." Then he's off, shouting at someone named Austin to mind their knife cuts, before I can murmur a thank-you.

I don't waste another moment. I pour my wine in the saucepan and add the spices, turning the heat on low.

The key is to warm the wine without letting it come to a boil, because that cooks off the alcohol, which, let's face it, takes the fun out of the cocktail.

While my wine is mulling, the spices mingling together like millennials at brunch, I grab a container that Reid prepped for me.

There are definite upsides to dating a chef—delicious food at the drop of a hat, getting to taste-test new recipes, and specially curated dishes to accompany my vino. Like these savory roasted nuts; pecans, cashews, and almonds tossed with oil, sea salt, and rosemary, and then roasted to perfection. It might sound like an odd combo, but the salty and earthy flavors balance perfectly with the orange zest and warm spices.

Before too long, stemless glasses are brimming with ruby liquid the viscosity of syrup, steam fogging the crystal bowls, and nuts glisten in a dish I commandeered.

Faster than I thought possible, Cash snags a handful of the nuts and pops them in his mouth, munching thoughtfully. "Savory, well seasoned, and with a satisfying crunch. You a chef, too?"

"I'm afraid I can't take credit for these," I answer vaguely, my voice pitchy and urgent as I imagine Akira searching for me in the dining room. "Any idea where I should set up?"

Cash takes pity on me again, flashing me a wink. "The four-top just outside the kitchen. We keep it open in case we need it for last-minute VIPs. And don't worry, Akira's a softy."

"Uh, thanks." *I think.*

I'm positioning the nuts and glasses around the roses when I sense rather than see someone appear at my elbow.

The new arrival is in her low thirties, with shiny black

hair pulled into a high ponytail, and chic octagonal wire-rimmed glasses. "Parker?"

"Yes," I say. "You must be Akira."

"Pleased to meet you. I'm glad you made it okay."

I wince. "Sorry I'm late."

"Better late than never." Her kind brown eyes twinkle as she directs me into a chair. "Let's get started."

"Right." I ease into my seat and rest my palms on the linen cloth, the lush cotton softer than my bedsheets at home. Somehow, I start to relax, start to feel like I might actually pull this off. I wave at a wineglass, diving into my spiel, "So, here we have—"

"Mind if I join," a smooth voice interjects. It's a voice I recognize, having heard it recently from behind a pillar. I look up, startled to see Annmarie Bauer is addressing me. *Me!*

Akira recovers first. "Of course, have a seat."

"Yes, definitely," I manage to sputter, reaching across the table to shake her hand. But I accidentally upend the dish of nuts, sending them scattering across the table and onto Annmarie's lap.

"At least it wasn't the wine," I say, scrambling to tidy the mess, my stomach plummeting with my pride.

With shaky hands, I scoop nuts from the tablecloth and dump them back in the bowl.

Akira helps, popping one into her mouth. "Tasty."

I shoot her a grateful smile.

Annmarie appears entirely unruffled. Maybe heated confrontations with strange men and being showered with herb-encrusted nuts are the norm for her.

"No harm done," she says, plucking one final cashew

from her pantsuit. "Although I was under the impression you would be pitching us wine."

"I am," I say. "These were just to pair with it."

Annmarie purses her lips and I catch a glimpse of the competitor who was such a force on the slopes she won not one, but *three* gold medals, and the savvy businesswoman who made Silver Creek one of the most successful ski destinations in the state. Her face is angular, cheeks and nose like the rocky side of a mountain. And her eyes are blue green, cold and calculating. It's clear she's remained in great shape—she's fit, lean, and strong.

At her continued silence, Akira steps in. "Let's move on to the wine, shall we?"

I wave to the two glasses on the table. I'd prepared one for myself in case Akira wanted company and because I could use a drink after the traffic on I-70. But I slide it across the table toward Annmarie, carefully so as not to spill the contents.

Besides, I've already tasted it. Many times. In the back of my winery among stainless-steel equipment—the crusher de-stemmer, state-of-the-art bottling system, and wine vats. At my apartment with my cat, Zin—short for Zinfandel—weaving between my legs. In the kitchen at Reid's restaurant, where we tasted and perfected his recipe for the spiced nuts.

"The—uh—I mean, my"—I flinch inwardly at my stammering and clear my throat, forcing myself to continue despite the butterflies in my stomach—"this is made from my Snowy Day Syrah, an exceptional red on its own with aromas of vanilla and a jammy cherry finish, paired with my trademark mulling spices. Enjoy." I finish with a flourish.

Akira swirls and sniffs before taking a sip, gurgling

like an expert. She cocks her head to the side while she swishes, her gaze cast over my shoulder. After she swallows, she nods, rolling her lips together.

Even though I suspect Akira is impressed, she doesn't say a word. Instead, she looks to Annmarie, ready to yield to her boss's opinion.

Annmarie takes an eternity analyzing the appearance—the color, consistency, how it clings to the sides of her glass—before smelling and finally sipping. And then she repeats the entire process: swirl, sniff, sip, repeat. At one point she even nibbles on one of the remaining nuts in the bowl.

To keep from fidgeting I fold my hands on the table, although my knees continue bouncing underneath, hidden from view.

Over the past year of owning Vino Valentine, I've learned people taste wine in different ways. There are the overly verbose, those who like to recite every whiff or flavor they detect, no matter how subtle. There are those who offer meager scraps of observations as they process, forcing you to piece together their opinion. And then there are those who say nothing at all.

Annmarie falls into the latter category, and I know better than to push. Instead, I study her—her smooth motions and unflappable face.

I remember watching her in the Olympics from the den of my parents' house, Liam and I excitedly cheering on a fellow Colorado native. To the chagrin of our neighbors, we'd run outside, ringing cowbells and whooping loudly after each of her medal-winning runs.

Annmarie is older now, obviously, and more sophisticated. But she has the same spark and complete focus I recall from the television screen.

Suddenly, while I'm watching, her eye twitches. It's just once at first, and Annmarie seems not to notice, but then it happens again. She takes another sip of mulled wine, touching the corner of her eye with her free hand, calming the spasming muscle.

"Well," Annmarie says, setting her glass down with a forceful *clunk*. "I think Akira will agree with me when I say your mulled wine is excellent and will be the perfect addition to our menu."

"One hundred percent," Akira supplies, happy to provide her opinion now. "Great flavors, especially considering it's a younger red."

I let out a sigh of relief, my shoulders slumping. "And it will only get better with age," I add with a wink.

Annmarie gives me a bemused smile and then turns to Akira. "You'll put an order in tomorrow?"

"Absolutely."

"Good," Annmarie continues. "And make sure Cash has this recipe." She gestures to the dish of nuts.

Reid for the win, again. Not that I'm surprised.

Akira flinches, so brief I almost think I imagined it. Then she nods, her ponytail swinging, her friendly demeanor back in place. And yet, she grits her teeth as she says, "Cash will be thrilled."

I wonder at her reaction, because from what I could tell, Cash *will* be thrilled. He's a bona fide food nerd.

Annmarie gets to her feet and I do the same, hungry (in more ways than one) to close this deal. She's taller than me—not uncommon given my five-foot-four-inch frame—but she must be near six feet, even without her heels. "In the meantime, I hope I'll see you on the slopes in the morning."

"You'll be skiing?" I ask, unable to keep the starstruck wonder from my voice.

Annmarie's phone buzzes with a text message. Her eye twitches again as she reads the screen. "Excuse me."

"Oh, wait," I say, snagging one of the extra bottles and spice packets from the box at my feet. I brought them along for just this instance. "A complimentary bottle and spice packet."

Annmarie kindly takes the gifts, tucking them under one arm, and mumbles, "I can tell I'll need it later." She purposefully strides through the doorway leading back to the lobby just as the first guests appear for dinner service.

"Well done," Akira says, clapping her hands together in a tiny applause before accepting her own bottle and spice packet. "Annmarie isn't easily impressed."

"Thank you," I say like it's no big deal, but inside I'm beaming.

Chapter Three

Toasting is universal. There's *cheers* in English, *santé* in French, *kanpai* in Japanese. Around the world, people come together to celebrate by clinking glasses. Just as my friends and I are doing now.

We're at the same table at the hotel restaurant where I pitched my wine, only now as guests, which I suppose makes us VIPs. Or airheads who didn't think to make reservations.

"To your success," Reid says, meeting my gaze over his own glass, his grin mischievous and his eyes twinkling with pride.

Reid's face—along with Liam's and Sage's—is flushed from the heat of the restaurant after the plummeting temperatures on the slopes. They were able to sneak in a couple of runs before dinner, which were apparently a blast. The snowstorm may have been hell to drive in, but it resulted in a layer of fresh powder, ideal for cutting down the mountain.

"I honestly had no idea if it was going to work out." I take a hard-earned sip, flavors of honeydew, nectarine, and, oddly, brioche bursting on my tongue. Akira recommended this white, a little-known varietal called Albariño, which has a delightful palate. She was spot on with her suggestion. "I mean, can you believe Annmarie Bauer—of *the* Bauer Power—sat in on my meeting?"

Bauer Power was what all the announcers used to say about Annmarie. *Think she'll bring the Bauer Power?* they'd banter while Annmarie dug her poles into the snow, rocking backward and forward at the starting gate. *There's the Bauer Power*, they'd say as she flew down the mountain, masterfully maneuvering every turn and mogul. *The Bauer Power*, they'd say, shaking their heads in disbelief at whatever record she'd set or race she'd dominated. *She's fearless.*

The nickname stuck.

Now it refers to her business acumen and financial boon in the hospitality industry rather than the slopes. Although I suspect she's still a force to be reckoned with on skis, which I very much look forward to verifying.

"*The* Bauer Power?" Liam asks sarcastically from across the table, widening his eyes in feigned surprise. "Because you haven't told us in the last thirty seconds."

"Oh, you're just jealous you didn't get to meet her," Sage says pointedly.

"There might be some truth to that," Liam admits with a wave of his hand. He had a mega crush on Annmarie back in the day as a hormone-charged adolescent. "Would it have killed you to send me a text?"

"No, but it would've been horribly unprofessional." I take another sip of my wine, the bouquet of flavors growing even more complex as it warms. "Besides, she mentioned she'd be skiing tomorrow morning so there's still a chance you'll get to meet her."

Liam perks up at this. Guess we never quite outgrow our childhood crushes.

"She is pretty awesome." Sage snags a piece of the dark-brown bread dotted with oats and slathers it with a generous portion of house-churned butter. "For a skier."

"I'll say cheers to that," Reid says.

It should be noted that Reid and Sage are both snowboarders, loyal to their sport, while Liam and I are devoted skiers. Not that I haven't tried snowboarding. I spent one very uncomfortable day in a lesson where the instructor tried to convince me it was like a leaf falling from a tree, a gentle zigzag across the run. Leaf, my ass. Which is coincidentally where I spent most of that day.

Liam scoffs and then takes a large swallow from his glass of cab. "I'll give snowboarders props for style, but what skiing has is speed."

Unlike me, Liam actually knows how to snowboard; he just prefers skiing, arguing that it's a skill that takes time to master. This is ironic on many counts, mainly because Liam has rarely stuck with anything in his life.

A reformed hobby-hopper who used to dwell in our parents' basement, Liam has only recently joined the ranks of adulthood, with a steady job working for the city and a passion he's ardently pursuing: photography. He even started his own freelance photography business, Valentine Photos, which has been getting some local buzz. I attribute his about-face to Sage and wanting to make himself worthy of her.

"Only because you haven't boarded with me," Reid says.

I turn to him, my foot hooking with his beneath the table. "Seriously, have you tried skiing?"

He leans in, so close I can smell the mint-and-pine aroma of his body wash. "It's like food—I'll try anything once to know if I like it."

"And?"

His lips twitch as he says, "I found it a little bland for my taste."

"I have to agree with my former client," Sage says, selecting another slice of bread.

Last year, when Reid was wrongfully accused of a murder and locked in the pokey, Sage came to my—and his—rescue, acting as his legal defense, something I don't think either of us will ever forget.

"And Sage is the smartest person I know, so . . ." Reid trails off with a faux grimace aimed at me and Liam.

At the compliment, Sage turns a shade of red that rivals her hair, which is artfully bedazzled with her favorite green lightsaber pin (Luke Skywalker's blade, Sage is quick to impart).

"Not that she isn't brilliant," I start, "but we all know that if Wonder Woman took up skiing, Sage would abandon her board in an instant."

"You've got me there." Sage nods and munches. "Luckily she has more important things to do, worlds to save, yada yada yada."

"And we have dinner to eat," Liam says, glancing at something over my shoulder. He rubs his hands together gleefully. "Good sir, your timing is impeccable."

I'm surprised to see it's Cash who deposits dishes in front of each of us, finishing with my shrimp scampi. The angel-hair pasta is coated in a delicious sauce and topped with succulent shrimp. Heavenly aromas of lemon, garlic, and Parmesan waft from my plate.

"Why, hello again," Cash says, lingering near my chair, a charming grin fixed on his face. I'm not sure if he usually delivers food, but the way our server stands behind him nonplussed tells me no.

Reid stretches his arm over my shoulder and clears his throat.

Cash takes in Reid's arm and then his face. If possible, his grin grows even broader—Cheshire. "Look what the cat dragged in."

As if on cue, the resort kitty, Madeline, struts through the entryway to the dining room, swishing her fluffy tail. She plants herself near one of the pillars, an advantageous location to scope out tables. Her nose twitches as she lifts her whiskered face to better sniff the delectable aromas. It's clear she's hankering for a stray bit of food. She and Zin would get along.

Fleetingly, I think of my feline counterpart. I can practically picture her snuggling up with Reid's cat, William, who's bunking at my apartment. My dad, whom cats are oddly fond of, agreed to stop by and check on them—and no doubt ply them with extra kitty treats.

"Cash Thiessen. I heard you were still here," Reid says, the cocky smirk that drives me crazy on his face. "I was gonna wait until after eating to track you down. That way I'd know how much flak to give you over the lack of seasoning."

The moment turns tense and I wonder what exactly transpired between these two. Reid worked as a sous chef in the kitchen here over one winter, right after he moved from New York City and before he landed in Boulder. I assume he must have worked with Cash, although whether they were nemeses or friends remains to be seen.

"And you're clearly still an arrogant jackass," Cash says, shaking his head, but then starts laughing. He gestures to Reid's tenderloin and roasted fingerling potatoes covered in butter and chives. "By all means."

Reid nibbles and ponders, an expression I'm accustomed to seeing spread across his face. I sit back and wait for his professional assessment. "Perfect. I expected nothing less."

The tension defuses and Reid and Cash do one of those handshakes that shifts into a shoulder hug.

"How are you, man?" Cash asks.

"Getting by," Reid says, although he's being humble, given his restaurant, Spoons, is all the rage in Boulder. "You?"

"Oh, you know," Cash says, shrugging. "Executive chef now."

"Congrats," Reid says, meaning it. "Who else is still here?"

While they descend into what's sure to be a lengthy conversation about the old times and what became of everyone, I tuck into my food, twirling a generous forkful of noodles. I'm munching, savoring the delicate angel hair and succulent shrimp, elevated by the garlic and citrusy flavors in the sauce when something brushes against my leg.

I look down to find Madeline, peering at me with pleading eyes that tug on my heartstrings. A master manipulator, this one. She's obviously decided my dinner is the crème de la crème.

Liam slouches over the table. "Psst," he hisses, his features shockingly earnest.

Reid is still occupied with Cash, so I glance at Sage, puzzled. She shakes her head, equally perplexed, her fingers wrapped around a giant turkey burger, pinky raised (we are ladies, after all).

"Do you need something?" I ask.

"I feel like it's my brotherly duty to warn you that Reid got you something for Valentine's Day."

"I'm aware." I spear another shrimp and gesture broadly with my fork. "This weekend, time together."

Liam holds my gaze. "But that isn't all. He got you something else."

"I'm sure Parker knows better," Sage says, shooting a warning look at Liam.

But the damage has been done. A seed of doubt takes root in my mind, tendrils of uncertainty creeping through my psyche like a strangling vine. I dab my lips with my napkin, my eyes cutting to Reid. He's laughing at something Cash said, oblivious to my mounting discomfort.

Reid doesn't know what Valentine's means to me. Correction, *used* to mean to me. And honestly, I'd prefer to keep it that way.

You see, my last boyfriend wasn't so understanding when I told him I didn't want to—nay, *couldn't*—celebrate Valentine's Day. This was two years ago, a few short months after my aunt's death, when I was struggling to process my grief, let alone explain it. We'd gotten into a huge fight because supposedly I wasn't appreciative enough of the candy and kitschy stuffed bear he'd given me. It was the first of many signs that we weren't meant to be, but the memory still stings.

Emotions well inside me, fighting against my carefully constructed dam. Worry, guilt, and sadness gnaw at my stomach, ruining my appetite. My chest squeezes and my face grows hot.

Come on, Parker, I tell myself, *it's just a holiday. You can do this—be romantic—for Reid.*

But the thing about logic is: it only goes so far.

"Thanks for letting me know," I say, my voice hoarse. I down the rest of my wine in one gulp.

Plucking a shrimp from my plate, I stealthily lower it to the ground, where a very patient Madeline has been waiting, as if sensing my emotional demise. She practically pounces on the morsel, which gives me a modicum of satisfaction. At least someone is enjoying the succulent shellfish.

The next morning, I fill my caffeine quota at the local café, a charming place called Chloe's.

The interior is homey with mismatched tables and chairs smooshed together between armrests and love seats. Specials are listed on a chalkboard in pinks and reds, complete with tiny hearts to dot the *i*'s and *j*'s, and cheery watercolors line the walls. The barista sports a frilly apron and chatters with customers, exchanging pleasantries about the weather forecast and the various hometowns of patrons.

It's not as eclectic as my haunt in Boulder, the Laughing Rooster, which is conveniently located next door to Vino Valentine. But my skinny vanilla latte is rich and delicious and perks me right up.

Like the *pop* of a cork coming out of a wine bottle, there's something distinct about the sound of snow crunching beneath a ski boot. It starts with a high-pitched squeak as your heel first meets the ground and transitions to a grating baritone as the rest of your foot follows. And, take it from me, there's no graceful way to walk in ski boots.

With my skis propped over one shoulder and poles clutched in my other gloved hand, I waddle through Silver Creek Village toward the base of the mountain.

It's a different culture here, completely acceptable to wear your gear while you munch on breakfast and sip coffee in the village's quaint café, as we did, or test equipment in one of the many sporting-goods shops, and wagons are totally a thing. Red wagons wait outside hotels and condos and near parking lots, free of charge, to help guests lug their stuff—or offspring—to the main event.

Even though I'm wearing thick snow pants over long underwear, a bulky winter coat, a neck warmer, gloves stuffed with hand warmers, and a hat with flaps that cover my ears, the bite of cold still makes me hiss under my breath.

The sun has just emerged from behind the mountain peaks in a blue-sky panorama, and while it's below freezing, I know in no time, I'll be sweating from exertion.

Reid walks beside me, looking decidedly more suave than I feel despite his equally clunky snowboard boots and gear. Tromping behind us, Sage and Liam are chatting about a show they binged the night before, something to do with a teleporting phone booth.

We join the throng heading toward the chairlift, a futuristic structure strung with benches that loop through a pulley system overhead. Adjacent to the lift is a bungalow that houses the controls, the operator of which is standing in the doorway, barking out a running commentary for those waiting to be whisked up the mountain.

"Parker?" a cheery voice asks from my left.

I spin around, careful not to accidentally whack anyone with my skis, to find Annmarie raising an arm in greeting, poles clutched in her hand. Her face is fresh and unadorned with makeup, and her trademark golden locks are in a braid down her back. She's emanating a glow of confidence that acts like a gravitational force.

"Good morning," I answer.

Reid, Liam, and Sage turn to see whom I'm speaking to, each stunned into silence as realization dawns.

Reid recovers first. "I'm sure you don't remember me, but I used to work here."

"Is that right?" Annmarie asks.

"I still remember a lunch I made you once." He breaks out the dimples. Oh, what I wouldn't do for those dimples. "Don't think I've ever been that nervous."

It's true. When I first floated my idea of selling mulled wine to a Colorado ski resort, Reid immediately suggested Silver Creek. He then regaled me with the story of how he cooked for the famed Olympian, had made a Greek quinoa salad and accompanying wheatgrass smoothie to her exact specifications. That's when I learned Reid basically has a photographic memory for food.

Annmarie laughs good-naturedly, although it's clear she has no recollection of the event. She sticks her poles into the deep snow and maneuvers her skis lovingly to the ground—very expensive, very long skis. And she's basically wearing the Cristal of snow gear, tailored to fit her to perfection, in red, white, and blue, just in case there's any confusion regarding her identity.

I sneak a peek at Liam, fearful he may have fainted

at the sight of his childhood crush. He's intact but in utter awe, his mouth hanging open. Beside him, Sage remains quiet, more out of courtesy, a patient and keen observer with her head tilted to the side and her eyes narrowed.

"Snow report is good for the morning," Annmarie says.

"Awesome sauce," I say, giving myself away for the nerd that I am. "So, do you ski here often?" Oh God, and now I sound like a bad pickup line.

I flinch at my awkwardness, but Annmarie doesn't seem to notice.

She beams as she dons her helmet. "As often as I can. It's good publicity." She clicks her heels into the fastenings of each ski. "Plus, I love it."

I can tell she means it. Just how I love winemaking, the art mixed with science, the nuances of flavor and how I can manipulate them.

Annmarie tilts her chin up, breathing in the thin air. "Well, enjoy," she says, pulling her orange-tinted goggles over her eyes.

She glides away and I'm amazed by the sheer smoothness—the fluidity—she achieves on nearly level ground. She's obviously still a master of the sport.

Eyes turn to watch her as she gets in line. That's right, no cutting for Annmarie. That would defeat the promotional purpose of her appearance today—better to take her time, let all her guests recognize her, observe her.

A figure I vaguely recognize joins Annmarie in line, looking almost as sleek and comfortable on skis as she is. The man is in head-to-toe black and silver, his jaw set in a determined frown. It takes me a split second to realize it's Hudson, abysmal driver and jerk extraordinaire, whom Annmarie argued with the night before.

Curious to hear their interaction, I click my boots into my own skis. "Come on, guys. The slopes aren't like wine."

"What's that supposed to mean?" Liam asks, finally coming to with a shake of his head.

Reid and Sage start at the same time, "They won't get better with age."

I crinkle my nose at my brother. "Let's go."

In a decidedly less graceful fashion than Annmarie, I lead the way to the chairlift.

Narrow strips of red carpet are nestled in the snow, flanked by cones and ropes to dictate where each line should be, all leading to gates that simultaneously swing open and shut to allow the next person through. Annmarie and Hudson are a few people in front of us, the zigzagging of the line working in my favor.

Reid has one foot in his snowboard, using the other to slide across the snow to my side. "So, Parks, are you ready to be dazzled by my supreme skills?"

I can't help the chuckle that bubbles out of me, even as I'm shushing him.

A cocksure grin spreads across his face as we scoot forward. "You might think I'm exaggerating," he says, and then winks at me. "But you should really prepare yourself because I'm just that good."

"Oh, I'm sure you are." I nudge his shoulder with mine and then bring a finger to my lips. "I mean this in the best possible way, but *shhh*, I wanna hear this." My breath swirls toward him as I nod toward Annmarie and Hudson, the strings dangling from my hat bobbing.

Reid follows my gaze. He narrows his eyes and cocks his head to the side like, *Okay, I'll play.*

Soon, Hudson and Annmarie will be just on the other side of the rope from us.

Hudson is talking in such a low voice it's clear he doesn't want to be overheard, and his cool-blue eyes plead with Annmarie's. He's as close to her as he can get without their skis tangling into a mess of fiberglass.

Over the rustling of jackets and clicking of equipment, I can only discern two words: *profit* and *development.*

Annmarie is shaking her head, but her forehead is creased and she's worrying the inside of her cheek. She hasn't said no yet, and Hudson seems all too aware that he's making progress in whatever disagreement they're in the middle of, winning her over inch by hard-earned inch.

Hudson starts talking again, more fervently this time.

Reid looks at me with his eyebrows raised. He doesn't need words to communicate his meaning: *You might be onto something.*

We lean forward but just then, a deep voice booms, "Hide your wallets, everyone."

This is such a bizarre statement, it wholly ruins any chance I have to discern more. I pat my pockets, blinking in confusion at the chairlift operator who expressed such a random warning.

When I refocus on my mark, Annmarie and Hudson glide through the gates where the chairlift bench wraps around, scoops them up, and whisks them up the mountain.

"Boone!" Reid exclaims. "You old liftie."

Liftie is a slang term for chairlift operators, individuals who, Reid tells me, are the best source of information at the resort—the scoop on gossip, events, and where the best snow can be found.

Boone is a rugged older man with leathery tanned

skin, an unruly beard, and a bright-red jacket that identifies him as an employee of the resort. He shifts comfortably in his boots, which are seemingly more an extension of him than footwear, and twists his mouth in a feral smile.

"Well, if it isn't Maverick," Boone says, his voice gravelly.

I cast a confused glance at Reid, who just smirks, a spark entering his eyes. Guess I know who the wallet remark was directed at . . .

"You guys still do a weekly poker game?" Reid asks.

"Not for the likes of you." Boone turns to where a pair of beginner skiers shuffle toward the lift. "Feel for the seat with your free hand and let the chair do the work."

The skiers do as they're told, securing themselves in the four-person bench.

A group of rabble-rousers snicker at the newbies, mocking their movements. When Boone sees them, he snaps, "Keep on like that and you'll be hiking up the mountain."

They stop midchuckle, realizing Boone is 100 percent serious.

"Come for the skiing, stay for Boone's colorful commentary," Reid whispers. "The guy's a legend, been here forever."

"Better watch yourself, Liam," I shoot over my shoulder, knowing my brother's tendency to open his mouth when he shouldn't.

"Hey," Liam says. "I'm an upstanding citizen—a gentleman."

"Sure you are, babe," Sage says, squeezing his upper arm. Her snowboard and helmet are covered in stickers from various fandoms, most from Marvelverse but with a healthy representation of *The Lord of the Rings* as well.

Truth be told, I'm still getting used to the new dynamic between my best friend and brother. But after witnessing Sage's engagement fall to pieces last year and then learning Liam has been carrying a torch for her practically forever, I couldn't be happier for them both. Besides, Sage and I had a heart-to-heart early on that no matter what happens with their burgeoning romance, our friendship comes first. And I know better than to renege on an agreement with Sage.

Not only does my friend have an acute sense of style, she's also a public defender for Boulder County, having followed her passion in criminal law. While I maintain Liam could do no better, I pity him for the many arguments he'll inevitably lose.

We ease forward and suddenly we're in front of the gate. I feel a surge of nerves as my mouth goes dry. Even though I've gotten on and off lifts since I was a kid, the first ride of the day always gets my adrenaline pumping. What if I suddenly forget everything I used to know? What if I completely biff? *And* take Reid, Liam, and Sage down with me?

It'll be more than my bum that gets bruised then . . .

The gate opens and I push forward with my poles, my breath hitching in my throat.

"Can't believe another girl fell for your dog-and-pony show," Boone says. The operator's eyes sear into my back, his hand resting on the side of the operating structure, ready to hit the emergency stop if needed.

"I can't believe it, either, but I'm really hoping she'll be the last," Reid says. "This is Parker."

My cheeks flush and next to me, Liam makes a gagging sound.

On my immediate right, Sage murmurs under her breath, "He sure is a sweet-talker, isn't he?"

"You have no idea," I whisper back to Sage.

"Nice to meet you, Parker," Boone says. "Hope you're able to keep this one in line."

"I'll do my best," I say.

The banter distracts me enough to get out of my own way. The chairlift scoops us up and away we go. My stomach flips as my skis leave the ground. Soon we're dangling twenty feet in the air and I'm struck by the majestic beauty. The cerulean sky, rolling mountain peaks in the distance like dollops of whipped cream, and pointed tops of pine trees. Below us skiers and snowboarders sail down the mountain.

Reid and Liam, the bookends of our ride, pull the safety bar down from above, securing it in place. I hold my poles across my lap, the fabric of my snow pants rustling.

Reid leans in, his breath warm on my neck. "You know I meant what I said, right?"

"What?" I ask, even though of course I know what he's referring to. I just want to hear him ship our relationship as endgame again.

He scratches his forehead with his gloved hand, his coppery hair barely peaking from beneath his hat and helmet, and his eyes search mine. "I have a surprise for you later tonight."

Liam's warning rings in my ears. I can sense him listening now, despite Sage chatting animatedly, theorizing the next era of *Star Wars*.

The catch about chairlifts: They're not very private.

It's not the best time to, say, spill your guts about all your unresolved issues with Valentine's Day. How you used to love it but can't even think of it now without memories bubbling to the surface that make your heart ache from sadness and throat constrict with grief.

It goes beyond the parties, too. Aunt Laura was whom I went to with broken hearts, whatever petty dramas were unfolding in my life, and my most fanciful daydreams, like Vino Valentine. She would listen, recognize when advice or silent companionship was the remedy, and, in the latter case, press a check into the palm of my hand. She'd give me a hug, engulfing me in a cloud of verbena. I can almost smell her perfume now, feel her arms holding me tight. She was many things to many people, but to me she was a pillar of support.

I try to keep my expression unreadable as I respond to Reid, "What sort of surprise?"

"It'd spoil all the fun if I told you," he says. "Though I should warn you, it's outside. Dress warm."

"But," I start, licking my lips, "we promised not to exchange—"

"I know, I know." He dips his chin, turning his gaze from me to his snowboard, dangling below. "I held to our bargain. You'll see."

I force a smile on my face, gripping my poles tighter. "If you say so."

Chapter Four

If I owned a ski resort, the runs would, predictably, be named after grape varietals: the Champagne, Torrontés, Sangiovese, Petit Verdot. The body of each varietal would correspond to the run's difficulty. Which means I would be sticking to the equivalent of a chardonnay, *maybe* rosé.

A large wooden sign on the summit displays a map with so many twisting routes it resembles the figure-eight knot I use when climbing. My eyebrows furrow as I puzzle over what Annmarie's motivation could have been for naming trails. There's the Turin, Lillehammer, Calgary, Innsbruck, Squaw Valley, Clymen, and more on the backside of the mountain.

"They're the locations of the Winter Olympics," Reid says, reminding us once again of his insider knowledge of Silver Creek. "All except for this one." He points with a gloved finger, hovering over the name *Clymen.* "I never did learn what that one was named after."

"Curious . . ." I say. Asking Annmarie about this would be an infinitely better conversation starter than my mindless drivel from earlier.

The crisp air, impressive surroundings, and bustling people provide a welcome distraction after the chairlift ride where Reid confirmed he has a Valentine's Day surprise for me and I sank into a vat of self-doubt.

I cast my gaze about for Annmarie, not wanting to miss the chance to see an Olympic champion ski in person. Over my shoulder, glass-enclosed gondola carriages deposit those who prefer to enjoy the sites in a more relaxed fashion. A simple lodge made of espresso pine offers hot chocolate, snacks, and warmth, steam spouting from a vent on the roof. There are racks outside to stash gear—the honor system strictly adhered to—and windows, fogged around the edges, promise spectacular views and ample people-watching opportunities.

And there, perched at the top of a steep mogul run that's intimidating to even look at, is Annmarie.

Hudson is at her side, still yammering away about whatever business—or hopeful business—they have together. From this distance, I can read between the lines of her stance, in how she leans away from Hudson, that she's finished with the conversation.

"Well, which one should we start with?" Sage asks.

"The Lillehammer looks like it'd make a decent warm-up," I suggest. It also happens to be parallel to the run Annmarie chose—the Clymen—so I can optimize my viewing.

"Why don't we make things interesting?" Reid asks. He looks like he belongs on the mountain, nonchalantly standing with one foot out of his snowboard, confident in his funky plaid pants, his gray hoodie protruding from under his coat.

"What do you have in mind?" Liam asks.

"Skiers versus snowboarders, we'll settle this once and for all."

"And how do you propose we settle the eternal debate?" I flutter my eyelashes at him through my orange-tinted goggles.

"First two to reach base win."

This is out of the question for multiple reasons. First, Reid is obviously the most skilled out of us and I know Sage can hold her own on the slopes. And second, I want to relax and enjoy my run, not stress out over a bet.

I start to shake my head, but Liam answers first: "What are the stakes?"

"Last one down gets drinks later," Reid says, his eyes sliding to me. "Unless you're scared."

I grind my teeth. Reid knows I can't resist a challenge—my pride won't let me.

"I'm in," I say, turning to Sage.

She exhales. "Well, if I must prove what a badass I am *again*, so be it." Then she crinkles her nose and starts toward the trailhead.

"If we get separated, I'll see you guys at the bottom," I say. "And by that I mean, if you can't keep up."

I use my poles to glide over to the edge of the Lillehammer. Having grown up in Colorado, I spent many a weekend skiing in the famed Rocky Mountains. But between opening a business and the demands of the grape harvest and winemaking, I haven't made it up here the last couple years.

Now, standing at the top of the mountain, anticipation courses through my body. It's a winding trail, lined on either side with pine trees. And it's crowded with people at various levels of experience, from the obvious tourists to essentially mountain goats. Beyond that, I can see the resort far below, the reservoir that doubles as an ice rink sparkling in the sunlight.

Out of the corner of my eye, Annmarie rocks backward and forward a few times, gathering momentum, before pushing off on her own run.

With a deep breath, I dig my poles in and push myself forward, over the lip of the hill, and down I go.

Skiing is like riding a bike. Muscle memory kicks in as I zigzag down the hill, shifting my weight from the inside to outside of each foot, flexing my calves to dig in with my edges. My head clears as my focus is fully on my twinging quads and the obstacles in my path. The chunks of ice, shifting slope, and orange-mesh fencing to help direct traffic.

I can't help the broad smile that spreads across my face.

Reid stays close to my side and catches my eye, mirroring my grin. Then, with a dramatic turn, he faces straight down and surges ahead. Sage and Liam are farther down the mountain, too, but I'm not worried. This specific run is almost three miles long; I have plenty of time to catch up.

Through the pine trees to my left, Annmarie masterfully tackles the moguls.

She might as well be soaring, the birds overhead having nothing on her grace and speed. Each mogul isn't so much a bump as an opportunity for her to increase speed, to give her leverage as she swishes from one side to the other, her poles tucked against her body. It's almost as if she and her skis are one.

I pause to fully appreciate the sight. Only, a dense thicket of pine trees obscures my view. I zig down a deep depression, lurching to the side and barely catching myself with my poles. The trees aren't as thick here, but I still don't have a visual on Annmarie.

That's when it happens.

A loud clamor erupts from the evergreens—a shout, deep and loud, but so short a second later, I'm not certain I heard anything at all. And then, out of the corner of my eye, I think I see a shadow. A dark figure moving between the tree trunks. I shake my head and squint to peer closer, but it's nowhere to be seen.

It can't be a good sign that I'm now seeing *and* hearing things.

I wait for Annmarie to emerge on the other side of the trees, my pulse racing, but there's no sign of her.

My stomach flips and I frown, gnawing on my lower lip in worry.

I glance down my own run. Reid, Sage, and Liam are mere specks in the distance now and I've no chance of catching up. But that's the least of my concerns right now.

Another minute passes and, still, no Annmarie.

Then I make a decision I hope I won't regret. Turning myself perpendicular on the slope, I push toward the tree line, venturing over to the black-diamond slope.

The terrain is far beyond my ability.

My heart hammers in my chest and I struggle to keep my breathing even as I traverse the banks of ice and snow, some obstacles nature-made and some constructed by man. It takes me forever, one leg farther down the hill than the other, both skis fighting against what I'm trying to make them do.

I weave between pine trees, clinging to my poles and using them to help me maneuver. At one point I hit a patch of powder and pick up speed.

Pizza slice, pizza slice, pizza slice, I desperately think, trying to pin the tips of my skis together in the signature beginner's move to bring you to a stop.

Finally, I emerge out of the trees and onto the black-diamond mogul run. While Annmarie handled each bump with ease, I flail over each and every one.

Curses fly from my mouth as my quads scream in protest and my calves burn in exertion. Needless to say, this is not the slope meant for someone trying to remember how to do this sport.

By the time I reach where Annmarie disappeared, the few people brave enough to attempt this run have already gathered. It's at a particularly tricky turn—called Lockdown Pass, from the wooden signage—before a thicket of pine trees, farther down from the one I cut through. The surrounding trees are lofty, soaring high into the sky, their gangly branches covered in needles and pinecones.

I slow to a stop, finding a gap between people. My blood freezes in my veins at the sight: Annmarie, crumpled on the ground, unmoving, next to a pine tree the width of my torso. She's on her back, her neck twisted at an awkward angle, face pale in the shadows and her eyes open and glassy. One leg is bent over her body, the ski still attached, and the other is beneath her. Her braid of golden hair is sprawled behind her, trailing out of her helmet.

I finally peel my tongue from the roof of my mouth. "Did someone call for help?" I ask the nearest bystander.

"Paramedics are on their way, but . . ." he trails off, shaking his head.

I negotiate with myself. Annmarie will be fine. She's far too skilled of a skier—far too determined—to go out like this. Any second now, she'll push herself up, like she did after her fall during the slalom run at the Olympics. Everyone thought she was out of the competition, but she bounced back, not only in that run, but she blew the competition out of the water in the others as well.

But she doesn't move.

There are few tracks in the snow, Annmarie's being the only set to have veered from the moguls and into the underbrush. Nothing more than a series of parallel indents in the powder, but there are strange marks among the trees, as if the wind blew patterns in the snow, and a there's a smattering of pine needles studded in the ground and surrounding Annmarie like an aura.

The paramedics arrive on skis. There are two of them, decked out in black apart from their bright-orange jackets, and one of them is hauling a rescue sled attached to their poles. They're all business.

"Move aside, please," one of them shouts, hurrying to Annmarie's side. "Back up."

I'm jostled by other concerned observers, one of them overlapping their skis with mine and almost causing me to fall. I shift my feet, gliding backward to extricate myself from the game of human dominoes, and watch with bated breath as the paramedics try to revive Annmarie.

Minutes pass and no one says a word. On other runs we can hear the *whoops* of skiers and snowboarders, a stark contrast to the solemn scene before us. If only they knew the woman responsible for their merriment was in mortal danger.

No, Parker, *don't think that way.*

The paramedics have an oxygen mask strapped to Annmarie's face and alternate between performing chest compresses and checking for a pulse. And still, nothing.

I'm no expert, but this can't be good. I would've expected Annmarie to regain consciousness by now. To bring the full force of the Bauer Power and finish her run.

Finally, one of the paramedics speaks. What he says makes my knees go weak and I can't help the shiver that snakes up my body: "Dead on arrival."

The waiting stretches on like a nightmare you've realized is a nightmare but can't wake from, no matter how hard you flail about or whimper.

I linger near Annmarie, trying and failing to make sense of what just happened. What I witnessed.

More people gather, initially drawn by curiosity to see what all the commotion is, and then stunned into statues at the sight. Clicks and shuffles of gear fill the air as swirling clouds amass from our collective exhales, a beacon marking our location.

The paramedics stand guard around Annmarie. I want to ask if there's any way I can help, and then feel ridiculous. What could I possibly do to make this better?

The sound of a snowmobile engine cuts through the tension, growing louder until a shiny black, white, and blue beast materializes from around the bend, an arc of snow trailing behind it like a rooster tail. The driver comes in quick—too quick, in my opinion—turning at the last second in a flashy stop.

"Show's over, folks," the sheriff says, disembarking from the mobile in a move that reminds me of the Wild West.

She unbuckles her helmet, draping it over the handlebar, and tromps toward the paramedics. Sporting a faux-fur-collared coat with the emblem of the sheriff's office on the sleeve, khaki pants, sturdy boots, and a no-nonsense expression, it's clear she's not one to be trifled with.

The paramedics greet the sheriff—Sheriff Scott, I manage to overhear—and they have a hushed conversation. Sheriff Scott squats on her haunches and drinks in the scene, absorbing every detail with steely eyes, before placing a phone call.

What ensues is more waiting. Torturous to the extreme, surrounded by strangers who are all equally as uncomfortable as I am—both physically and emotionally. I have no idea how much time has passed . . . minutes, hours, days? More officers arrive on snowmobiles and the area is taped off.

Finally, Sheriff Scott pinpoints the pair who first reached Annmarie, which, thanks to my slow reaction and even slower skiing, is most definitely not me. The rest of us are dismissed with instructions to give our names and phone numbers to a waiting officer.

I do so, teeth chattering as I recite my phone number. Then, with one last glance at Annmarie's crumpled body—so small compared to the entrepreneur and ski goddess I'd chatted with not long ago—and the trees and strange windblown marks in the snow, I make my way back to my own run.

There's nothing for it but for me to continue down Lillehammer.

It seems ridiculous that the resort is operating per usual when the world has shifted. Back among the revelers on the slope, I force myself to focus, even as every move I make, every flex of my muscles, feels surreal. Because if an accident can take out an expert skier like Annmarie, no one is safe.

I swish back and forth across the mountainside, breathing in through my nose and out through my mouth.

Finally, I near the final descent, a plunging slope that leads back to the main chairlift and, beyond that, Silver Creek Village.

I steady myself, quelling my panic, and wait for an opening. I seize my chance. The crisp air whipping my hair and majestic backdrop hold no joy for me. When I finally come to a stop, I find that I'm shaking.

"There she is," Reid's voice says. I turn to find him tromping toward me, his snowboard propped over one shoulder. "We were getting ready to send out a search party."

I drink in his presence, willing it to ground me. I want to run and throw my arms around him, disappear into his warmth and scent. But, alas: skis. And I don't trust my balance enough to twist and push the fastenings behind either heel so I can step out. Instead, I go into statue mode.

My brother and Sage trail close behind Reid.

"No referee needed to say: you lost," Liam says. "So, you know, thanks for giving skiers a bad name."

I open my mouth to respond, but no words come out. A lump has lodged itself in my throat. The ski world has lost so much more than our stupid bet today.

"Don't take it too hard," Sage says, thinking my silence is from shame. "We can't all be perfect at everything, and you come about as close as one can get."

"It's not that," I croak, my throat drier than a New Zealand sauvignon blanc. I take a shuddering breath, my eyes filling with tears that cause my goggles to fog.

Reid is the first to realize something is wrong. "What happened? Are you hurt?" Where a moment ago, his tone was playful, it's now serious. He sets his board on the ground and gently moves my goggles to rest on top of my helmet.

I grip his arms, my gloved fingers digging into the crinkly polyester of his jacket.

"I'm fine," I manage to say. "Really. But Annmarie . . ." I trail off, shaking my head.

"What about Annmarie?" Reid asks, his gaze anchoring me to reality.

"There was an accident. She's gone."

The blood drains from Reid's face and his jaw falls open in shock. He has history with Annmarie, too, so it's no wonder he's taking this news hard. Even though he'd only met her the one time he made her lunch, the interaction left a mark.

Sage comes over and wraps an arm around me. "Let's get you inside and you can tell us what happened."

Thoughts swirl through my mind like wine in a glass. Something isn't settling in my gut, and until I pinpoint what it is, I won't able to move on.

It's then I realize what's bothering me: Annmarie's accident might not have been an accident at all.

Annmarie is—was—one of the best skiers in the world. It doesn't make sense that she would get in a fatal accident on a joyride. She'd even been wearing a helmet. How could this have happened?

I shake my head. "No, there's something I need to tell the sheriff."

Reid furrows his eyebrows. "Are you sure you're okay? We can call later to report whatever it is."

"This could be important," I say, chewing on my lower lip.

Reid gives me a penetrating look. We've come a long way in the last nine months we've been dating, so much so that I easily interpret the question in his gaze. I've surprised Reid with my—we'll call it grit, although it's probably more akin to stubbornness—and apparently this is another one of those instances.

To prove just how okay I am, I twist around and click out of my left ski and then my right, hardly wavering at all. Still, he seems unconvinced.

"I saw something, and heard something," I explain. "Right before"—I gulp, urging saliva back into my parched mouth—"it happened."

"You were there?" Reid asks, his pallor taking on an ashy hue.

"Close enough. I stopped to watch and then . . ." I trail off with a sniffle.

"I'll go stash my board and be right back," Reid says, giving me a shoulder squeeze before disappearing.

"Me too," Sage says, following Reid.

Liam, however, stays by my side. There's concern painted on his face and, if I'm not mistaken, disapproval. "Is this really the time to be inserting yourself in an investigation?"

"What are you talking about?"

He balances his forearms on his ski poles. "Aren't you and Reid supposed to be having a romantic getaway?"

"I thought you didn't want to hear any details about

my relationship," I say blandly, calling back to Liam's requirement when he gave me his proverbial blessing to date his friend.

"That's still true." He feigns a wince. "What do you need to tell the sheriff that's so important, anyway?"

"That's between me and the sheriff." That he's even challenging me on this is proof he doesn't understand the situation. "Besides, wasn't Annmarie your childhood idol? Don't you want to find out what really happened?"

"Of course." Liam exhales, showing a sliver of empathy. He rubs the back of his neck where his raven hair, the same shade as mine, peeks out from beneath his hat and helmet. "It's just, haven't you been through enough? You're not some honorary detective."

"Thanks for your concern," I say, jabbing my poles into the ground with slightly more force than necessary. "But you should probably focus on your own Valentine."

"Oh, I plan to," he says with a wink. "Unlike you, I actually got *mi amor* something to show her how much I care."

I feel as though I've been slapped. I grind my teeth. "I hardly think that matters now."

It's absurd to think a bit ago I was stressing over something as benign as an unreciprocated gift. Because the thing about facing mortality, even indirectly: it provides perspective.

"You were distracted before this," Liam says, rocking forward on his ski poles. I'm tempted to knock them out from under him. "And look, I know this time of year is hard on you—"

I cut him off, leveling him with my best withering glare. "This is about Annmarie. You weren't there, you didn't see." My breath catches and tears sting my eyes afresh.

This is a new level of ignorance for Liam. To attack me now, after something like *this* happens? It's completely off base. "Sometimes there are things going on with people you can't begin to comprehend."

He snorts. "Hate to break it to you, Parker, but you're not that mysterious."

"Oh, so suddenly you know everything?"

"All I'm saying is there's a chance you're sticking your nose in other people's business as a way to—I dunno—get some sort of closure for Aunt Laura."

This strikes a chord deep in my core, but I would never admit that to Liam. "I told you, this isn't about me," I hiss, "and pretending everything is peachy isn't going to solve anything."

"I'm only trying to watch out for you."

That's rich coming from my brother, whose primary solution to problems is to ignore them. "Yeah, well, you have a weird way of showing it."

Concern flickers in his eyes and he says, so quietly, I almost miss it, "If you need to hash anything out, I'm here."

I hitch my skis over one shoulder and stalk off before he can make any other empty offers.

Chapter Five

Liam's words rattle me more than a crusher de-stemmer does a bunch of grapes.

Which is why, when Reid returns to my side, I find myself asking, "Am I out of line waiting to talk to the sheriff?"

We've found a spot near a fire pit, rays of sunshine warming us almost as much as the flames dancing beneath the metal grate. Emergency vehicles are parked along the street separating the main village from the parking lot and the chairlift, their lights flashing blue and red. An officer prowls near the chairlift, which is shockingly still running.

Sage and Liam have since disappeared inside the lodge in search of food, it being nearly lunchtime, not that any of us really has an appetite. But I've learned, sometimes people need to feel like they're doing something to help.

So, when they offered to track down provisions, I readily accepted.

Reid's arm is draped behind my back as he lounges. It's unfair how effortlessly attractive he is. With his hat resting in his lap, his hair is mussed with streaks of caramel running through it, and even in the many layers he's wearing, you can tell he's in shape. I catch the way other women eye Reid and sidle closer to him.

"Why would you be out of line?" he asks, his thumb forming small circles on top of my shoulder.

That's another thing about Reid: He's hardly ever still. It serves him well in the kitchen, and when I'm craving his touch like I am now. I lean into him.

"Because we're supposed to be on vacation. We should be, you know, vacaying."

"We are vacaying." The corner of his lips twitch into the tiniest of smirks.

"But do I really want to involve myself with the police again? *Another* investigation?"

Reid leans forward, pulling his arm away. He rubs his chin in thought. "You have to do what you feel is right."

"What is that?" I stare at my boyfriend, the man who has done so much for me—from helping save my business, to making me an incomparable amount of chocolate truffles, to proving he's there for me. We both work such long hours, we deserve—nay, *need*—this time together. "Because I honestly don't know."

Reid's voice is low and deadly serious when he speaks. "Parks, we both know how important witness statements can be."

Reid rarely references his time behind bars, nor the witness who falsely landed him there. He's the type who prefers to live in the present. Even so, I know his family continues to dredge up everything that happened last fall. There isn't much hope of repairing his relationship with his father and older brother, Tristan, but the same can't be said for his mom and other brother, Ben. They even flew out for the holidays to be with him, to show him they want to be a part of his life.

"If you think you can make a difference in discovering the truth of what happened, then you have to try. For Annmarie. And for you." He heaves a sigh. "We both know you won't let it go until you do, anyway."

I lean my head on his shoulder. "Ugh, I hate it when you're right."

"I know." He presses his lips to my forehead.

Shadows linger in the lines of his face, in his eyes, which are usually sparking with mischief. It's clear he's as haunted as I am by what befell Annmarie. And yet, he's the one comforting me—here for me.

"I'll wait with you," he continues. "However long it takes."

The least I can do is be there for him. I take his hand in mine and give it a squeeze. "That's not necessary. Why don't you take care of yourself while I talk to the sheriff? We'll meet up later."

The relief that washes over his face lets me know I made the right call. "If you're sure, I'll go find Cash. Someone should make sure he and the kitchen staff know."

I give him a peck. "I'm sure."

Reid's absence leaves me chilled and hollow. I give in to my emotions, letting myself replay everything—Annmarie expertly maneuvering moguls, her disappearing into the woods, the horror when I realized something was wrong, and my inability to get there fast enough to help. I wallow in the shock and sadness until my mouth fills with bile. Then I turn my focus to the base of the mountain, watching for the paramedics, the sheriff, anyone really, to emerge.

While I'm keeping my vigil, I see two people I recognize.

One is Hudson Gray, whom I haven't seen since he and Annmarie were locked in their battle of wills at the top of the Clymen. He's about twenty feet in front of me, still in his skis, although he seems completely unaware of his surroundings or that he's being observed. He's staring at the mountain with reverence, and though I only get a look at his profile, I can tell from the glistening around his eyes that tears are streaming down his face.

A realization dawns on me—I didn't see him anywhere near Annmarie when she was going down her run. He'd been hard pressed to let her out of his sight before that; is there a chance he opted for a different trail back to base? Or was he MIA for a more malevolent reason?

The other person is, surprisingly, Paisley Moore, resort manager and resident sourpuss. She disembarks from the gondola, which has just returned from the summit with a group of people.

Once she's free of the crowd, Paisley straightens her navy peacoat, buttoned all the way to her neck, and stomps snow from her laced boots. A great deal of snow, actually. Far more than a trip to the summit by gondola warrants. Her mousy hair hangs limp around her face, and there's something strange in her expression. She casts her gaze about furtively, arms crossed over her chest, almost as if she doesn't want to be seen.

I frown, shifting slightly on the hard, limestone bench.

Paisley catches me watching and, pretending not to have seen me, pivots on her heels and books it to the lodge.

I hardly have a chance to puzzle over her or Hudson's behavior. The rumble of a snowmobile reverberates through the air as the sheriff returns to base.

I've dealt with my fair share of law enforcement officials. In fact, my favorite climbing buddy happens to be a detective with the Boulder PD. And yet a jolt of nerves surges through my body and sucks my mouth dry faster than a tannic cabernet sauvignon.

Sheriff Scott has since parked her snowmobile and is speaking with officers. She directs them to where the paramedics move the rescue sled to the back of a waiting ambulance, a sheet covering Annmarie's body.

A shiver snakes down my spine, radiating outward to my fingertips. From the cold, shock, and the feeling of eyes boring into me, a disconcerting combination.

I approach the sheriff with a wobbliness rivaling that of a baby deer standing for the first time. Wringing my gloves in my hand, I go with the brilliant conversation starter of clearing my throat. When that doesn't get her attention, I try actual words, "Um, excuse me, Sheriff Scott."

Removing aviator sunglasses, she turns to me. "Jenny, please," she says.

Her light-brown hair is pulled into a loose bun at the nape of her neck, wisps escaping and blowing across her face. With faint lines in her freckled skin and inquisitive hazel eyes, she poses a striking figure. I would call her lovely, but she doesn't seem like the type to put weight in such things.

"Did you need something?" she prods, radiating an unapologetic assertiveness.

I peel my tongue from the roof of my mouth. "I was on the run next to Annmarie's when she had her accident, and I saw and heard something. Just before."

Jenny shouts over her shoulder. "Sullivan, get the evidence logged. Mark, find out when the postmortem will be."

The officers hop to and I can't help but feel a surge of admiration at her leadership savvy. Then I remember that sheriff is an elected position; she must be popular in the community to have been voted in. Especially as a woman in a small mountain town.

She takes a notepad from her jacket pocket and takes down my name and contact information. "Okay, shoot."

My toes are frozen in my ski boots as I shift, snow crunching beneath them. "There was a shadow in the trees—"

"What kind of shadow?"

"Something large, an animal maybe. It was there one second and gone the next."

Jenny jots something down, and I see the ghosts of other cases—other deaths—flicker across her features, a tangled web of connections. "And the noise?"

"It was loud, a shout."

"Was it coming from where you observed the shadow?"

"Hard to say," I answer. "Sound travels differently on the mountain."

Her eyes snap to mine, but she doesn't ask me to

elaborate. Truth is, in Colorado, we're well versed in temperature swings and how it can manipulate the senses. Sounds travel farther through the thin mountain air, clinging to curves and echoing off trees.

"Were you paying especially close attention to Annmarie?"

"Me and everyone else," I say with a shrug. "It's not every day you get to see an Olympian perform their sport in person."

"Ah, another fan," she says, eyebrows raised. "Yet, no one else reported witnessing a sound or seeing anything in the trees."

"R-really?" I stutter, sweating beneath all my layers.

Now that I'm off the slope, with my skis tucked away, the veil of time creates a cloud in my mind like bacteria in wine. My confidence wavers. Could it have been a trick of the light? Could I have simply heard another skier or snowboarder? I replay the memory in my mind, goose bumps rising on my arms.

"Really." Jenny tucks her notepad under one arm, flashing me a side smile. "Which is why I appreciate you bringing this to my attention."

I sag with relief that she believes me.

Then Jenny continues, "Annmarie's death was under suspicious circumstances."

Under suspicious circumstances. That's code for "murder." I blink rapidly, taking my hat off to fan my now-overheating face.

Annmarie murdered. It's as inconceivable as serving wine from a can—far-fetched until it becomes a reality.

I pull my hat back on my head and let out a long exhale, both cheeks puffed out. "Well, you'll probably find this interesting, then. It wasn't on the slope, but I overheard an argument between Annmarie and a man, Hudson Gray."

A gleam enters Jenny's eyes. Faster than I can pour a taster of vino, she has her pen out again, at the ready. "Any idea what they were arguing about?"

"I didn't hear much. Just the words *profit* and *development*, but he's over there if you want to ask him." I gesture toward where Hudson is still standing, staring transfixed at the mountain.

I'm not sure why he's lingering. No doubt mourning the loss of whatever he'd hoped to gain from Annmarie. Or perhaps he's wrestling with guilt. He definitely had a motive if he thought she'd unlawfully backed out of a business agreement. Maybe he'd had enough talking and resorted to a more menacing approach.

The gondola draws my attention, depositing another group of tourists at the base. "And then there was the resort manager, Paisley Moore."

"She was arguing with Annmarie, too?" Jenny's words are laced with excitement, like she's unexpectedly struck gold.

Apparently, during my short time at Silver Creek, I've compiled quite the dossier on Annmarie.

"Not arguing, per se," I amend. "But she was acting funny a bit ago. Twitchy. Like she didn't want anyone to see her."

"Are you well acquainted with Ms. Moore?"

"No."

"Then how do you know her behavior was abnormal?"

"I guess I don't," I admit, feeling slightly chastised. But Jenny's shown herself to be a professional, eager to find out who did this, so I try to explain. "It's just a gut feeling, you know?"

"I put a lot of stock into gut feelings." She assesses me. "Anything else you noticed?"

"The pattern in the snow. At first I assumed it was the wind, but now I'm not so sure . . ." I think back to the markings, how they'd almost looked natural, curved in a sweeping motion. Almost, if not for the whole murder thing. "And then there were the pine needles around her body."

"What about the needles?"

"Well, they were reddish brown. The tree she was lying next to was green."

She tucks her notebook away, appraising me with newfound interest. "If you think of anything else, call the sheriff's station."

Jenny returns to her waiting vehicle, rubbing her hands together, whether from cold or excitement, I don't know.

I tromp toward where my skis are waiting and then on toward the lodge. My feet and fingers might be frozen, but my core burns with hope that maybe there will be justice for Annmarie.

My phone rings when I reach the hotel lobby and I have to set all my things down—poles, skis, helmet, hat, gloves—to dig it out of the inside pocket of my coat. The caller ID shows that it's my mom. I slump into a leather sofa near the central fireplace, startling Madeline, who's curled up on the adjacent cushion, a smoky ball of fluff. I let her sniff my fingers before scratching behind her ears and she relaxes again, turning on her side and kneading at my snow pants. Maybe she remembers the shrimp I snuck her last night, or maybe she's used to snuggling up to guests.

"Hi, Mom," I say, careful to keep my voice light and cheery. My mom is like a master sommelier for my life, able to suss out even the subtlest hints of trouble.

"Just calling between tastings at Vino Valentine," she says, an excitement in her voice that makes me smile.

It wasn't long ago that my mom and I were at odds over my choice of profession. But after we both gave an inch, we found common ground: chemistry. My mom is the lead chemist at NIST Laboratories in Boulder and was wowed during the fall harvest by the sheer amount of science involved in winemaking. After that, she volunteered to help in my shop, which worked out well for this little trip.

"How's it going?"

"Gladys stopped by and she is a hoot!"

I first met Gladys during a last-ditch-effort party to save my business where she intimidated me silly, but since then I've learned she's a marshmallow. A velvet-clad marshmallow who happens to be one of my most enthusiastic supporters.

"How is my favorite customer?" I lean back, reveling in the simplicity of this conversation. I continue stroking Madeline's silky fur, a low rumble emanating from her throat.

"Feisty. She wanted me to tell you to enjoy your time with your sweetheart and that if she were younger she'd steal him away."

"That sounds like Gladys."

I can hear the telltale jingle in the background of a new arrival entering my shop. My mom adds, "I don't have long but wanted to let you know things are going great here."

I can just picture it—the oak-barrel tables, wine-bottle lanterns, pillar candles (unscented so as not to interfere with the aromas of the wine), and vases of fresh flowers. My heart squeezes. This will be the longest I've been away from my winery since it opened last May and, to be honest, I hardly know who I am without Vino Valentine.

"Thanks for checking in," I say. "I appreciate all your help. And Dad's. I hope Zin isn't giving him too much trouble. Or William, for that matter."

"Your dad's enjoying spoiling the little furballs, and there's nowhere I'd rather be," she says, meaning every word. "What about your big meeting? Did you get the deal?"

I freeze midpat on Madeline's head, a lump forming in my throat. For it's dawning on me that my deal may not go through. There was nothing official, no contracts signed. All I had were Annmarie's verbal agreement and Akira's promise to put an order in today. And I know this is the last thing I should be worrying about. A woman died, for chrissake. But it's an insult added to injury, like cork debris floating in a vinegary glass of wine.

I force myself to swallow and answer, "It went well." Even I can tell the cheeriness in my voice is forced. Best to get off the phone stat. "I'll let you go. Love you."

"Love you, too. Be sure to have some fun."

"I'll try." I hang up before I say something I'll regret.

Movement off to the side attracts my attention. It's Paisley, standing at the end of the wooden desk and warily talking with a fellow guest. The lodger is an older woman who looks like she's here for the shopping more than the skiing, based on her cashmere turtleneck, leggings, fashionable boots, and collection of retail bags at her feet.

Paisley is swimming in her blazer, this one a tweed chartreuse that clashes with her skin tone. Her hair hangs around her face, the layers reminiscent of a nineties sitcom, and there's a sour expression on her face. Absently, I notice she's changed out of her boots and into pumps, though clumps of melting snow still cling to her slacks. She's poised, the twitchiness I observed earlier gone.

The guest speaks to Paisley with a Southern accent that becomes stronger as her voice rises. "I don't know what to tell you, but it was in my room this morning and now it's gone."

"Ma'am, like I said, you can check the lost and found, or, if you wish, file a complaint."

"I want to speak with your manager."

No wonder Paisley always looks like she's just bitten into a lemon. I mean, I've certainly had my fair share of persnickety customers, but this is verging on nightmare behavior. Madeline and I look at each other in companionable shock. She twitches her ears as if to communicate, *See what I have to put up with all day?* We both turn back to the desk.

"I'm afraid that won't be possible," Paisley answers. The cool way she says this makes me wonder if she knows about Annmarie, and if so, who would have told her.

"I want my necklace back," the woman says, gesturing wildly with both arms. "The sapphire pendant belonged to my grandmother. Someone must pay for this."

Gotta hand it to Paisley. She doesn't give an inch. Ice enters her voice as she replies, "I'll call you if it turns up, Mrs. Landry."

Fumes practically pour from the woman's ears as she

tosses her bleach-blond locks over one shoulder and threatens, "You haven't heard the last from me. Wait until I tell my husband the way I've been treated."

"Of course, we're always open to feedback." Paisley gives what can only be described as a self-satisfied smirk. Maybe she doesn't detest her job as much as she lets on.

The lady storms out of the lobby.

First a murder, and now a missing precious necklace . . . while one crime is clearly more serious than the other, it makes me wonder: What sort of place is this?

Chapter Six

The hotel room Reid and I share is a mixture of rustic decor and modern comfort. Log paneling with accents of pine green, large canvas prints of nature stills, and a luxurious bed with clean white linens the color of snow. In the corner, a granite fireplace gives off glorious radiant heat. But above all, we have an enviable view.

Our private balcony overlooks the village and giant ice-skating rink below, and beyond that the snow-topped peaks and expansive blue sky. The majestic surroundings bring me a moment of peace, a drop of calm in the tumultuous sea.

After I trade in my clunky ski boots for thick wool socks and strip down to the leggings that serve as long underwear, I find Reid on the balcony. He's resting his forearms on the railing and taking in the sights as if they were giving him life, as they did for me. The sun is at just such an angle to bask our small space in warming light.

At the sound of the sliding glass door opening, he turns to me, dazzling me with a smile. He's in worn jeans and a long-sleeved shirt that's just the right amount of tight. "There you are."

"Here I am."

He gestures for me to sit down in one of the Adirondack chairs and passes me a sandwich wrapped in paper and a bottle of water. My mouth waters and my stomach rumbles at the savory aromas wafting from the food.

"I can't take credit, it was all Liam and Sage," Reid says. "Sage said to text her or"—he pauses to sit down in the other chair—"she'll come hunt you down."

And she will. I make a mental note to text her after I get sustenance. I didn't realize it until I sat down, but after skiing and, well, everything else this morning, I'm famished.

I peel the wrapper away and find a toasted sub, still warm, with oozing mozzarella, peppery arugula, roasted bell peppers, and creamy hummus. There are even briny olives dotted in the ciabatta. I take a bite, leaning my head back as I let out a tiny moan.

"Want me to leave you two alone?" Reid asks, gesturing with his finger between me and my sandwich.

"Not necessary," I say. "Did you eat already?"

"Right before you got here," he says. "And right after a painful conversation with my mother."

I swallow my sandwich, focusing entirely on Reid. His relationship with his family has always been fraught, but it's even more so now. "Painful how?"

"She wants to *start over*." He says these last two words

with air quotes, and obvious sarcasm. "She's filing for divorce from my dad, which I completely support—"

Understandably so. Even though up until now she's played the dutiful upper-crust wife.

"—but she wants to begin again in Colorado. She was asking what sort of place Celestial Seasonings would be to work at."

I chose a bad time to take a sip of water because I almost do a full-on spit take. Once my coughing and sputtering calms down I ask, "Are you serious?"

"It took me by surprise, too." A haunted expression crosses his face. "Colorado is where I made a home for myself. It means a lot that she accepts that and, I guess, wants to be a part of it. Maybe wants to find something for herself. I want to be supportive."

"Of course you do." I take his hand in mine, which means setting my sandwich down, a true sign of love. "We'll figure it out, and if not, there's always the peppermint room."

The peppermint room is a closed-off space at the Celestial Seasonings tea factory. The peppermint leaves prove to be so strong they need to be separated from the other more delicate tea leaves. During tours of the facility, you can step inside and breathe in the potent aroma. It's a great way to clear the sinuses. I have a hard time picturing Reid's mother—with her pearls, cardigans, and coiffure—lasting more than a minute in there.

He chuckles and squeezes my hand. "Thanks."

I return to my sandwich and more graceful hydrating. "So, don't hold back, let's hear your critique." Reid is such a flavor nerd, I've grown accustomed to, and appreciate, his analysis of nearly every meal we consume.

He pulls my feet into his lap and proceeds to give me a foot massage. That's right, a *foot massage.* Do you see how lucky I am?

"It all comes down to the bread, and they must bake theirs in-house every day because it had just the right texture. Crusty on the outside, soft and flaky on the inside," he says, his mind churning through details my palate—adept as it is—could never discern. "Decent, fresh ingredients. Maybe could have used a touch more seasoning, but all in all, a winner."

"Reid's stamp of approval, that means a lot," I say. "Were you able to talk with Cash?"

"And then some." He massages my toes, which go as gooey as the mozzarella dripping out of the back of my sandwich. "One thing I forgot about this place is how fast news travels. Cash had already gone through shock, denial, and was on his way to acceptance when I left, with the help of the lunch rush. And a shot of liquid grain."

"I wonder who he heard it from?" I ask, frowning.

"You've got me." He shrugs a full-bodied shrug. "How'd it go with the sheriff?"

I swallow the rather large and unladylike bite of sandwich and take a sip of water, trying to figure out how to answer. "I said what I needed to say. The sheriff can do with it what she wants."

"That good, huh?"

Silence follows as I fiddle with the paper wrapper, buying time. There's no great way to deliver this news. "Annmarie was murdered." The word rests heavy on my tongue.

His hands still on my feet. My eyes flick to Reid's, studying his response. He looks thoughtful but, oddly, not alarmed.

He heaves a sigh with a small shake of his head. "Then what you said must have helped." Reid turns his gaze to the mountain—to the resort Annmarie created after she'd already made a household name for herself as an Olympian.

"Any idea who could have done such a thing? Who would've wanted her out of the picture?" I ask, my sandwich forgotten. If I focus on the facts, the emotions welling inside of me subside to a bearable level.

"No, but I've been out of the loop for years. I'm shocked Cash and Boone are still here, to be honest. Well," he amends, "maybe not Boone. That guy will probably outlive us all on this mountain."

"Did you ever work with Paisley?"

"She's still at Silver Creek?" he asks, genuinely surprised, as if he hasn't waltzed by her half a dozen times already.

"Yeah, she's the manager of the hotel."

"Huh." He tilts his head to the side, eyebrows raised. "Didn't even recognize her, but that name can't belong to many people."

Now I'm even more intrigued. "What do you remember about her?"

"Very little. We worked in different circles and she never made much of an impression, unlike you."

I smile, but my mind is whirring through what I've observed in the last twenty-four hours. From Hudson's argument to Paisley's weird behavior to all the other unknown reasons someone would have it in for Annmarie. "Maybe it was someone Annmarie bested."

"That would be a lot of people," Reid says. "Annmarie Bauer was competitive in every aspect of her life, as I understand it."

We fall into the companionable silence of two people who don't need words to communicate. The grim downturn of our lips spoke to our sadness, the bewilderment in our eyes to disbelief, and the lines on our brows to the questions consuming us both: Who would do such a thing? And how did they pull it off?

As a self-proclaimed internet enthusiast, I think I've shown great restraint by waiting this long to check email and social media.

I give in to the urge now, propping my laptop on my lap on the balcony, enjoying the warmth of the last rays of sunshine.

The first thing I do is navigate to the website for the Colorado Wine Festival. It's the biggest vintner event in the state, taking place in Palisade at the end of July, a celebration where winemakers showcase their craftsmanship and aficionados discover new labels. I knew it was a long shot when I applied for a booth, Vino Valentine still being on the come up, but I'm going to take it as a good sign that my application hasn't been denied. Yet.

That means there's still hope. Which I very much need right now.

The next thing I do is check social media. I'm curious to learn if word of Annmarie's death has spread outside of Silver Creek. Imagine my surprise when I find *#BauerPower* trending on Twitter. I scroll through the feed, reading messages to rest in peace, notes full of shock, sadness, and injustice at her dying so young. But most are personal comments on what the skier meant to people, how she inspired the world.

I find the source that first leaked the story: a local paper who published a bare-bones article just an hour ago. It stated that Annmarie perished in a ski accident at her resort. It mentions her business holdings, all that she accomplished at the Olympics and since. What it doesn't mention is her family. Or murder.

Chewing on my lower lip, I glance through the wrought iron bars enclosing the balcony and down to the street below. People are meandering to and fro on the cobblestone walkways, the occasional vehicle cruising along the parallel street, searching for a coveted parking space. Tomorrow this place will no doubt be swarming with journalists vying for the inside scoop, but for now, it's peaceful—calm.

I lean back and search for one more name: *Hudson Gray.*

The first hit is for his LinkedIn profile and below that, bingo, his website.

A professional headshot is in the upper corner, the pointy chin and smug smile telling me I have the right guy. Gray Developments focuses on sustainable real estate development, with a foothold in the mountains.

The properties listed are mostly LEED-certified condos, conveniently located near popular ski destinations, and überexpensive. These are not built for the likes of me but for another class, those who don't mind dropping a spare million on a vacation home.

This information sheds new light on the arguments I overheard between Hudson and Annmarie, especially the words *profit* and *development*. It's obvious Hudson was hoping to develop some of his fancy-schmancy condos in Silver Creek. What's less clear is why Annmarie was so hesitant, and what Hudson felt she'd owed him.

Reid leans against the sliding glass door to the balcony, his flannel rolled to his elbows and arms crossed casually over his chest, the picture of nonchalance. He nods toward my computer screen. "Looking for a new investment opportunity?"

"Ha," I answer, shutting my laptop, stretching my hands over my head. "With all the spare cash I have lying around."

"Come on, Parks, you know no one pays cash anymore."

"What do they deal in, then?"

"Credit." He rubs the scruff on his chin in thought, continuing, "Or in your case: truffles."

I snort but then rub my arms. The sun has disappeared behind the mountains, leaving a chill in its wake and casting the village in a dusky blue. I shiver and follow Reid inside.

While I wouldn't consider myself high maintenance per se, I do enjoy primping. A hint of blush on my cheeks, a swipe of mascara on my lashes, occasionally dramatic lipstick. And then, of course, there's the actual ensemble. Which is why I told Reid to go ahead and meet me in the lobby.

Because whatever surprise Reid has planned is outdoors and—spoiler alert—dressing for the elements and dinner will take finesse.

Eventually, I land on my favorite pair of skinny jeans, tucked fashionably into my snow boots, and a thick wool sweater the same shade of blue gray as my eyes. I finish with my beaded necklace, a fine chain dotted with tiny bunches of grapes, a gift from Aunt Laura.

I clench the silver chain in my palm, right over my heart. Taking a deep yoga breath—in through my nose and out through my mouth—I try to calm the emotions churning through me.

As painful as it is to admit, there was truth in what Liam said to me earlier. I was distracted before Annmarie's nonaccident. And I do want closure for Annmarie and those dear to her, because I know what it's like when you're left wondering; how it can consume your thoughts. But I need to find a way to move forward, to live in the moment instead of dwelling on the past. Not only do I owe it to Aunt Laura, but I owe it to Reid.

So, I give myself a little pep talk. I can be happy, witty, and romantic tonight. Go with the flow and enjoy the surprise my incredibly thoughtful boyfriend planned for me. Right? My reflection in the mirror doesn't imbue me with confidence.

Draping my winter gear over one arm, my purse hanging from the other, I head for the door.

I jump when I discover I'm not alone in the hallway. Madeline the cat is outside the neighboring door, sniffing at a room service tray laden with dishes of partially consumed food, her tail flicking back and forth.

"You'd better hope Paisley doesn't catch you," I whisper. "I don't think she'd approve of you sneaking leftovers."

Madeline appraises me with her pale-gold eyes, tilting her furry head to the side in challenge.

"You know it's true." I kneel down and scratch behind her ears. "How did you get up here anyway?"

She purrs and mews in response, an adorable garble of kitty-speak.

"I'm heading back down to the lobby. Why don't you tag along and we'll see about getting you some real dinner?"

Madeline doesn't move and instead resolutely sets her rump down on the floor, her gaze still fixed on me. No stranger to staring contests with cats, I maintain eye contact, narrowing my eyes. A few seconds later, she forfeits, trotting over and rubbing up against my leg in approval.

In case it wasn't obvious: I'm a complete sucker for cats. Even the grouchiest and shyest felines weasel their way into my heart. Just like my cat, Zin, managed to do when I first saw her at the rescue shelter. She'd peeked her furry face out of a play tunnel and, sensing a kindred spirit, immediately claimed me. At least, that's how I see it.

So, even though it will mean long white and gray cat hairs clinging to my ensemble for the rest of the night, I pluck Madeline up. Arms full of cat and winter gear, I continue down the hallway, cooing soothingly.

The elevator door opens into the lobby. Lingering skiers and snowboarders clomp inside, trailing salt and pellets of snow behind them, and parties congregate around the dual fireplaces, deciding what to do for dinner. My group, however, is nowhere to be seen.

"Looks like you have a new friend," Akira says. Her eyes are gleaming behind her wire-rimmed octagonal glasses, and she's dressed in a professional, yet hip, style. Linen collared shirt over a long-sleeved tee, and wide-legged trousers. Her hair is in a high ponytail, highlighting cuff earrings on each ear.

"I found her upstairs outside my room." The subject of our conversation wriggles free and leaps to the floor, proceeding to weave between Akira's legs, a look of pure adoration on her face. "I think she's hungry."

"It is suppertime, huh, girl?" Akira says to Madeline, who mews in response.

"For her and me both."

"Let me get Madeline situated and then I'll walk you to the lounge, where your friends are waiting."

Akira disappears through a door behind the desk fashioned from a tree with Madeline leading, as if her charge might have forgotten the way. She returns a moment later with a scoop of kibble in one hand and a very excited kitty trotting behind her. Madeline wastes no time tucking into her kibble after Akira deposits a generous scoop in the dish next to her plush bed. I can't help but smile, thinking of Zin.

My smile falters as an itch forms between my shoulder blades that has nothing to do with an inconvenient tag. I rub my hand over the back of my neck, goose bumps rising, and glance subtly over my shoulder. The elevator doors have just shut and none of the guests in the vicinity are paying me any attention. And yet, I can't shake the sensation that I'm being watched—studied.

Eyebrows narrowed, I spin on my heel, taking a closer look at my surroundings. But just as quickly as the sensation came, it evaporates.

Still, I'm grateful when Akira returns to my side. I try to shake off my unease as we start toward the lounge, located just off the main dining room.

"I was actually hoping to speak with you," Akira starts.

"About putting a wine order in?" I try to mask the hopefulness in my voice.

"In a sense."

The rustic motif of the rest of the resort continues into the lounge, located next door to the restaurant, antlers interspersed with sepia wildlife photographs adorning the walls. The tables are wooden and full of character, knots, grooves, and interweaving colors of caramel and espresso, and decorated with flickering tea lights and coasters fashioned from trail maps. There's a musky scent—spirits mixed with pine—that suits the atmosphere.

Akira gestures to a secluded corner near a window where Reid, Liam, and Sage are occupying a high-top, but she doesn't proceed into the lounge. "Before we talk business, why don't you pick a bottle of wine." She snags a wine list from the hostess stand and hands it to me. "My treat."

I eye her skeptically, shifting my purse and winter coat to my other arm. "You sure?"

"Absolutely. It's the least I can do."

I peruse the list, not wanting to admit that in my stalking of the lodge prior to our meeting, I'd basically memorized their suppliers. I feign indecision for a moment before saying, "If you insist, I'll take a bottle of the Bend It Red, please."

Akira nods in approval. "Excellent choice. Theirs is one of my favorite blends."

"Mine, too," I say with a wink.

The winery that produces the Bend It Red is Vino Valentine's prime competition in Boulder, and also happens to be owned by my friends Moira and Carrick, an attractive older couple who have turned into quasi-mentors. The fact that they secured Silver Creek's business gave me confidence to go through with my pitch here. That perhaps I could do the same.

Akira presses the tasting menu between her palms. "I have a confession to make."

My ears perk up at the word *confession*. "Oh?"

"The complimentary wine was also to ease the sting

of having to put our order on hold." She purses her lips to the side. "After what happened to Annmarie"—she pauses as sadness flickers in her eyes—"we're temporarily freezing spending."

The blow stings, leaving me numb. My visions of expanding my business, making a name for myself outside of Boulder, evaporate. As if from a distance, I hear myself mumble the words I know I'm supposed to say: "I understand."

"While I loved your mulled wine—and I mean, *loved*—and think it would be a great fit here, everything's up in the air, and no one is sure who's in charge. Silver Creek is in a tither."

"I totally get it," I say. "Really." And this time, I mean it. Honestly, hadn't I suspected our unofficial agreement might be scrapped? Still, nothing about this situation is fair.

"I'll go get your Bend It Red and four glasses," Akira says before striding away.

I continue to the high-top table where my friends are waiting, draping my purse and coat over the back of a barstool next to Reid.

"Everything okay?" he asks, seeing the look on my face.

"Peachy." I force myself to smile, even as my insides are hollowed out. "The round of drinks I owe you guys is on the way."

Liam finishes whatever cocktail he was imbibing, smacking his lips. "Excellent timing."

"Huzzah," Sage says.

"You know you don't have to do that, right?" Reid grips my hand beneath the table.

Of course he isn't fooled by my act. "I know," I say,

the words difficult over the lump rising in my throat. "You really have Akira to thank."

I fiddle with a coaster, tracing a winding blue line across the map with my finger until it abruptly veers to the side and off the laminated cardboard. The Clymen, and its treacherous turn: Lockdown.

"Licorice and strawberries," Sage surmises after taking a swallow of wine.

"Dried cherries and leather," Liam offers.

Both have swirled, sniffed, and swished with such savvy that pride warms my heart. To think, last year neither of them knew their way around a tasting room. I hold a hand over my chest.

"And how exactly do you know what leather tastes like?" Sage challenges. She's in a Sailor Moon hoodie with corduroys tucked into knee-high laced boots.

Liam doesn't miss a beat before responding, "I really was lost before I met you."

Akira chuckles as she finishes pouring me a sizable glass of red wine. The ruby liquid is translucent when held to the light, with thin legs trickling down the sides of the crystal bowl. Familiar aromas of summer berries, vanilla, and tobacco ease the knot in my stomach.

I'm perched next to Reid, who's dapper in a black sweater and forest-green khakis, his hair the perfect kind of disheveled—the kind that makes me want to run my hands through it. I refrain, barely.

"I'll be in touch when the spending freeze is lifted and we know more about the new ownership," Akira says, setting the diminished bottle in the center of the table.

"Or you could suck it up and ask Paisley," Cash says, suddenly appearing beside Akira.

His eyes sparkle playfully as he takes in Akira. The black curls atop his head are fashionably gelled, giving way to the faded sides and the single earring dangling from one lobe. He's in a chef's coat and slacks, a platter with steam rising from it balanced on one hand.

A frown tugs at Akira's lips, her cheeks taking on a rosy hue. "Why would I do that? It's not like she knows more than us."

"For starters, whether we like it or not, she's probably going to take over." He tilts his head and shrugs, but the grim expression on his face betrays his attempt at nonchalance. "For another, don't you think she knows more than you about the business side of things?"

"She likes to think she does," Akira mumbles under her breath.

Cash either doesn't hear her or chooses not to respond, depositing the platter in the center of the table with a flourish.

Liam's and Sage's befuddled expressions mirror my own, keenly aware we didn't order anything, our dinner destination being elsewhere.

"What do we have here?" Reid asks.

"A little something from our family dinner tonight," Cash explains, referencing the meal kitchen staff traditionally prepare prior to evening service. It's usually more free-form, experimental, often resulting in deliciously creative dishes. "Flatbread with roasted root vegetables, winter greens, chèvre, and topped with candied hazelnuts."

"Careful, or the other guests are going to want to order this," Reid says.

Sage shushes him from across the table. "Don't mind my friend here." She flashes Cash a winning smile that has my brother rolling his eyes, already helping herself to a slice. "What he meant to say was, thank you."

No one comes between Sage and free food.

I help myself to a slice of flatbread, savoring the hearty root vegetables, creamy cheese, freshness of the greens, and little pops of sweetness from the hazelnuts. I chase it with a sip of wine, the luscious fruity notes and hint of smoke pairing perfectly.

Through my munching, it doesn't escape my notice that Akira is shooting metaphorical daggers at Cash, and her arms are crossed in a way that tells me she's feeling defensive.

Reid takes a bite, his gaze distant as he chews. "Exceptional. I hope you'll put it on the menu."

"That's the plan." Cash winks, flashing us a half smile. Then he blanches, his voice laced with sarcasm as he continues, "I still can't believe you're abandoning us for Tourist Village."

"Give me more credit than that." Reid brings a hand to his chest in mock pain. "We're going to Cheeky's."

Reid picked the restaurant we're going to tonight, apparently the best dive in town, renowned for their street-style tacos so hot they'll melt you into a puddle of goo. Perfect after a day playing in the snow and ice.

"I take it back." Cash nods in approval. "Wish I could tag along."

"Likewise," Akira says.

"Can we circle back for a minute?" I interject, running my fingertip along the rim of my glass. "You think Paisley is going to take over running Silver Creek?"

I try to picture the sullen-faced woman in charge. She

already seems so out of her element, like a toddler given access to her mother's closet. Either my observational skills aren't up to snuff or the future of Silver Creek is even more dire than I realized.

Sage and Reid lean back in their chairs awaiting a response, clearly as curious as I am. But Liam just shakes his head at me, snagging another slice of flatbread.

"She already does whenever Annmarie is away on business," Cash says. "Plus, she's been gunning for a promotion for ages."

"No matter the cost to herself or others," Akira adds.

Cash squeezes her shoulder but Akira shrugs him off, a silent message passing between them. It's clear Akira is one of the "others" Paisley has used as a stepping-stone. Akira's frustration speaks volumes, especially given how little Annmarie's micromanaging seemed to bother her.

She lets out a shuddering breath. "How was the snow this morning?"

As far as segues go, that was a pitiful attempt. I decide to let her off the hook about Paisley, redirecting my needling, but Liam beats me to the punch.

"It was ideal," he says, shooting me a warning look to back off. "I'll have to get some shots tomorrow." Liam pats his camera bag, stashed at his feet.

Not one to be deterred, I plow forward, staunchly ignoring my brother. "Wouldn't it be up to whoever inherits Silver Creek—Annmarie's family—to decide who would be running the resort?"

If this was some fanciful mystery novel, an estranged family member would emerge, claiming the right to her assets. But this isn't a mystery novel. This is real life. And I'm curious to hear more about Annmarie's history.

"It would be if she had any," Akira says, clinging to

the new conversation topic like legs to a wineglass. "Her parents died in a plane crash, a fluke, when she was a girl, and she doesn't have any siblings that I know of."

The tragic story comes back to me through the foggy veil of time. The media had been obsessed with it during the Winter Olympics Annmarie took part in. They showed childhood photos and repeated the tale as a lead-in to every one of Annmarie's appearances, marveling at her bravery and perseverance. Despite all the attention, she never made any comments on her parents' death.

She'd been brought up by her kind, aging grandmother, who followed the one wish of Annmarie's parents: that she continue skiing.

Cash interrupts my waltz down memory lane. "There's only Boone."

"Boone?" Reid asks, sitting forward, dropping his arm from the back of his chair to his lap. "As in head liftie and grizzly bear?"

"Yeah, he and Annmarie were like this." Cash crosses his fingers to elaborate his point.

Akira jumps in to explain, "I always figured Annmarie saw him as a sort of father figure."

Cash snorts, shaking his head.

"What?" she admonishes. "He's a good listener, and authentic, which she probably needed."

I file that piece of information away for later, pivoting our conversation again. "What about Hudson Gray? Do either of you know him?"

Reid shoots me a questioning glance and I squeeze his hand beneath the table, my way to communicate, *I'll tell you later.* I take a sip of wine to camouflage my heightened interest.

"He's been here a few times in the last couple months," Akira says. "But I couldn't tell you more than that."

"Anyone interested in a poker game?" Cash asks.

"Is that really appropriate?" Akira challenges, moving her hands to her hips. "I mean, I know your weekly game is basically a physical law in your universe but under the circumstances, maybe it should move to tomorrow night."

Hurt dances in Cash's eyes, in the way they turn down at the corners from his frown. "Some of us cope best by being around others, by talking and mourning together." He stands up straighter, dusting a nonexistent speck from his sleeve. "So, the offer stands: Hold'em, twenty-five-dollar buy-in."

"As much as I'd like to take your money, I'm gonna have to pass," Reid says, lifting our clasped hands and bringing them to his lips for a kiss. "I've got other plans."

My face warms.

"We'll pass, too," Sage says. "We've got a season of *Doctor Who* to finish."

"Is that what we're calling it now?" Liam jokes, causing Sage's cheeks to flush the same shade as her hair.

A fire alights in Akira's eyes as she says, "Count me in."

The grin slides from Cash's face, leaving him looking stunned and slightly frightened. Can't say I blame him. Although there's far more to fear at this resort than a poker game.

Chapter Seven

The village looks like something out of a snow globe—rooftops gleam against strands of twinkling lights, giant ice sculptures in the shape of hearts line cobblestone walkways, and interspersed fire pits glow with warmth, their flames licking the moon and stars overhead.

Reid and I stroll with arms linked down the salted sidewalk. We've just finished an exemplary dinner at Cheeky's. It was standing room only in the dive when we first got there, but Reid, having an in with the owner, immediately got us a table.

After sampling nearly every taco on their menu, from carne asada to spicy corn with cotija to shrimp with a citrusy cabbage slaw, the walk is welcome for both my stomach and scorched mouth. Reid wasn't kidding when he said Cheeky's was known for their heat.

"Does it involve chocolate?" I guess. I've been badgering Reid about what his surprise is since we parted ways with Sage and Liam.

"No," Reid says through a low chuckle. His coat is zipped and he's wearing his hat, gloves, and a dapper scarf. He seems so at ease here, navigating between the locals and tourists as if they weren't completely different worlds. "Shocking as it might be, the surprise does not involve food."

A large group coming from the opposite direction makes us scoot closer together. We pass beneath an archway that spills into a roundabout. Behind the snowbank and bordering trees, spotlights shine down on the frozen lake where ice skaters glide in circles, their laughter ringing through the air.

"Are we going ice-skating?" I venture.

He just shakes his head, a smirk playing on his lips.

I grip his arm tighter. *See*, I tell myself, *you can do this. Be romantic—be normal.*

We turn and suddenly I stop in my tracks, a sharp exhale of breath sending swirls of fog around my face. Because parked curbside is a horse-drawn carriage.

The sleigh is deep maroon with four rows and a perch for the driver. The other passengers—mostly couples, with one family—are already cozy in their seats beneath plaid, fleece blankets. Two massive chestnut Clydesdales shift in their bridles.

"You didn't."

"I did." He leans in and deposits a light kiss on my cheek, whispering in my ear, "But there's more."

He greets the driver and nary a minute later, we're tucked into the last seats in the carriage and off at a brisk pace. The clopping of hooves and jingle of bridle bells serenade us as we cruise along a narrow snow-packed frontage road. It runs parallel to the skating rink before zigzagging up the mountain. The temperature drops the higher we climb, making me pull the fleece blanket up to my chin and snuggle close to Reid. Dense pine trees line either side of the road and there are so many twists and turns, it's impossible to tell where we're going.

Despite my initial reservations, excitement and curiosity course through me. I haven't thought about Annmarie, murder, or the loss of Aunt Laura and our bygone traditions. Only, I totally just did. *Ugh.*

I refocus on Reid, determined to be the Valentine he deserves. "You know, this is going to wreck your bad-boy reputation."

He adjusts his knit cap and wraps an arm around me. "Eh, it was on its way out anyway."

I cock an eyebrow at him. "Really? So what was with the tattoo you got last month?"

"Had to commemorate the occasion."

The "occasion" he's referring to is the wild success of his restaurant, Spoons, which he honored with a tiny image of a ladle—identical to the ones used as handles to the doors of his establishment—on the inside of his wrist.

He continues, "Besides, I thought you liked my tattoos."

"Oh, you know I have no qualms with your ink." I pat his forearm where, among oven-burn scars, are impressive designs celebrating his passions for cooking and music.

Honestly, I've considered getting a tattoo myself. Something small and tasteful and of the feline variety, probably on the outside of my ankle, where Zin likes to trip me up. But I haven't taken the plunge yet.

The carriage slows to a stop in the middle of nowhere and the driver glances meaningfully at Reid.

Reid nods, hops off, and offers me his hand. In the middle of nowhere.

I look from side to side, gripping the blanket with white knuckles. "Um, I don't think we're there yet."

The other passengers eye us curiously, a couple muttering under their breath.

"Come on, Parks, where's your sense of adventure?" Reid asks, flashing me a roguish wink.

And despite my apprehension, frozen fingertips, and the fact that there's a killer at large, I take his outstretched hand and follow him into the unknown.

The snow is so deep it reaches the tops of my boots. I follow in Reid's footprints, prancing like a very awkward deer through the pine trees, their branches skeletal in the pale moonlight. I'd hate to think how complete the darkness would be if the moon weren't full. Sounds of the wilderness surround us: wood creaking, snow tumbling from foliage, and a howling on the wind.

A shiver snakes up my spine, making my teeth chatter. It'd be enough to set anyone on edge.

"How much farther?" I ask, my voice shaky.

"Having a hard time keeping up?" Reid goads.

Damn my pride, and Reid's intimate knowledge of it.

"Hardly." I press forward, keeping my complaints—and worries—mum as we march through the forest.

Gotta hand it to Reid, his surprise is proving to be an adventure, much like life with him. An adventure I'm keen to continue.

The cold closes in around me, even more chilling after the warmth of the blanket. We fall into a steady rhythm, our footfalls keeping to the same inaudible beat.

There are layers to the snow, a crust on top that yields to powder beneath, much like cracking into a ramekin of crème brûlée. Only this metaphorical custard will freeze rather than sustain.

My thoughts drift to Annmarie in her final moments. Did she feel a stab of fear before she died or was she lulled into contentment, the snow and fragrance of pine and frost like home to her? Did she get a look at who killed her? Recognize the individual who betrayed her? I recall the way her eye twitched during our brief meeting, an unmistakable sign of stress and exhaustion; is it possible she felt threatened, suspected she was in danger?

The shadow I'd seen and the shout I'd heard reel through my mind until I find myself glancing over my shoulder.

That had to have been the killer. They'd been so close, and yet I'd observed so little. How did they do it? Take down an Olympian at her pièce de résistance? With so many eyes watching, to boot?

Reid navigates around a tree trunk and I do the same, gripping the rough tree bark for balance, my lungs aching from the frigid air.

It was the turn—Lockdown Pass, an eerily apt name. Annmarie had been out of sight for a split second, just long enough for the murderer to make their move. They had to have known which specific run she would be on, and the exact spot to take her down.

That thought alone, so primal and brutal, is enough to make my blood run cold.

I let Reid's silhouette, the sound of our boots squelching in the snow, and the scents of pine trees and sap ground me.

Voices reach my ears, high-pitched cries that make

me worry my subconscious has manifested into a full-fledged nightmare.

That is, until Reid says, "Almost there." He snags a tree branch and pulls it aside for me, almost like a gentleman holding a door open. "After you."

I nod at him in thanks and traipse through, a nervous laugh bubbling out of me. I stumble out of the underbrush and come to a stop at the top of a hill, stunned. I'm not sure what I expected, but it certainly wasn't this.

Night tubing. That's the surprise.

I can't contain the grin that spreads across my face. The mountainside below us is doused with pinks, turquoises, and violets, like luminescent tie-dye from spotlights overhead. Grooved trenches are etched into the mountainside, creating distinct lanes for sledding. The voices I heard were nothing but the cheers and hollers of merry sledders.

Reid glances at me, his expression unusually vulnerable as he tilts his head to the side. "Since this is an experience, I figured it doesn't technically count as a gift." He closes the distance between us, his footing uneven among the piles of snow.

"That's some loophole." I lift my chin to look at him. The cosmic lighting casts us in a surreal glow, accentuating Reid's sculpted cheekbones and faint stubble.

"I wanted to do something for our first Valentine's Day together." He takes my gloved hands in his, heat traveling through the layers of fabric. "Because I love you."

That's when it hits me: this is a big deal for Reid.

Reid was a perpetual bachelor before we met. Which

means there's a decent chance he's never had a Valentine to celebrate this holiday with. And now I feel like garbage. Worse than garbage. Like wasted grape skins that no longer add anything to a batch of wine and, in fact, have the potential to ruin everything. Even being consumed with my own baggage, I should have recognized this.

"You still with me, Parks?" Reid shifts, his jacket crinkling.

"Of course," I manage to say, my throat dry. "I love you, too."

He brushes his lips over mine. They're cold and hot all at the same time, and send a jolt of electricity through my body. I pull him into a deeper embrace, letting the world fall away as our mouths move together in delicious harmony. The chemistry between us has always been there—has always just worked. But right now, it's not enough to calm the waves of guilt and anxiety roaring in my mind.

I pull away abruptly. "I—I didn't get you anything, didn't think to do anything for you. And you did all this." I wave back toward where the sleigh dropped us off and then toward the hill ahead. "I completely suck. I'm the worst."

For an instant, the spark in Reid's eyes diminishes, replaced with unmistakable hurt. If only I'd heeded Liam's warning last night, I could have cobbled something together. A shoddy homemade card would have been better than nothing.

Reid recovers quickly and tries to brush it off. "You're not the worst, and you definitely don't suck."

I lick my lips, desperate to help heal the hurt I've caused, even if it means peeling back layers of my own skin. “Look, there’s something you should know.” I pause, bracing myself for the words.

“You don’t have to explain anything, Parks,” Reid says, wrapping an arm around my shoulders. “Really, I just want for us to enjoy ourselves tonight. Unless you’re embarrassed about your tubing skills.”

I rock forward on the balls of my feet, the truth I both want and don’t want to share thick on my tongue. And then I hesitate, swallowing the words.

“Bring it,” I say with a small smile, because what else am I supposed to do?

I trail my fingers down the side of his face until my palm is resting over his heart. His disappointment lingers in my psyche like a bad aftertaste, but silently I vow to make it up to Reid, starting with not telling my sob story and bungling the fun he planned.

We walk in tandem to where the giant inner tubes are stacked at the top of the hill. The slope is more forgiving than those for skiing and snowboarding, ending in an open area that gently flattens, allowing sledders to come to a gradual stop near a magic carpet that will carry them to the top for another go.

And far below is Silver Creek. It appears so small, insignificant compared to the enduring mountain peaks rising around us. The bridge over the river for which the village is named glimmers with lampposts, and the restaurants and hotels glow warmly. Barely visible to our right are the runs open for night skiing.

“You know your way around here pretty well,” I muse, casting a glance back the way we came. No doubt there were more direct ways to get here, but Reid’s always been one to take the less-traveled path.

"The trails are all connected around here, if you know the way."

"Which you clearly do. From your time working here?"

"Sure, it's part of the culture. Even working in the kitchen, I spent a lot of time that winter exploring the backcountry."

We select tubes from the nearest pile, red for me and blue for Reid. The rubber is thick and the diameter so wide as to be unwieldy. We drag them behind us to a relatively quiet lane, leaving matching depressions in our wake.

"Together or separate?" Reid asks, pulling me back to the present. He raises his eyebrows, holding up a bungee cord we can use to connect our two tubes.

There's only one answer: "Together."

The anticipation makes me giddy as we climb onto our respective sleds, nudge ourselves right at the edge, and then count down.

"Three, two, one."

We tip forward and go down, down, down. The wind whips our faces and I emit a loud *squee.*

Maneuvered by the grooves in our lane, our tubes spin around. I catch Reid's eye and he mirrors my goofy grin. In that moment, I experience a surge of pure joy. From the stars and neon lights overhead, the crisp mountain air filling our lungs, and the sheer fun and innocence of this activity. But above all, it's that I'm here with Reid.

My smile falters and Reid's does the same. Snow passes beneath us, bumpy and uneven. The bungee holding our tubes together is taught with tension. We make it to the bottom still attached, but only just.

Snow is like a map of what has happened since the initial storm. Animal or human footprints, tire tracks, snow angels—every indentation tells a story. And there's no going back to the pristine sparkle after snow has been tampered with. No matter how hard someone might try, there will always be marks.

Like the ones made by this tube and, more important, the ones around Annmarie.

Two things become crystal clear: Someone tried to change the story of what happened to Annmarie—either by covering up their tracks, or hers. And whoever that was has an impressive knowledge of the mountain.

My muscles positively sing as I sink into the Jacuzzi later. It's been a marathon of a day. From naively taking on the slopes and witnessing Annmarie's murder to chatting with the sheriff and fighting with Liam to dinner on the town followed by surprise night tubing, it's no wonder my mind is as drained as my body.

Hot water laps at my neck and steam swirls around me, the temperatures between the surface and open air in stark contrast. The Jacuzzi is located on the rooftop patio of our hotel, surrounded by a slated privacy wall, heat lamps, and a breathtaking view of the night sky.

I let out a contented sigh. "I'm never leaving."

Reid pokes me in the side. "That so?"

If Reid can manage to look attractive in baggy snow gear, there's no way to describe him in a swimsuit. His toned abs are on full display, corded arms with their sleeve tattoos glisten with water droplets, and green eyes spark mischievously. Basically I can't look directly at him for fear of drooling.

"We could totally live here," Sage says from across the way. She and Liam were already near-prune when we got here. My brother soaks away the scant amount of stress in his life, our disagreement from earlier tabled in lieu of relaxing. And Sage, legitimately in need of letting her hair down, has done just that, her strawberry-blond locks bobbing around her shoulders.

I raise my foot to give her a high five. "Roomies again?"

Sage and I met when we were assigned as roommates freshmen year of college at CU Boulder. There were plenty of nightmarish cohabitation situations, but I'd hit the jackpot. We were polar opposites in our educational pursuits, styles, and hobbies, and yet we shared a perspective of the world that allowed us to understand each other, to be there for each other through thick and thin. Which remains intact today.

Sage taps my foot with hers. "I'll negotiate the lease."

Liam maneuvers himself onto the ledge of the tub, steam wafting from his body. His hair is slicked back and, while he usually gives off a carefree vibe, it's nice to see him genuinely happy. "I'm not sure you two realize the sort of dedication required for constant relaxing." He presses his hands together in front of him and bows. "Don't worry, I'll show you the way."

"Much as I approve of this idea," Reid says, pouring water from one palm to the other, "I'm not sure how Zin would feel."

I think of her pawing at the water curiously, her ear with the tip missing twitching, and smile softly. "Guess I'll have to settle for visiting."

Sage points vaguely around her, her blue eyes twinkling. "A mini fridge there, a desk over there."

"A desk," Liam scoffs. "Now you've taken this too

far. Come on, Bennet, that *Doctor Who* finale won't watch itself."

In a gentlemanly move, my brother takes on the frigid breeze to retrieve his and Sage's fluffy towels. After she hops out, he wraps it around her shoulders with such tenderness, I avert my eyes.

"See ya," Liam says with a salute.

"We'll continue planning my new digs tomorrow," Sage says.

They hurry inside with their teeth chattering, the fogged glass door clicking shut behind them.

"Finally," Reid says, scooting closer, the thin fabric of his trunks brushing my thigh. "I thought they'd never leave."

I turn so we're facing each other. "I thought you liked them."

"Sure, it's just that I can't do this in front of your brother." Reid leans in and places a lingering kiss on my cheek. "Or this." My pulse hitches as his lips graze my neck.

"Good point."

With steam swirling around us, I take his face in my hands and kiss him properly. Our lips meet and it's as if the remaining tension leaves my body. We melt into each other, our arms entangled and the taste of him a glorious palate on my tongue.

That's when I hear it: the telltale click of the dead bolt.

I pull away, startled, my eyes darting around. I can't make sense of the darkness and shadows through the curls of steam. "Did you hear that?"

"Hear what?" Reid follows my gaze.

"The door." I try to keep the panic from my voice. "I think it might be locked."

Reid frowns, his eyebrows furrowing together, his hair in utter disarray. Without a word, he heaves himself out of the tub, dripping water that will soon turn to ice onto the deck. He tugs on the door handle and when it doesn't budge, holds his hands around his face to peer inside. "There's someone in there."

Hope swells in my chest like champagne bubbles.

"Hey, let us in!" Reid shouts, banging a fist against the door. "There are still people out here!"

There's no response.

After one final bang, Reid inspects the entrance while I scan the vicinity looking for an intercom or something that might help us call for help since both of our phones are floors below in our room. It's no use. The patio is annoyingly devoid of any connection to the rest of the world and perched atop so many stories the only way down is through the steadfast door.

Rubbing his arms, Reid jogs back to the warmth of the Jacuzzi. His entire body is covered in goose bumps and his lips are pale from the cold.

Silence presses in around us and my anxiety ticks up a notch. "What are we gonna do?"

Reid drapes an arm over my shoulder and kisses my forehead. "Don't worry, Parks. There are worse places to be stuck."

Right, sure, I think to myself, *worse places like . . .* only, none come to mind. Because this is bad. Very bad. I tell myself to remain calm even as dread chips away at my resolve.

I nuzzle into Reid, yearning for an iota of his optimism. Surely someone from the hotel will come close the rooftop patio for the night, make sure the lid is secure, and no belongings were left behind. I feel myself start to relax. Until then, Reid and I have each other and the breadth of the Colorado sky overhead to enjoy.

Then the power goes out and we're plunged into complete darkness.

Chapter Eight

In winemaking, there's a process called cold soaking. Essentially, grapes are purposely kept at a temperature too low for fermentation so that colors and flavors can be extracted without tannins. It works well for varietals like pinot noir, merlot, or Syrah. You know what cold soaking doesn't work well for? Me.

The heat lamps are dark and the hum of the Jacuzzi pump is ominously missing. A gust of wind chills my damp hair and I dunk deeper in the water so it covers my chin.

While my understanding of thermodynamics is primarily limited to viticulture, even I know we're in a precarious situation. Without electricity, the heat of the water will transfer to the air, effectively turning the Jacuzzi into an ice cube and us into human Popsicles.

"Don't worry," Reid says. "The backup generator will kick on in a minute."

Knots unravel in my stomach, the sensation of impending doom lightening. I nod, my chin dipping in the water. But one minute passes, and then another, and the power remains out. To be sure, I count to sixty in my head, silently reciting *hippopotamus* between each number. Still, nothing happens.

"Why isn't the generator coming on?" I ask.

"I don't know." Reid clenches his jaw.

The lack of lights at our hotel enhances those in the surrounding village. The yellow luminescence of the shops and restaurants transition into a pale glow of muted blues and greens of the moon and stars overhead. Which brings something to my attention.

"Why did the power only go out here?" I ask.

Reid's eyes are wide with panic, his brow dotted with condensation. "It can't have been because of the weather. It's a clear night, and that would've impacted the whole village."

"Maybe that means it'll come back on soon." Or maybe that means we're done for. The hotel staff will be too busy to check the roof now. "Did this ever happen when you worked here?"

"Never."

I breathe in through my nose and out through my mouth, releasing bubbles in the otherwise still water. Then I turn my attention to Reid, who, apart from succumbing to panic, is looking around for something to get us out of this mess.

"The heat will stay in longer if we put the lid on, at least partway," he says, nodding toward where the hot tub cover is resting against the privacy wall.

"I'll help," I say. "We should try to get someone's attention, too."

On the other side of the cover is an open railing overlooking the village. I figure, if we're going to freeze our bums off, we might as well see what's happening on the street below.

"Ready?" Reid asks.

There's no reason to prolong the inevitable so I nod.

I follow Reid up the stairs, the fabric of my swimsuit suctioning to my skin. The air is so cold it almost feels like a physical punch. I let out a hiss that would make Zin proud and hug my arms to my chest, dancing on my tiptoes.

From the ledge, we have a view of the entirety of Silver Creek. It's odd to see people still going about their lives—dining, sneaking in final runs, or congregating around the warmth of fire pits—while we're in such a tizzy.

"Help!" I shout, and then remember the word that's more effective in garnering attention: "Fire!"

My voice is desperate and screechy and not enough. Beside me, Reid adds his shouts to mine and together, I feel a surge of hope that perhaps someone might hear our cries. Goose bumps coat my bare arms and legs, and my hair hardens into icicles.

Finally, we're rewarded with a response. It's so faint I have to strain my ears to make sense of the sounds traveling back to me. And it's howls of partygoers. Because they think Reid and I are boisterous partyers having a blast up here.

We try again. "Send help! We're stuck up here! Fire!"

But our yells are only met with more howls.

Frustration and fear roil in my bloodstream until it's

impossible to know if I'm shaking from adrenaline or the cold.

"Come on, Parks, let's conserve our body heat." Reid takes my hand and pulls me away from the metal railing.

We each take an end of the Jacuzzi cover. It's light but a cumbersome rectangular shape with slippery grips. Between the two of us we're able to maneuver it onto the hot tub, despite the shivers making us twitch uncontrollably.

I practically leap back into the water, my pulse rising, with Reid hot on my heels. I could cry in relief, even as needlelike pinpricks tingle in my fingers and toes.

Reid's gaze is appraising. "Okay?"

"O-okay," I stammer.

He tugs the lid farther on so it's more secure and almost covering the entirety of the tub. We're wedged in a corner, huddled together, our breath mingling in swirls, which isn't nearly as romantic as it sounds.

"We'll just stay like this until . . ." Reid trails off, grazing his thumb over my cheek.

"Until we need to hide under the cover," I supplement, not wanting to vocalize my fear.

The corner of Reid's lips twitch into the ghost of a smile. "Yeah."

"At least we're together. Usually when I'm in a life-threatening situation, I'm alone."

He snorts and leans his head back, rolling his neck to the side to face me. "If we were going to be in danger this weekend, you'd think it'd have been when we were flying down a mountain on a piece of plastic, not lounging in a sauna."

I can't help the laugh that escapes my throat, nor the

way Reid and I descend into giggles, feeding off each other in a slaphappy delirium.

The door to the hotel opens and both Reid and I turn so fast we bonk heads. I shield my eyes from the intense brightness of a flashlight, hiccuping from the bout of laughter, eager to see our rescuer.

That's when the power finally comes back on, illuminating Sage in the doorway. "Am I interrupting something?"

I can't be certain, but I'm pretty sure a hairpin saved my life. A blue lightsaber bobby pin, to be exact.

We're just inside the hotel door, Reid and me drying off with our towels, rubbing warmth back into our limbs. Sage is in a hoodie, leggings, and Uggs, her prized accessory clutched in one hand and a flashlight in the other.

"I can't believe you came all the way back up here for that," Reid says to Sage, shaking his head in wonderment.

"Hey, it's a collector's item," Sage says defensively. "Besides, I didn't come *just* for that. I came to make sure you guys were okay with the power outage."

"And it's a good thing you did," I say.

I can't even think about what would've happened if my friend had waited until morning to search for her missing hairpin or left us in the dark.

"Did you see anyone on your way up?" Reid asks. He cranes his neck to search both directions of the hallway.

There's nothing but an unmarked door—probably some sort of maintenance or storage room—elevators, and the stairwell. The lights flicker ominously overhead but remain on.

Sage frowns, lines forming between her eyebrows. "No. Who was I supposed to see?"

"Someone locked us out." Reid shifts his focus, casting me a meaningful look. "After what happened to Annmarie, we need to tell the sheriff."

This takes me aback. I wrap my towel around me like a cape, my teeth still chattering. "They must have thought the roof was empty. It was a fluke, completely unrelated to Annmarie."

"I saw someone inside when I was banging on the door," Reid argues. "Whoever it was had to have heard me and did nothing. Then the power went out for no apparent reason."

Dread seeps through my veins, leaving me feeling shaken and exposed. I'd been too consumed with panic to consider the possibility this wasn't random. That perhaps we were targeted. My skin crawls at the thought.

I look from my boyfriend, whose face is uncharacteristically serious and, even worse, scared, to my friend, whose attention is peculiarly fixed on the ceiling. Sage paces the length of the hallway, her freckles standing out against her pale skin, her eyes taking in every detail overhead.

"Missing another hairpin?" I ask.

"No, checking for cameras." Sage shakes her head, her lips downturned as if she'd just lost a significant case. "Too much to hope for, I suppose."

"Good thought." I give her hand a squeeze. And suddenly, I can't be in this hallway, in nothing but my swimsuit, for another second. "Let's get out of here."

With a promise to text Sage with an update, Reid and

I head back to our room. I change into the coziest clothes I packed, all layered together—long underwear, sweats, wool socks, CU Buffs hoodie, and even a fleece jacket. I'll be roasting in no time, but the fear of freezing is still too raw.

Reid dresses much more reasonably, donning a pair of jeans, flannel shirt, and unlaced boots. He perches on the end of the bed. "I'll make the call if you want."

It's a tempting offer since, like most millennials, I have an aversion to the telephone. You'd think owning a business would have forced me to overcome this quirk but honestly, it remains an uncomfortable part of the job for me.

I exhale as I take a seat next to him, tucking a loose strand of hair behind my ear. "Thanks, but it should be me. The sheriff will remember me." Which might not be a point in my favor.

The duvet is so soft and cushy, it morphs to my body like a marshmallow. All I want to do is sink into the folds and pretend this day never happened. Instead, I search for the phone number to the sheriff's office and, given my cell service is patchy here at best, dial it into the hotel's receiver.

"Summit Sheriff's Office," an efficient voice answers.

"Yeah, hi, I need to talk to Sheriff Scott?" It comes out like a question, like I have no idea what I need. Which isn't far from the truth.

"What is the reason for your call?"

Where to start, I muse. Reid drapes an arm around my shoulders and I flash him a grateful smile.

"I'm a guest at Silver Creek and talked to Sheriff Scott earlier about Annmarie Bauer's accident, or non-accident, as the case may be." I chuckle nervously and get on with it. "Anyway, something just happened that I think she'd want to know about."

Thankfully, the dispatch lady needs no further convincing. "Can you give me your location and contact information in case we get disconnected?"

"Room 408 at Silver Creek Lodge, and my number is 303-555-8542."

"Please hold."

I fiddle with the zipper of my hoodie and mouth to Reid, *On hold.*

A minute later, the lady returns. "Sheriff Scott is on the premises and will meet you in the lobby."

"Perfect," I answer. "We'll head down there now."

Despite the late hour, the lobby is hopping with guests milling about the game room, loitering near the lounge, and coming or going from the village. There's a charged energy in the air, as if some sort of benign current was released through the space when the electricity came back on.

The buzz of laughter and chatter is the embodiment of revelry. I can't help but feel a pang of envy. That was supposed to be me this weekend, dammit. Instead, I'm seeking out the sheriff for the second time today.

I give Reid's hand an extra squeeze, a signal for him to stay by my side. From the steeliness in his gaze, he's not going anywhere. My heart swells and then shrivels with shame. The emotions are too much, like trying to swirl a glass of wine filled to the brim.

There's a fire crackling in the dual fireplace and I tug on Reid's arm. We drift toward it. In the chair closest to the fire is Madeline. She lifts her furry head as I draw near, the flames reflected in her pale-gold eyes. She emits a satisfied purr as I pet her with my free hand. My throat constricts at how badly I wish I could snuggle with my own kitty, who never fails to make me feel better.

"Have you seen the sheriff?" I coo at Madeline. "Because I don't see her anywhere. No, I don't."

Reid flashes me a bemused smile. He talks plenty to his own cat in various voices, so has no room to mock.

Madeline mews in response and I give her ear one last scratch.

Sage and Liam emerge from the archway that leads to the dining room, each carrying two ceramic mugs. Sage hands me one of the mugs and I breathe in the wafting steam, the aroma floral and soothing.

"Chamomile?" Reid asks after Liam passes him a mug. "Really, man? Couldn't you find anything stronger?"

"Blame this one," Liam says, nudging Sage with his shoulder. "She said it would be calming." Liam turns his attention to me. "You okay, sis?"

All jibing and bickering aside, Liam has always viewed himself as my protector, and I catch the spark of retribution in his eyes now. We may not agree on everything—or anything, really—but when push comes to shove, he's got my back. Just like I've got his.

Not wanting to worry him even more, I force a smile on my face. "Just be glad you two left when you did."

"I tried to warn you: relaxing is serious business." Liam slips his free hand into the pocket of his joggers, his shoulders hunched forward. A shadow darkens his features. "It wasn't all sunshine inside, either. After the power'd been out for a while, I came down here to see what was going on and that lady at the front desk basically drop-kicked me for even asking."

"Paisley?" I surmise.

He grunts in the affirmative.

"She's in the wrong profession if that's how she treats guests," Sage says, rubbing my brother's arm reassuringly.

"Too true," I say.

I hear Sheriff Jenny before I see her. She's chatting animatedly with Cash, strolling from the direction of the dining room. "Akira cleaned you out good." She chuckles, no doubt referring to the infamous poker game we'd been invited to.

"Don't remind me." Cash exaggerates a wince, pulling a knit cap over his curls. "I've gotta go lick my wounds."

Jenny snorts. "She'll take more than that if you're not careful."

"What are you going on about now?"

"Oh, nothing."

Cash shakes his head as he shrugs on his winter jacket over his chef's coat. "Next week, can you please not grill my players? Puts a damper on the whole scene."

"Part of the job." She claps Cash on the shoulder and continues, with a wink, "As is this." She strides over to where we're congregated as Cash disappears into the night.

Even though Jenny has presumably had a very long day, she appears just as energetic and capable as when we spoke this morning. Her hair is slightly more disheveled, and her coat is draped over one arm, showcasing her khaki sheriff's uniform and gleaming gold badge.

"I'm glad you're still here," I say by way of a greeting.

"Parker." She takes in me and my posse, an amused

expression on her face. "Fortunately, I was here for another matter."

"The poker game?" I ask.

"That, and a reported theft." She leans her hip against the chair, not blinking twice at the cat in the lobby. "It seems that someone saw the power outage as an opportunity to help themselves to a tennis bracelet. Although my guess is it'll turn up on the wrist of the husband's mistress." She shoots us a look that tells us she's not entirely kidding. "I'd keep your rooms locked if I were you."

I think back to the lady I overheard chewing out Paisley for jewelry that was supposedly missing from her room. At first, I'd dismissed the lady, but now I wonder if there's something to her claim. And if it's possible the thefts are related to Annmarie's murder.

"A murderer and a thief," Liam interjects. "This will definitely ding my Tripadvisor review."

Jenny regards him coolly. "Don't judge Silver Creek by all this," she says, gesturing broadly. "We're really a good town."

I see the pride in her eyes; the rush to defend her hometown makes sense. I feel the same way about Boulder.

She brushes a wisp of hair off her cheek. "But you didn't call me for my two cents on local accommodations."

Hastily, I make introductions, ending with Reid. "Reid was with me when it all went down."

"And what exactly *went down*?"

With Sage and Liam offering their silent support, Reid and I take turns explaining about getting locked on the roof, seeing someone in the hallway, and the electricity then going out. To her credit, Jenny listens attentively to every word, pulling her notebook out at one point to jot a thought down.

"If it hadn't been for my friend, I hate to think how long we would've been stuck up there. Or what might've happened."

After we grow quiet, Jenny scratches her nose and shuts her notebook. "Honestly, it doesn't sound malicious to me. It sounds like you two were in the wrong place at the wrong time."

After what happened to Annmarie—what I'd witnessed—this doesn't sit well in my gut. I chew on my bottom lip.

Reid isn't satisfied, either, which is surprising, since being overly suspicious is usually my MO. "It doesn't seem like too much of a coincidence to you?"

"Not with Valentine's Day being this weekend. Resorts are always nutty around holidays. But I want you to call me if anything else comes up." She pulls a card from her cell phone case. "Here's my direct line."

The sheriff's calm centers me, gives me a small piece of my composure back. Enough to realize that with Annmarie's killer at large, I'll always be looking over my shoulder, wondering what—or who—could be lurking around the next bend. And there won't always be a hairpin to save me.

Chapter Nine

When tragedy strikes, society has this pesky inclination to return to normal, even if *normal* is no longer achievable. Such is the state of Silver Creek the next morning.

The café, sporting-goods shop, and runs are open, the chairlifts rotating in their constant cycle while visitors queue up for tickets. The mountain, of course, remains unchanged, reaching toward the majestic blue sky, as it's done before us and will continue to do long after us.

But that's where the normalcy ends.

The resort is ridiculously crowded, even for a Saturday. Cars are already being directed into overflow lots as swarms of people pour in from every direction. They're sporting Bauer Power T-shirts over their jackets; red, white, and blue accessories; and waving tiny Olympic flags in Annmarie's honor.

It's as if she transcended from legend to myth.

I shouldn't be surprised. I'd checked this morning to find *#BauerPower* still trending online. There are headlines galore, tugging at the heartstrings as they recount Annmarie's life, her woes and triumphs, and how she died too young doing something she loved. There was only one article that referenced her passing being under investigation in Summit County, the briefest hint that maybe, just maybe, there was more to her accident.

Soon, other news sources will follow suit and sniff out the story. I can't even imagine what sort of circus will descend on this quaint village when that happens.

To be honest, I'm not in the mood to strap on skis. But it was either this or mope around the hotel room, oscillating between sorrow, self-pity, and lingering stress from the Jacuzzi debacle. So here I am. Bright-eyed and bushy-tailed thanks to the copious amounts of coffee I consumed at breakfast.

Reid doesn't share my misgivings about today, wanting to make the most of our time here and, I suspect, to pay homage to Annmarie in his own way.

Reid, Liam, Sage, and I cross the bridge over Silver Creek, the water bubbling despite the thick layers of ice and snow coating each bank.

I find myself jostled by the parade of mourners, dodging stray ski poles and unwieldy snowboards. By the time we get to the end of the significant chairlift line, I'm twitchy and grouchy and about ready to call it quits.

Reid must sense my unease, because he waves for us to follow him. "I know a guy."

Envious eyes drill into us as we bypass the line, squelching in our boots along the outside of the zigzagging rope and cones. Reid continues past where the chairlift rotates through the pulley system and continues to the adjacent bungalow.

The door is open a crack, allowing the crisp air and sunshine to pour in. Reid knocks on the doorframe.

"Told ya I'm on my coffee break," Boone growls, swiveling around in his chair, thermos in hand. It's clear we've interrupted a private moment. He wipes at the corners of his eyes, but not before I see glistening traces of tears.

Then I remember that Boone and Annmarie had been close. How, as unlikely as it might seem, he was the nearest thing to family she had. Perhaps she was the same to him.

And suddenly I feel terrible for intruding on his space and time to—what?—cut in line. Shame sets my cheeks ablaze.

When Boone registers our—mostly Reid's—presence, his lined face breaks into a lopsided smirk that, with his slumped shoulders and elongated sigh, comes across as unbearably sad. "Missed you last night, Maverick."

"That so?" Reid asks, the catch in his voice suggesting he's as aware as I am of our imposition.

"Aye," Boone says, sounding distinctly pirate-esque. "You might've stood a shot against that wine chick."

I recall the words I'd overheard last night between Jenny and Cash. Apparently Cash wasn't the only one Akira cleaned out during the poker game. I stifle a grin, silently cheering for Akira. *You get yours, girl.*

"Akira did well, then?" I ask.

"Beginner's luck." He tries for good humor but dips his chin.

While words sometimes feel empty and like they

can't begin to alleviate the pain of grief and loss, they can at least let someone know they're not alone.

"We're all so sorry for what happened to Annmarie." I shake my head and swallow, momentarily overwhelmed. "You have my condolences."

Boone nods in thanks, his face grim. His hand trembles and there's a beat where I fear he might completely break down; I wouldn't blame him. Beneath his scraggly beard, he works his jaw back and forth.

"I still can't believe it," Reid adds, resting his chin on the top of his board. "Annmarie seemed so . . . infallible."

"It's a damn shame." Boone sniffs, rubbing his nose with the sleeve of his shirt. "If I ever find out who did this, there'll be hell to pay."

"Did the sheriff talk to you?" I ask, even as Liam digs his ski pole into the back of my calf. I shoot him a dirty look over my shoulder, rubbing my leg. Just because he doesn't want me to investigate doesn't mean he has to leave a bruise.

"Sure," Boone says, resigned. "Jenny questioned everyone, said it was routine. She was especially interested in the chairlift rotation, who was working where and at what times. I told her all that's on the schedule."

"Was anyone not at their post yesterday?"

Boone pierces me with his blue eyes, clear and undiluted like the Colorado sky. "It's my job to keep the young pups in line. If one of them wasn't—which I'm not saying they weren't—it'd be on me as much as them."

So, I'll take that to mean yes. But who? I scan the inside of the shed for a hint. It's minimalistic, like a cross between an office and a break room. There are controls for the chairlift—nobs, levers, buttons, and receivers. A color-coded wall calendar, lists of rules, and emergency phone numbers line the walls. A microwave and hot plate rest on top of a mini refrigerator. But no handy list of employees.

"Your bark really is worse than your bite," Reid says. "Don't worry, we won't tell."

Sage and Liam shift behind us, Liam's pole bumping into my calf again, not on accident. I shuffle forward to give him more space.

"I don't want to get anyone in trouble." I swish words around in my mind, evaluating their poignancy and flavor. "I want to figure out what happened to Annmarie, to get her the justice she deserves." *Before anyone else gets hurt.*

Boone's chest heaves, my words bringing him both hope and pain. "Micah Bugrov," he concedes huskily. "New kid. Still figuring out how things work. He was having a tough time, so I relieved him early."

The letters of that name sear into my mind: Micah Bugrov.

"But that's not why y'all stopped by." Boone coughs and clears his throat, shifting his focus to Reid. "You here for what I think you're here for?"

"The lines are awfully long," Reid says sheepishly, adjusting his knit cap.

"Punk," Boone grumbles, but then gets to his feet. He grabs his red coat from the back of his chair. "Come on, then."

As I lift my skis and make to turn around, something catches my attention. There, on a table on the far side of the small space, among papers and a lost-and-found basket containing mostly ear warmers and single gloves, is an empty wine bottle.

I immediately recognize the Vino Valentine logo—crisscrossing grapevines punctuated by the sun. It must be the bottle of Snowy Day Syrah I gifted Annmarie, but what it's doing here, I can't even begin to guess.

"See something you like?" Boone asks, towering over me.

"No," I say quickly, and realize I'm blocking the doorway. "I'll just . . ." I trail off, gesturing behind me. I back up, cursing my clumsiness with my ski boots and bulky equipment.

Boone clicks the door shut and stomps past. "Good. Now, let's see about getting you four on the mountain."

If your friends jump off a cliff, will you blindly follow them? This question has plagued parents and adolescent children for ages. The answer for me today is embarrassingly: yes.

Despite my better inclinations, when my friends suggested we do the Turin, an intermediate blue that should probably be classified as a black, I found myself agreeing.

And now here I am, perched at the top of what can best be described as an icy cliff. Liam and Sage are already speeding their way down, Liam swishing back and forth on his skis and Sage gracefully carving the trail with the nose of her snowboard at a breakneck pace.

"You sure about this?" Reid asks, his goggles resting on top of his helmet. "We can do an easier run. It'll be more relaxed that way."

My heart is hammering in my chest and I swallow the lump in my throat. "No, this will be fine." At least I hope it will.

Because I saw the spark enter Reid's eyes when Liam

pointed to this run on the map, at the promise of a thrill. And the last thing I want, especially after everything Reid has done for me this weekend, is to stand—or rather, ski—in his way of fun.

"Let's do this." I force a smile on my face. "See you at the bottom."

"If you say so, Parks." His eyes flicker with amusement.

To show him I'm serious, I pull my goggles over my eyes, effectively applying an orange filter to the world. The surface of the slope shines like glass, the snow having hardened into ice from the combination of melting and refreezing and being compressed by the skiers and snowboarders who have traversed this bluff. There's no going back now.

I tip forward and launch down the mountain. My first thought is: *This isn't so bad.* The wind rushes against my face and the view is exquisite—rolling mountains, expansive robin's-egg-blue sky, and the picturesque Silver Creek Village far below.

Reid flies by me, a broad grin on his face. The sunlight glints off the silver accents on his coat and the pearly white of his teeth. Even if this proves to be a colossal mistake, it's worth it to see him happy.

Then I pick up speed.

I dig the edges of my skis in the mountainside. It's so slick I barely manage to shift my weight and redirect the tips of my skis. My breath puffs out in foggy swirls from the exertion, but there's no time to recover. The entirety of my focus is on the slope—the slight changes in gradient, the shimmer of especially icy patches, other people zipping by me.

My quads burn from effort as I approach a sharp turn that funnels into a steep bowl, pine trees providing a border to the neighboring run. I take the hill at an angle, hoping to leverage the gentler slope but hit a chunk of ice that sends me flailing.

I try to make purchase with the edges of my skis, but the ground is too hard, too slick. I drill my ski poles into the ground but the straps slide right off my wrists. The only way to avoid a fate similar to Annmarie's is to intentionally fall.

I go down. Hard.

If I thought walking with skis was awkward, it's nothing compared to falling. I go head over butt, leaving a trail of equipment behind me.

When I finally come to a stop, I take a moment to do a yoga breath—deep inhale, long exhale—before taking stock. My neck is sore, my left wrist is tender, and my pride smarts, but other than that I'm in one piece. At least my body is. My poles are at the top of the ravine while one ski is about halfway down, the other, by some miracle, still strapped to my foot.

Through the haze of shock and adrenaline, shouts of skiers and snowboarders reach my ears.

"Watch it!"

"Move to the side!"

I prop myself up on my elbows and use my free boot to kick at the lever of the other to release my ski. After a few dismal attempts, I finally manage to click free. I struggle to my feet and, shielding my eyes from the glare of the sun, glance up the hill, swearing under my breath. Even harder than going down this run might be hiking back up it to retrieve my gear.

"That was quite the spill," Reid says. His snowboard is under one arm and he's balanced sideways on the hill. "You okay?"

I wince. It'd been too much to hope that my fall would go unnoticed by my extremely suave and talented boyfriend. "You saw that, huh?"

"It was one for the books." He drops his snowboard off to the side. "Let me help you out."

I can only nod, tears stinging the corners of my eyes in relief, embarrassment, and frustration.

Reid dodges oncoming traffic as he tromps up the hill and collects my wayward poles and ski. He makes it look easy, effortless, which for some reason makes me want to cry even more. I swallow my emotions, bile coating my mouth, and force myself to get a grip.

"Thanks," I say quietly as Reid hands me my poles. He sets my ski on the ground parallel to the other one.

"If we cut through over there"—Reid points to a narrow trail I hadn't even noticed that slices between two thickets of pine trees—"we can take Lillehammer the rest of the way down."

So, this is what it feels like to be between a rock and a hard place.

I look wistfully between the steep slope and the gentler run. Normally, this would be a no-brainer. I mean, duh, you go with the one most likely to allow you to hobble out at the bottom. But this decision isn't so simple.

Because the Lillehammer passes right by where I saw Annmarie die, and I'm not sure my fragile psyche can handle that. Except, perhaps seeing the space again will dislodge any remaining ghosts, untangle the ambiguity of what I witnessed. Damaging as it might be to my well-being.

With a fresh surge of determination, I press down with both heels until my boots clip back into my skis. "Lead the way."

* * *

There's a minuscule aphidlike insect called *Phylloxera* that's a blight to vineyards. They move from plant to plant, sucking the sap from grapevines until the root structures completely collapse. The only remedy, if it can even be called that, is to graft resistant roots to the old vines, essentially regrowing the entire vineyard.

I wonder what sort of infestation is at the center of this crime, how long it had been feeding on Annmarie, and what chance there is of eradication.

Reid and I are perched at the edge of the Lillehammer. Sprawled before us is the dense wood that leads to the Clymen with its many moguls, and, of course, Lockdown Pass.

I don't know if visiting the place where Annmarie fell will be fruitful, but I have to try.

Reid keeps his board perpendicular to the gradient and shifts his weight to remain stationary. To his credit, he didn't ask questions when I asked him to stop. He just nodded and veered to the side, seeming to understand my motivations, maybe even better than I do.

"I was right about here," I say, skiing forward a few more feet.

My breath hitches as I dig my poles into the ground. I don't like being here. In this place, where I watched naively as someone I respected met their demise. I'm not sure I'll ever be able to ski without feeling this dread.

Sometimes facing fears makes sense. Like when I started feeling twitchy about heights, I climbed the famed Bastille Crack in Eldorado Canyon, a 350-foot sandstone wall. And, while it didn't cure my fear, it gave me confidence that I could manage it. Live my life without being impeded by that phobia.

I don't know if any victory can be found in this case, but I have to try. For Annmarie.

My pulse quickens as I drum up memories—her position as she flew down the adjacent run, the shadow, the shout, which was sharp and three syllables, almost like Annmarie's name, come to think of it, but not quite. I try to overlay my recollections with reality but am only moderately successful.

"Let's get closer," I say.

Reid hops forward and skids on the edge of his board down the gradual incline to the trees. "What exactly are we looking for?"

"I'm not sure." I lick my lips. "Anything that stands out."

I peer into the thicket. The strange markings in the snow I'd noticed yesterday aren't there anymore, having been obscured by the sun or wind since then. The quiet of the trees seems to absorb sounds, filtering the yelps and cheers of skiers and snowboarders behind us into dulled white noise.

I gesture with my pole to a space between two tree trunks. "That's where I saw the shadow."

While I could explain away the shout I heard as belonging to someone on the neighboring slope—or even a figment of my imagination—the shadow bothers me. Someone, or something, was here right before Annmarie crashed.

Reid gazes around, his green eyes soaking in our surroundings, wary, curious, and, as always, unpredictable. "There are elk, deer, bears, mountain lions around here."

My exhale sends a swirl of fog into the air as tangled

as my thoughts. "It could have been an animal, I suppose. Maybe it surprised Annmarie, frightened her."

"Maybe it was intentionally there to surprise her," Reid surmises, leaning back, his arms draped at his sides for balance. "The run she was doing would have required focus, especially at Lockdown Pass, even for an Olympian. Any distractions at the wrong time could prove deadly."

"Now that's food for thought."

"Well, food has always been my specialty," he jokes, though his face harbors no humor.

"Naturally." I try for a smile, my teeth cold against the air.

An unsettling feeling washes over me and, beneath my fleece gaiter, the hair rises at the nape of my neck. I look around, trying to determine the source of my unease, why it suddenly feels like we're not alone.

The runs on either side of us are crowded, but no one pays us any attention, and the woods are barren. On the other side of the Clymen, gliding diagonally overhead, an auxiliary chairlift carries skiers and snowboarders from a smaller checkpoint farther down the mountain back up to the summit. Maybe it was one of their gazes I sensed, but if that's the case, why isn't the feeling alleviating?

The wind picks up, swaying the branches of the trees.

That's when I realize there's something missing from the scene. Reddish-brown pine needles.

Obviously the ones I'd seen yesterday, dotted in the snow and circling Annmarie, would've been long buried, blown away, or possibly even collected by forensics. But where had they initially come from? The nearby trees are all healthy and green with no sign of dried or dead foliage.

"Do you see any brown evergreens? Even ones just starting to turn."

Reid does a cursory scan and then shakes his head. "No. Should I? That'd be a bad sign, right? Of drought or pine beetles."

"A bad sign for the tree, true, but a promising sign for the investigation." I take one last look, shivering in my boots as a gust of wind whips against my face, chapping my already-dry skin. A wall of dense clouds is forming over the western peaks, a storm brewing—or rather, fermenting. "Let's keep moving."

My twitchiness grows as I follow Reid to the base until I feel exposed and vulnerable, as if the world can see what lies beneath my skin. I don't know how to voice my concern that someone had been watching us on the mountain—following us. Because I have no proof.

We find Sage and Liam polishing off Clif Bars near a rope separating the lengthy chairlift line from the freestyle snowboarding area. From the looks of it, they've been waiting a good while but not without entertainment. Snowboarders fly around the man-made terrain like bees around a hive, following their own set of unspoken rules. They slide down rails, jump on and off boxes, and strike poses in the air over the half-pipe.

We glide to their side, me leveraging my poles and Reid with one foot unfastened to help maneuver through the crowd. It's only grown since this morning, a sea of red, white, and blue.

"Thinking of going out there?" I ask Sage, by way of a greeting.

"As if," she scoffs, eyes wide.

"You guys take a detour?" Liam asks. He crumples his wrapper and tosses it into a trash bin.

"Something like that." I click out of my skis and clasp them together with the brake prongs. "Actually, I'm going to head back to the lodge." Truth is, after essentially feeling like stalked prey, I can't bring myself to face the mountain again.

Sage furrows her eyebrows, instantly on edge. "Is everything okay?"

My brother, however, crosses his arms over his chest and ribs me. "I knew it'd been a while, but I didn't think you were in *that* bad shape."

"It has nothing to do with my fitness level, thank you very much," I retort. "I'm just not in the mood and don't want to kill your guys' buzz. Really, go have fun and I'll see you for lunch."

"Oh, I see," Liam continues. "You have more unofficial sleuthing to do."

Liam's comment heightens my resolve to keep mum about my so-called *unofficial sleuthing*. I'm not in the right headspace for a tête-à-tête with him, or to psychoanalyze my compulsive need for closure. Especially when it's painfully obvious he doesn't understand, or care to. Instead, I go for my favorite brand of avoidance: denial.

I roll my eyes. "You see nothing, as always."

Reid rests his goggles on top of his helmet and turns the full force of his green eyes on me. His cheeks have a healthy flush from exertion and his mouth is set in a concerned frown. This man I've come to love is full of so much passion and adventure, I can't help but worry I'm letting him down.

He squeezes my shoulder and says quietly, "You can't let one fall shake your confidence."

"What fall?" Sage asks.

"I took a spill on Turin." I try to alleviate my friend's

concern, as if my tumble is all that's bothering me. "My ego is more bruised than anything."

"It's a tough run," Liam says. In his face, I see flashbacks to the times I'd tried following in his footsteps as a kid, despite being two years his junior. When I split my chin trying to climb up the slide after him, was double-bounced off the trampoline with him and his friends, or crashed my mountain bike on a trail he'd recently mastered.

I hate his pity most of all.

"Normally I'd get back on the proverbial horse, but I just can't." I feel like an empty bottle of wine—what used to be merry now just a reminder of a better time.

"I get it," Reid says, and the wild thing is, I think he does. Even though I haven't been exactly forthcoming with all my emotional baggage. "Take some time. Maybe this afternoon you'll feel like getting back out there."

"Yeah, maybe," I say, my voice pitchy and weirdly hopeful.

Reid clears his throat and says, mostly to Liam, "This is your PDA warning."

"'Nuff said. See ya, sis." With one last wave, he and Sage snag a spot at the end of the chairlift line, already perusing the map for their next run.

Reid leans in and brushes his lips over mine, his fingers tangling in the hair that's escaped my ponytail and hat. His lips are soft and reassuring, and gone too soon.

"I'll text you when we're ready for a break." He pushes with one foot, gliding away.

I can't help the feelings swelling inside of me—the guilt that I'm letting everyone down, the sadness I can't seem to shake this weekend, and a tickling of fear.

Chapter Ten

The lobby is rife with drama when I arrive. Given the conflict in my own life, I soak it up like wine does oakiness from a barrel.

"This can't be happening," Paisley says. She tears out of a room behind the lobby desk, showing more life than I've seen out of her yet. Her cheeks are splotchy and her chest is heaving. "There must be some mistake."

A dignified man in a suit pursues her. "I'm afraid there's no mistake," he says in a practiced, calm manner. He's in a polished navy suit and grips a leather ledger in his hands. "Ms. Bauer was clear in her desires for the future of her estate. Mr. Rufus Clymen Billingsly inherits everything."

My ears perk up at that. As quietly as I can, I lean my skis against the log siding and slink toward a nearby armchair, the back of which is at an angle that will hopefully hide my shameless eavesdropping. Needless to say, my clunky boots and rustling snow pants don't help. Still, somehow I manage to settle into the chair, avoiding detection.

The only other person in the lobby apart from me is the sheriff. She's in her tan uniform with her badge clipped to her belt and her light-brown hair pulled into another messy ponytail. She's leaning against the doorframe of the recently vacated room, an amused expression on her face. She might as well be at dinner theater.

"Mr. Rufus Clymen Billingsly," Paisley shrieks, her voice laced with disbelief. "*Mr. Rufus Clymen Billingsly!*"

There's a niggling in the back of my mind. I've heard that name before, but where? I chew on my bottom lip and narrow my eyes, willing my brain to spit out the answer. An image of the summit flashes through my mind—the rudimentary lodge, gondola carriages, and large wooden trail map. Reid's voice comes back to me like a whisper in my ear. He'd explained the nomenclature of the trails on the map, how all but one were named after places the Winter Olympic have been held: the Clymen.

"I'm afraid so," the man I can only assume is a lawyer says.

"But there must be something I can do." Paisley tugs at the sleeves of her blazer, which reach midpalm without any extra stretching. "I'll contest it, argue Annmarie wasn't of sound mind. I mean, Boone!" The last word reverberates through the open space.

Even as my brain struggles to reconcile what I've just learned, my jaw drops in shock. Boone is the mysterious—and now very wealthy—Mr. Rufus Clymen Billingsly? It makes sense that Annmarie would name a run after someone she considered family, her only family, but leaving her entire estate to him? That takes a level of trust I'm not sure I've ever experienced.

Paisley continues, pacing in heels that make her ankles wobble, "Boone running Silver Creek . . . it's inconceivable."

Jenny turns her head and murmurs something into the room behind her—there must be others present for the reading of Annmarie's will—and waltzes out from behind the refurbished-log desk.

She prowls toward Paisley, reminding me very much of a mountain lion. "Ms. Moore, this is what Annmarie wanted." She speaks succinctly and punctuates every word. "It will hold up in a court of law. Get yourself under control, unless there is something you need to tell me." The insinuation hangs in the air, unfiltered and harsh, like a cab that needs to breathe.

Paisley swallows, a sheen of perspiration appearing on her forehead. "Nothing."

"Good." Jenny somehow manages to look down the bridge of her nose at Paisley, even though they're practically eye level. "Because Boone is going to need your help."

Paisley nods, running a hand through her mousy hair, stunned into silence.

Jenny stares at the jilted manager for another second before cutting her eyes sharply to me. "Do you have something else to report, Parker?"

I jump at being caught snooping, straightening my back. "No, ma'am." For some reason the *ma'am* feels appropriate.

"Okay, then." Jenny addresses the lawyer, who's watching this spectacle with an air of tedium. "Is there more to discuss or can we wrap up this rodeo?"

"We're just about done," he responds, leading the way back to the room.

Jenny follows and closes the door behind her, but Paisley remains where she is, as if the soles of her shoes have taken root in the hardwood floor.

I study her now, a frozen statue, staring into the flames of the fireplace, hypnotized.

She'd been so skittish after Annmarie's nonaccident, had practically tried to make herself invisible after disembarking from the gondola.

From my time serving guests at Vino Valentine, I've learned a thing or two about reading people. Differentiating the oenophiles from the newbies, determining which patrons are social butterflies and which prefer minimal interactions, and even predicting which varietals customers favor. But I can't get a pulse on Paisley.

Then there's the tidbit Cash and Akira divulged about her being desperate for a promotion.

Well, if Paisley killed Annmarie to gain control over the Olympian's empire, it rather blew up in her face.

I struggle to my feet and wince, my hip sore from my fall earlier. But I've had worse. I stretch my arms over my head and gingerly make my way toward Paisley. The fireplace gives off a warm radiant heat, making me sweat beneath my many layers.

Paisley doesn't acknowledge my presence. Her face is sallow, emphasizing the dark bags beneath her eyes, flames dancing in her irises.

"I couldn't help but overhear . . ." I trail off.

Paisley pivots toward me, blinking in surprise to find someone beside her but doesn't initiate further conversation.

I've never been one to take a hint. I let out a whistle.

"Boone running Silver Creek—that's quite the upgrade, going from running the chairlift to running the whole resort."

She shoots me a glare that would wither a grapevine. "Did you need something?"

"Yeah, I was just wondering what you were doing on the mountain yesterday."

Paisley crosses her arms over her chest. "I don't know what you're talking about."

I tap my pointer finger against my chin, trying to make my voice conversational rather than accusatory. "Here's the thing: I saw you get off the gondola, and I'm pretty sure you saw me." What I really want to ask is: *Why are you pretending otherwise?*

"Were you checking on something at the lodge? Taking in the view?" *Tromping through the woods?* Because how else would she have encountered the amount of snow I'd seen on her boots?

"I don't have time for this." Paisley nudges my shoulder with hers as she storms past. She continues out the main entrance, scattering a group of chattering skiers like a rogue bowling ball, and into the frigid air with nothing but her ill-fitting pantsuit and impractical footwear.

I rub my shoulder where she bumped me, watching Paisley through the window until she disappears around the corner. Despite her dismissal, she spoke volumes by evading a simple question. Whatever she was doing on the mountain, she doesn't want anyone to know about it.

Curiosity has a strong pull that ensnares more than cats. People flock to conflict like moths to a lightbulb. Which is why I shouldn't be surprised to find Akira has drifted into the lobby.

She's wearing a flannel number with utility pants that taper around her laced ankle boots. Her long black hair is coiled into an extravagant knot on top of her head and behind her wire-rimmed glasses, her eyes are wary. Nipping at her heels is Madeline, her smoky-gray, bushy tail twitching with indecision. And in her mouth is a knitted kitty toy, a tiny mitten that is so fitting I can't help but smile.

"I heard shouting, all the way in the dining room," Akira says. "Is everybody okay?"

"Yeah, everyone's fine." I cock my head to the side, amending, "Although Paisley's had better days."

Her reaction is almost imperceptible, a slight crinkle of her nose and twitch of her lips. "Glad to hear it." She strokes Madeline's back, the latter raising her bum in the air in appreciation. It's obvious Akira is her favorite human, although I know how fickle feline loyalties can be. The only way to retain them is constant attention. And vittles.

"I hear you came out on top at the big poker game last night."

"A few lucky hands and"—her eyes take on a mischievous glint as she smiles innocently—"I guess everyone thought I was too nice to bluff. Pity, though, I don't think I'm invited back."

I chuckle, prepping for a little bluffing of my own. "Who all was there?"

"Cash, obviously, and Austin, one of his sous chefs." She continues, counting the names off on her fingers, "Micah, a new liftie, Jenny, the sheriff, and Boone, at least until the pot got too rich for him."

My attention snags on Micah, the one who was supposedly relieved from his post early and then disappeared. I make a mental note to track him down later and ask where exactly he was during Annmarie's final run.

"That won't be a problem for Boone anymore. The pot getting too rich, that is. You were right. Annmarie must've seen him as family because she left him all of Silver Creek."

Madeline drops her toy mitten at Akira's feet. The latter tosses it for her and the cat goes careening after it, her paws struggling to find purchase on the smooth floor. "Boone loves the mountain and knows what Annmarie would've wanted." She tilts her head to the side, clicking her tongue. "Paisley must be crushed. All she ever wanted was for Annmarie to trust her and give her more responsibility."

"Time is a painful investment to waste." I think of the precious time I poured into trying to hock my mulled wine; at least it was only a meeting and not a decade.

Madeline trots back with the glove in her mouth and proudly deposits it before Akira, who scoops it up and tosses it again. It lands near a rug with tassels, which add extra amusement to Madeline's game.

I smile at the cat pawing at the fringe, even as my spidey senses tingle. I know better than to ignore my gut, so I ask, "What do you have against Paisley?"

"Apart from the obvious?" Akira retorts, and then flinches. "Sorry, just slipped out."

Behind her remorse is an emotion I recognize: hurt. I focus on that, giving her an opening to vent. Because with venting often comes information. "She is a little difficult to swallow."

"She wasn't always like this." Akira lowers her voice, even though there's no one else in the lobby with us, and the door to the office behind the desk remains firmly closed. "You know, she was my first friend when I started here a couple years ago."

I can't keep the surprise from my voice. "Really?"

"Yeah. I moved here from Chicago and didn't know anyone and she took me under her wing. Showed me around town, the hidden gems only locals know, the best places for a quick bite, where the night scene is, which ski trails to take to avoid the crowds. She even saved me from making a huge mistake."

"What sort of mistake?"

"A guy I thought was okay turned out to be a complete tool." She shakes her head, a strand of long black hair coming loose from her updo.

"Ah, that kind of mistake. Gotta appreciate a friend who's got your back in the love department." I was put in that position once for Sage with her former fiancé, and it was brutal. It almost destroyed our friendship, but we've since promised to be honest with each other no matter what and that no guy will ever come between us. "So, why aren't you friends anymore?"

"Because six months ago, she ghosted me."

"Why would she do that?"

"Wish I knew," Akira says, chewing her lower lip. "It started the day before the resort opened for the season. It's a tradition that employees get a free pass and the run of the mountain. We were supposed to go together, but she stood me up, without any warning or explanation." She looks at me sadly, giving the tiniest of shrugs.

"That's not cool." I shift my weight, my feet aching in my boots, which are meant for skiing, not idling. "Did you ever figure out what happened?"

"I tried talking to her about it the first couple months.

Do you know how awkward it is to be ghosted by someone you see on a daily basis?" She lets out a huff. "Anyway, she always brushed me off, made it seem like it was all in my head. Eventually, I gave up." Along with the hurt is a sheer desperation to understand and, if I'm not mistaken, loneliness.

I can't imagine how I'd feel if Sage pulled something like that on me. Romantic breakups are terrible in their own right—heart-wrenching and life-altering—but the end of friendships can arguably be worse. Without closure, the regret can linger, damaging your soul and making you question your entire person.

"The next thing I knew, she traded in her hipster wardrobe for those awful pantsuits." She blanches; can't say I blame her.

"You and Cash mentioned Paisley wanted a promotion. When did that start?"

"Since I first met her, really, but last year it became sort of an obsession."

Obsession is an interesting term to use. It implies more than a dream or desire but to be consumed to the point of madness. The sweat under my many layers turns to ice.

"Did she ever strike you as being dangerous?"

"I keep asking myself the same question and . . . no, I don't think so. At least I hope not." The more she speaks, the less convinced she appears. "I just can't imagine anyone doing that."

"Me, neither." Sensing I've pried enough, I give Akira what I hope comes across as an encouraging look. "I don't know either of you that well, but for what it's worth, it sounds like whatever's going on with Paisley has more to do with her than with you."

"Thanks," Akira says with a grateful smile. "At least

I have a furry friend, even if it is only because she wants food." Madeline has since stashed her toy mitten in her plush bed and returned to rub up against Akira's leg, a loud purr emanating from her.

"My cat is the same way. Sometimes it feels like in her eyes, I exist purely to fill her food dish." Zin's face flashes in my mind—her gray silky hair, green orblike eyes, and the tip of one ear missing. I owe my dad a check-in text later. To make sure Zin and William are being sufficiently supplied with kitty treats, though I really have no cause for concern.

A group of well-to-do ladies bustle past us, their arms laden with shopping bags, chattering happily about their purchases. "I'd better get back to inventory," Akira says with a nod at them. "Something tells me that lot will be thirsty later."

"Hey, did you enjoy the bottle of Snowy Day Syrah?"

"I'm saving it for my day off so I can enjoy a cup of mulled wine with a good book."

"Now, that sounds like an excellent pairing." I throw her a wink as we part ways.

My last question might have seemed like fishing for a compliment—a last-ditch effort to secure a sales contract—but there's more to it than that. Akira confirmed what I'd already suspected: that it was Annmarie's bottle I'd seen in the chairlift operator's stand. How it got there escapes me.

Even though I'd rather jam my hand in an operating crusher de-stemmer than put off changing out of my ski gear for one more second, I pause in the corridor outside the elevators.

Located at the base of the central tower, down a lengthy hallway from the lobby, rec room, and dining area, the space is cloaked in silence. It has a hallowed atmosphere, almost like a museum with a series of framed photographs adorning warm, butter-yellow walls and a table holding maps, to-go menus, and advertisements for tourist attractions.

But none of this is why I stopped.

There's a shadowed figure, studying the pictures on the wall. With his slow footsteps and one finger studiously on his pointy chin, Hudson Gray gives me the impression of someone deep in nostalgia.

I set my skis on the ground with a *thunk*, leaning them into the crook of my elbow. The tops of my boots cut into my calves, my snow pants and coat crinkle with every movement, and my hair is matted to my forehead. I imagine how I must look—disheveled, crazed, and slightly desperate. Perhaps it will work in my favor.

The clunking of my boots against the hardwood gets his attention, even as I ask, "Hudson, right?"

There's an absurd amount of gel in his hair, but strands still stick out as if he couldn't be bothered to finish styling it, and one of his eyes is stark red with a recently burst blood vessel. His gray half-zip fleece makes me wonder, absently, if his entire wardrobe matches his car.

He barely turns to me, his suede boots still firmly facing the wall. "And you are?"

I reach out a hand. "Parker Valentine."

He ignores my offer of a handshake and goes back to studying the photographs.

I follow his gaze. The photos are of Annmarie's medal-winning runs from the year she was in the Winter

Olympics. There's a picture of her bent at the torso, her body tucked with her ski poles facing straight back, the downhill race where the speeds get upward of ninety miles per hour. Then another of her on the edges of her skis, snow spraying behind her as she dodges a flag, her teeth bared. The next is a shot from far away where she's nothing more than a speck taking on the expansive run. And still one more of Annmarie atop the podium, smiling brilliantly at the camera in a blaze of glory.

The last picture doesn't quite fit with the others—it's of a youth-club team. Kids are perched in rows of graduating height, half smiling and half caught blinking or with their attention fixed elsewhere. At the bottom of the matte border, it reads: DILLON SKI SCHOOL 1997–1998. A small town not far from here, Dillon's picturesque lake and proximity to ski resorts put it on the map.

Hudson breaks the silence, surprising both himself and me. "I knew her back then." He nods at this last photograph, our reflections gleaming in the pristine frame. He points to the front row. "That's Annmarie in the middle—she was always front and center."

Even back then, Annmarie evoked a confidence and manner that set her apart. Whereas her teammates were distracted or smiling goofily, she peered straight at the camera, her lips pursed together.

Hudson continues, "And that's me on the end." He shakes his head, a small smile tugging at the corner of his lips.

The young Hudson Gray wasn't even pretending to look at the camera, and instead stared unabashedly at the girl in the spotlight. I know a mega crush when I see it and he was clearly smitten, although from what I overheard, there was no love lost between them.

"You were on a team together?" I ask.

"Only the local club team," he says. "I was never good enough to compete at the same level as Annmarie. Hell, no one could. Even our coach had a hard time keeping up with her." He gestures to the only adult in the picture, a man with a receding hairline, broad shoulders, and a frown that says things in his life hadn't gone according to plan.

"You've known Annmarie a long time," I muse.

"I'm probably one of the few she's kept in touch with, though I wouldn't say I know her."

I shift on my feet, easing the burning in my calves. "Did you stop by to see her often?"

"Only for our business dealings together."

I furrow my eyebrows; from what I overheard, it sounded more like he *wished* they had business dealings together. "Is that what you two were arguing about?"

Hudson shoots me a quizzical glance, his eyes flitting over me as if he's only now taking in the specifics. Maybe it's a good thing I'm in my snow gear; I'm practically incognito.

"Who are you again?"

"Parker Valentine, owner of Vino Valentine in Boulder," I say proudly. I flutter my eyelashes faux-sweetly, making myself as nonthreatening as possible. "I heard you and Annmarie talking in the dining room before a wine tasting—it sounded intense."

Hudson clenches his jaw, which emphasizes his pointy chin—a weak chin. "We were discussing a venture that doesn't concern you." The sharpness of his tone reminds me of when he'd told Annmarie *You owe me.* She'd coolly brushed him off, an act she may have come to regret.

Hudson is a skilled skier—maybe not as skilled as Annmarie—but he could clearly hold his own, and he'd been at the summit with Annmarie before her fatal run. I don't remember seeing him near her when the Olympian met her demise, nor in the crowd that waited while the paramedics and sheriff secured the vicinity.

"Right, totally get it." I backpedal as if I couldn't care less about his withholding intel. "You went down the Clymen with her yesterday morning. That must've been tough."

"I wasn't anywhere near Clymen," he snaps.

"But I saw you at the top of that run."

He shakes his head as if I were an impertinent child. "Annmarie didn't like to share the spotlight."

"What does that mean?"

"It means I left her to her adoring public and took a different route. I didn't find out about her accident until I was back at base." His shoulders slump and ghosts flit across his features.

Whether that's true will be almost impossible to prove since he was skiing alone with no one to verify his whereabouts.

"Which run did you take?"

"Calgary," he says wearily, dropping his head back, the light enhancing the ghoulish red of his bloodshot eye.

"Then how did you injure your eye?" I ask, because sure, it could simply be from exertion, or it could be a defensive wound.

"You ever heard of a little thing called stress?"

I click my tongue. I've almost worn out his patience. Honestly, I'm shocked he's been this forthcoming. But I'm not done yet. It was time to push his buttons, see how loud his bark is and, subsequently, if he has any inclination to bite. Plus, maybe he'll let something slip.

"Why did you keep harassing Annmarie after she told you no? Having trouble with your finances?"

Hudson seethes. "I don't have to explain anything to you."

"Well, actually, there is one thing I deserve an answer to. You see, I was in the jeep you ran off the road on Thursday." From the clueless expression on his face, he has no idea he almost crashed into us. Fumes practically spout from my ears. Admittedly, there's a chance I've been looking for an opportunity to chew this guy out since we first arrived. "You must be familiar with the roads up here. Why not drive a car you can handle in the snow?"

His nostrils flare with his temper. "I'm not going to stand here being insulted by some girl who doesn't have the faintest idea what she's talking about." He gives the childhood photograph one last lingering stare. "That's enough of a march down memory lane for me, anyway." He grips his hands into tight fists behind his back as he walks away.

I wait for his elevator to close and whisk him away before pushing the call button, questions swirling through my mind.

Chapter Eleven

It helps to have an in with your local police department, although ideally one wouldn't need to tap that resource as often as I do.

Back in my room, I call my old high school acquaintance and current climbing buddy.

"Detective Fuller," he answers on the first ring.

"Hey, Eli, it's Parker." I hold the resort receiver to my ear.

My cell service is on the fritz, barely sufficient to send a text. Which I discovered when I pinged my dad about Zin. Apparently she and William are having the time of their lives. While the owners are away, the cats will play. Or indulge gluttonously in laser-pointer pouncing and overflowing food dishes.

I also seized the opportunity to check the status of my application to the Colorado Wine Festival. You know, because I've been worrying about every other aspect of my life—why not throw my business in the mix, too? Of course, as with all ardently watched pots of water and fermenting tubs of grapes, there's nothing to report.

Given the cellular dead zone, I'm relegated to the landline, which at least is positioned on an end table next to a comfortable armchair. I nuzzle back into the cushions and prop my feet on the ottoman. I changed out of my snow gear and into more pedestrian attire—jeans, sweater, and boots with such a thick sheepskin lining they might as well be slippers. Feeble rays of sunshine cascade through the sliding glass door that leads to the balcony, covering my legs like a threadbare blanket. Outside, the wind howls and snowflakes have started falling from the sky. This will be a full-blown blizzard in no time.

There's a lot of commotion on Eli's end of the line, muffled chatter, scraping of earthenware, clinking glasses.

"Is this an okay time?" I ask.

"Yeah, sure, just give me a sec." He must cover the speaker because his words are muffled.

I can envision him: perfectly slicked-back hair, warm eyes the color of caramel, pressed navy suit and tie. He's come a long way since our adolescence when he was the renowned stoner of the Boulder Cineplex, leaning on pot as a way to cope with a lousy home life. He works hard to maintain his upstanding reputation as a detective, which I'd like to think I helped boost. First by solving the murder in my winery, and then identifying the real culprit last fall when Reid was wrongfully accused.

"Okay, what's up?" Eli asks, slightly breathless.

"I hope I didn't take you away from a crime scene or something."

"No. At least, I hope not," he says with a low chuckle. "I'm on a date."

"Oh." I sit up a bit, a knot unraveling in my gut. Eli asked me out once and, after I politely refused, it took some time for us to recover from the awkwardness. And really, he's such a great guy, he deserves to be happy.

"It's new, but with it being Valentine's weekend and all . . ." he trails off, as if this is something I would obviously understand.

Which I should. My heart sinks, straight down into my empty, gnawing stomach. Not only did I let Reid down, but what would Aunt Laura say if she saw me now? Flouting the holiday she loved. And now I'm pulling Eli away from his date. I can hardly stand to be in my own skin.

"Of course." I swallow my guilt and remind myself why I called—for Annmarie. To weed out the malicious presence at Silver Creek. "I promise I won't keep you long, I was just wondering if you'd look into someone for me."

"What happened?" His tone immediately grows serious. "I thought you were out of town this weekend."

"I am. There's just a guy here giving off weird vibes." I think of my charged interaction with Hudson Gray. It's only gotten weirder the more I replay it in my mind, like a bad aftertaste you can't shake.

"You're gonna have to give me more than vibes. What specifically has this individual done?"

"It's what he might have done. To the owner of the resort."

I gaze out the window, the sky so blindingly white I

almost need my sunglasses. While my friends are unquestionably making the most of their time on the mountain, you couldn't pay me enough to get back out there. Only, you totally could. What can I say? I'm cheap.

"What aren't you telling me?" Eli asks.

I squirm in my chair, letting out a long exhale. "There was a murder."

"How is it you wind up involved in so much homicide?" Eli asks in disbelief. "I'm beginning to think it's you."

I know he's mostly joking, but the implication cuts deep. Especially since it's not dissimilar from Liam chiding me for inserting myself into the investigation.

"Wrong place, wrong time," I say, brushing it off, although the coincidences lay gritty on my tongue like sediment.

"Now you're bothering some other perfectly capable detective by interfering in an investigation."

"Sheriff," I correct. "And she is completely capable. I promise I'm not stepping on her toes, just trying to be smart, stay on guard, all that jazz."

Eli doesn't respond immediately, which I'm going to take as a good sign. A no from him takes far less consideration than a yes.

"Text me the guy's name and I'll do what I can," he eventually says. "But, Parker, seriously, stay out of it. Enjoy your weekend getaway, your time with Reid. Leave this one to the authorities." His voice is placating, but I get he means well.

"Scout's honor." I hold up three fingers—or was it two? Truth be told, I wasn't in Girl Scouts long enough to have it ingrained in my subconscious.

"I know what that's worth," Eli says with a snort. "A big goose egg. But hey, I've gotta get back. I'll let you know when I have something."

"Thanks, Eli. And have a good date."

I end the call, pull my cell out of my pocket, and text Eli the name *Hudson Gray.* Or at least, I attempt to text him. I watch as my phone struggles against the Wi-Fi and lift it higher in the air to, I dunno, get closer to the satellites. Eons later, my message finally goes through and Eli shoots back a thumbs-up emoji.

Leaning back, a warmth spreads through my chest, a feeling of accomplishment, of having done something.

I drop my feet to the floor, ready to meet up with Reid, Liam, and Sage and track down some lunch. Then maybe I'll spend the afternoon at the shops and find something thoughtful and perfect to give Reid for Valentine's Day. Something to show him how much he means to me. As my grandiose plans come together, I crinkle my nose.

I smell smoke.

It's acrid and strong and makes me gag and cough. I pull my sweater over my mouth and turn to find dark plumes pouring into the room, the hotel door consumed with flames.

My time in the Girl Scouts may have been short, but I learned two important things. One, that Samoas are indisputably the best cookie; and two, what to do if there's a fire.

I mentally run through the list. First, check the nearest exit.

Bright red-and-orange flames engulf the door, crackling and spitting sparks onto the carpet and walls. Grayish-black smoke billows around, making me cough again, and my forehead beads with sweat from the heat. The fire alarm triggers, its siren blaring so loudly it hurts my eardrums and its lights flashing like a strobe, making me see stars. Sprinklers kick on, dousing the flames with water. It makes no difference.

I'm not getting out that way.

Plan B it is. I stumble forward and into the bathroom, my eyes burning from smoke. I shut the door behind me and, with shaky hands, douse a towel with water and jam it in the crack beneath the door. I grab another towel and repeat the process, filling in the rest of the space. Then I slide to the tiled floor and lean back against the porcelain sink, allowing myself to take a deep gulp of air.

My damp hair clings to the sides of my face and my sweater is laden on my shoulders, smelling of wet wool and a wood-fire oven.

I'd thought this bathroom marvelous when we first checked in—the clawfoot tub of my dreams, a waterfall shower positioned overhead, heat lamps that transform it into a sauna, a dual-faucet sink with a gilded mirror. Now this space is my saving grace.

I gather my wits about me. The towels will only protect my lungs, and not for long. As luxurious as this bathroom is, it's missing some very important features. Namely, a window, ceiling fan, or any other means of escape. I grapple for my cell phone, thankfully still tucked in my pocket and mostly dry. Frantically, I dial 911 and curse. Because there's no signal.

I push myself to my feet, coughing into my elbow, and go to every corner of the room, waving my phone wildly, pressing redial over and over, until finally it picks up the Wi-Fi.

"Summit County 911. Where is your emergency?"

"At Silver Creek Resort," I say. My throat stings from smoke and my voice is hoarse.

"I didn't catch that, where are you?"

I press myself against the wall, my entire body pulsing along with my heartbeat. "Fire," I shout into the phone. "Silver Creek Resort." I succumb in a fit of coughing and have to breathe into the sleeve of my sweater before I try to speak again, "Room 408. There's a fire at Silver Creek—"

Three beeps alerts me to the fact that my call dropped.

I try redialing. Again, and again, to no avail.

With sweaty, clumsy fingers, I type frenzied texts to Reid, Liam, and Sage, pressing send and praying to the internet gods that my pleas for help somehow go through.

Desperation gnaws at me. I sink to the floor and hug my knees to my chest, burying my face in the crook of my elbows, tears streaming down my face. Time stretches so I can't tell the difference between a second and a minute.

My thoughts drift to Reid, who will never know what he means to me. To my brother and Sage, my constant supporters and compatriots. My mom, who's looking after Vino Valentine, perhaps permanently, and my dad, who may be unwittingly adopting Zin.

At the thought of my loved ones, a fresh surge of determination courses through me.

I peel off my sweater, which leaves me in a tank, and wrap the sweater around my face so it covers my nose and mouth. If I can just get to the receiver I left on the armrest of the chair, I can dial the front desk—how surreal that my life depends on such a simple thing.

I grab a hand towel from the shelf and ready myself to turn the doorknob. I count down under my breath, giving myself little pep talks in between each number.

Three. *Come on, Parker, you can do this.*

Two. *Really, you'll be fine.*

One. *Okay, so you might not be* fine, *but you have to at least try.*

Just as I'm ready to burst through, there's a commotion on the other side of the door. My heart leaps in my throat.

"Stand back," a deep voice shouts.

I scuttle to the far corner of the bathroom and shout, "I'm out of the way."

A second later the door is forced open and a firefighter stands before me, a knight in fluorescent-yellow shining armor.

Mercaptan is the sulfur compound responsible for those unpleasant burnt-rubber and skunky aromas in wine. A scent eerily similar to this clings to my clothes, coats the inside of my nostrils, and leaves a bitter aftertaste on my tongue, even now that I'm safely two floors below in a conference room.

It turns out the authorities were already en route to Silver Creek when I called, the fire alarm triggering an immediate response, and the 911 operator understood enough of my frantic phone call to pass along my room number.

After my rescue, another firefighter who doubled as a

paramedic checked me out, testing my oxygen levels and smoke inhalation. Deeming me healthy—and incredibly lucky—I was then directed to await the sheriff.

The conference room is modern, if a little generic, meant for corporate retreats and upper-echelon business meetings. Posters featuring Silver Creek are mounted on the walls. The long table is made of the same pine as the logged siding and outfitted with the latest technology—video conferencing, projectors, and charging stations for various devices. I focus on these details now, letting the commonplace of it all soothe me.

Years ago, I worked at a marketing company while I saved and scraped enough money together to open Vino Valentine, a feat eventually accomplished with Aunt Laura's financial backing. I remember that time well, the routine, camaraderie, and security. Quitting and venturing out on my own was one of the hardest things I've ever done, and even though it's involved extra stress, uncertainty, and some less-than-stellar predicaments, I don't regret it for one second.

The door opens, jolting me back to the present. Sheriff Jenny strolls in and sits across from me. She leans back in the chair and swivels back and forth, her eyes never leaving my face. "We sure are seeing a lot of each other."

I tug my hands into the sleeves of my wrinkled sweater, reclaimed after its stint as a face mask. I quip, "What can I say? I have a magnetism."

"Of some sort." She snorts and pushes a clear bag across the table. "This was the source of the fire."

Eagerly, I lean forward and study the contents. It's thin, roughly the size of a sheet of paper, and charred beyond recognition. "What is it?"

"We'll have to wait for forensics, but it looks like a bit of scorched cardboard to me. One that was lit and slid under your door, which had been doused in accelerant."

A cold sweat breaks out on my forehead and my hands grow clammy. I wipe them on my jeans. I don't need confirmation from Jenny to know this was an intentional fire.

"Can you think of anyone who might want to harm you?"

"No," I answer, befuddled.

I mean, sure, Reid's family still aren't my biggest fans, and my former assistant no doubt has qualms with me. But they're hardly in a position to do harm, especially at a remote mountain resort.

Then I think of who *is* here that I might have offended. Hudson Gray and Paisley Moore. I'd prodded both earlier, thrown accusations at them, Hudson about his abysmal driving and the fight I'd overheard, and Paisley about how I saw her on the gondola yesterday morning.

I tell Jenny as much.

She jots a few notes down. "I recommend you lie low."

As if I haven't been doing that, or at least trying to.

I lick my lips, chapped from the dry air, made even dryer by smoke. "Do you still think the Jacuzzi incident was a coincidence?"

"I'm reevaluating in light of recent events."

So, someone has it in for me. Fire and ice; what I once thought a cute party theme is now the drama by which I'm living my life.

I glance outside at the snowflakes, which have grown fatter and more condensed since I last looked, blanketing the ground in a fresh layer of snow.

"Could it be related to Annmarie?"

"Possibly," she says, although it's as clear as a crystal flute she absolutely thinks it is.

"Did you ever find where the discolored pine needles came from?" I ask, not expecting an answer.

"As a matter of fact, we did." A fervor that I hope means she has a solid lead enters her eyes. "A large tree branch with reddish-brown needles was discovered approximately fifty feet from the scene of the crime, with a single strand of blond hair attached. We won't have confirmation until the DNA analysis comes back, but I'm willing to wager that was what actually killed Annmarie."

"Not the tree."

"No, the forensic botanist said there was no sign of impact, no damage to the bark, nada."

I blink slowly, absorbing the fact that forensic botanists are indeed a thing along with new pieces to the puzzle. "The markings in the snow weren't just to disguise footprints, were they?"

She shakes her head, watching me steadily as I draw my own conclusions.

My pulse ticks up and goose bumps form on my arms. "They were also to camouflage repositioning her body."

"That's my guess."

"All we have are guesses, huh?" I prod.

Admittedly, uncertainty isn't my forte. The ambiguity in winemaking is alleviated by science—by testing the Brix (the amount of residual sugar in the fruit), titratable acidity, and pH of the grapes every step of the way. The same is usually true in a murder investigation. *Usually* being the operative word.

"Between us, I don't expect to get much more than

that. Yours is the only witness statement, and everyone wears gloves and enough layers on the mountain that I doubt we'll find any DNA apart from Annmarie's at the crime scene." She scowls, this fact clearly grating on her. "There's one thing I know: You got very lucky. Fires up here are no joke."

"They're no joke in Boulder, either."

Colorado is notoriously plagued by fires. In the height of summer, temperatures soar, humidity drops, and rainfall becomes a thing of the past. You get used to seeing smoke on the horizon or rolling down the mountains, an orange tinge to the gray. When everything is that dry, a stray ember—a strike of lightning, a campfire, a firework—can catch and destroy thousands of acres in mere days. And while February isn't typically considered wildfire season, flames can be just as detrimental.

"This isn't the city," Jenny says, folding her hands on the table in front of her. "You're in the wilderness. There are different rules."

My mouth goes tannin dry. "What exactly are you saying?"

Jenny gets to her feet and paces across the conference room, pausing at the window, arms crossed over her chest. When she speaks, her voice is hollow, haunted.

With her eyes fixed on the falling snow outside, hypnotized, she starts, "There was a deadly fire at H Basin a couple years ago."

H Basin is a neighboring ski resort, the only other one located off the frontage road we took from I-70. I don't recall hearing about a fire there, but it's far enough from Boulder it wouldn't necessarily make the news.

I listen, transfixed, as she continues, "There were plans to expand, add new runs and a chairlift that would've been located right by a luxury development going in. A private entry point for the upper class."

I raise my eyebrows. *My, doesn't that sound nice? And wholly unnecessary.*

"Not everyone was happy about it. Most around here agreed it'd be better to build something that would benefit the local community, not just tourists who visit for a week at a time."

Real estate in the mountains is like Dom Pérignon—highly sought after and extremely pricey. I was astounded when Reid told me what it cost to live up here for a season. I'd thought renting in Boulder was expensive, but it's not even in the same orbit as a place like Silver Creek.

"Makes sense folks would be upset," I say.

"Yeah, but not enough to do more than whine and pass around a petition. Until the Coalition to Save Earth got involved." Jenny pauses and swallows. "They were a radical environmentalist group who saw themselves as crusaders, set the whole place ablaze."

Debates over land—whether to preserve or exploit its natural beauty—can get intense, especially when money is at stake. I peel my tongue from the roof of my mouth. "What happened?"

"An entire wing of the main resort lodge was destroyed and a couple was killed due to the group's recklessness." She dips her chin in respect but then cocks her head to the side. "The expansion went forward as planned, just slightly delayed."

"And the environmentalists?"

"They were apprehended and charged, their group

disbanded." She turns toward me, a pained smile on her face. "Well, all but one of them."

I give her a pleading look, too tired for mind games. "Why are you telling me this?"

"Might be the wilderness, or that we're on our own up here, but the mountains have a way of making a bad situation worse."

Understanding your environment is part of knowing your adversary, essential in business and in life. "Do I have to stay in town?"

"No. In fact, if I were you, I'd get the hell out of Dodge, and step on it. There's already a storm warning in effect and I-70 will close soon, all the way to the Eisenhower Tunnel, and the back roads will be almost impossible to navigate."

I condense what she's saying into a harsh statement: "We'll be stuck here."

"Hey, I'm a sheriff, not a meteorologist." Jenny gestures to the flakes falling, a knowing look on her face. "But yeah, unless you hightail it outta here."

Chapter Twelve

If our old hotel room was posh, our new one is the pinnacle of extravagance. Someone on the resort staff must have taken pity on me and upgraded our accommodations to a suite. In addition to a private balcony, fireplace, and luxurious four-poster bed, we also have a sitting area and a small kitchenette. None of it is enough to entice me to stay.

By some miracle, our luggage survived the fire. The same can't be said for my skis, the melted fiberglass looking more like giant misshapen corkscrews than sporting equipment. It's okay, though; I wasn't planning on skiing more this weekend, anyway.

I plop my suitcase on the end of the bed and, a testament to my distraught state, I think I hear the mattress let out a meow.

You're losing it, Parker.

I press down on my suitcase again and detect another, more distinct meow. Giving in to my better judgment, I kneel down and lift the bedskirt. Two pale-gold orbs stare out at me.

I fall backward, crab-walking until I bump into the entertainment center, my heart racing.

And then I feel ridiculous. Because Madeline traipses out as if this were her room and I were the intruder. Her bell collar jingles merrily as she stretches her back languidly, front paws extended, tail high in the air.

"Did you sneak in here for a nap?" I ask her. "Because you have a perfectly good bed downstairs."

She gazes at me adoringly, a purr radiating from her chest.

"Okay, you can stay," I say. Seeming to comprehend my meaning, she leaps onto the bed and begins what's sure to be a lengthy process of making herself comfortable. "I won't be here much longer, and then you can have the room all to yourself again."

And I'm talking to a cat when I should be packing. Great. I shake my head and refocus on my task.

I'm a tornado of action, pulling on fresh skinny jeans, a tank, and cropped cable-knit sweater—clothes that don't have the stink of smoke stuck to them. Überplanner that I am, I packed extra clothes for this trip, not really knowing what to expect in terms of dress. I'm grateful for my preparedness now, if not for the reason.

It's funny how, whenever I try to rush, even the simplest of tasks can take twice as long as it should. Like tying my hair into a ponytail.

Reid finds me in a state of frustration and panic, my hair tie getting the better of me. He drops his snowboard by the door and hurries to my side. He scoops me into his arms, pushing stray locks out of my face and raining kisses down on my cheeks.

"I'm fine," I say. "Really."

He scans me, his eyes full of worry and disbelief.

To prove my point, I give him a deep kiss, something I feared I'd never be able to do again when I was huddled in the bathroom. I savor the feeling of his lips pressed against mine, our mouths opening against each other in ecstasy. I only pull away when I need air.

We drink each other in, our foreheads resting against each other, our fingers tangled together. His scent envelops me in calm, washing away the last lingering traces of smoke.

"I came as fast as I could when I got your texts," he explains. "Reception on the mountain is shit. If I could've come sooner—"

I shush him, holding a finger to his lips. "You're here now, which is all that counts. Because we have to go."

"Where?"

"Home. Boulder."

Reid clenches his stubbled jaw and nods, casting a glance at the walls as if they might be watching us. His attention snags on Madeline, who's perched at the end of the bed in what I affectionately refer to as bread-loaf pose. With her paws tucked underneath her, she could pass for a boule.

His eyebrows furrow in confusion, but he ultimately doesn't question my insistence that we flee while we can, nor the feline's presence. Maybe there was a resort cat when he worked here, too.

"You're right," Reid finally says. "It's not safe here."

He peels off his jacket and the fleece underneath, a sliver of his abs visible as his T-shirt is tugged up. Despite our urgency, I take a second to appreciate that inch of skin and the smooth muscles beneath.

A knock at the door interrupts my blatant ogling. Of course, it's my brother and best friend. They've shed most of their bulky gear but are still in their snow pants.

"Would you please stop getting yourself into life-threatening situations?" Liam asks. "It's really cutting into our vacay." Beneath his carefree facade, annoyance flickers in his eyes. No doubt he blames me for the fire, for not heeding his warning.

Tension simmers between us, unspoken yet palpable, at least to the Valentine siblings. The thing about tiffs between Liam and me: they have to run their course. And any progress made in the last twenty-four hours has been wiped away.

"I'll do my best." I punch him mildly in the upper arm, equally aggravated. "I'm fine, by the way."

"Glad to hear it," Liam says. His shoulders slacken and he throws me the faintest head nod, a movement that signifies a momentary truce, his relief at my safety trumping our disagreement.

Sage gives me a tight squeeze. "What happened?"

"I'll tell you guys on the drive. For now, get packed. We need to vamoose before the road closes."

Sage gets an unreadable expression on her face, one I haven't seen since she admitted she wasn't sure she could get Reid out of jail following his arrest. She'd been right then; it'd taken my finding the real culprit to free him. I hate to think about what she's afraid to tell me now.

As the silence drags on, my anticipation builds until it becomes painful. That's when I realize I've been holding my breath.

"Spit it out," Reid says, not harshly but as someone who doesn't shy away from hardship. Which is good since he's dating me and I apparently attract trouble.

"We're too late," Liam answers. He doesn't frown often but when he does, he looks like my dad, scholarly lines forming around his jaw and eyes. "We heard the lady at the front desk talking to guests when we came in. The storm shut everything down outside of Silver Creek Village."

I push my bangs off my forehead and maneuver around the bed, pressing my palms flat against the window. The snowflakes are large and falling fast, and so dense I can't even see the ice-skating rink below. Sure enough, the storm has morphed into a full-fledged blizzard, just like I suspected it would, back when it would make for a pleasant afternoon instead of a death trap.

An icy sweat breaks out all over my body and my throat constricts as the terrifying realization settles in: we're trapped.

We all have different reactions to this news.

Mine is to stare numbly out the window, calculating the odds that whoever is trying to hurt me will be deterred by this snow, too.

Reid's is to console me. He wraps his arms around me from behind, whispering into my ear, "Some Valentine's, huh?"

And now, if possible, I feel even worse. My afternoon plans come back to me—how I was going to slip out and go shopping for my boyfriend extraordinaire.

"It's not Valentine's Day yet," I counter. "Technically it's not until tomorrow."

Which means perhaps there's still a way I can salvage this holiday.

Aunt Laura wouldn't have been deterred by a few snowflakes. In fact, one of her most memorable soirees was during a heavy snowstorm. For those who managed to wade through the three feet of accumulation to her place, they were met with open arms and plenty of open bottles of wine. There hadn't been many of us that year, but those who attended were full of warmth, laughter, and love, which could be why it remains one of my favorites.

Although, to be fair, Aunt Laura never had a homicidal maniac to contend with while planning her festivities.

Sage's reaction is to research alternate routes home, forgotten backroads or even trains that might be able to pass through the Rockies. When that fails, she scours the internet for other, safer lodgings, although we all know none exist. Between the day-trippers and flood of fans who came to mourn Annmarie, there are more people than accommodations. Everything is booked up.

Liam's response is to think of his stomach. "Let's order room service." At our scoffs, he continues defensively, "Come on, it's lunchtime and we're all approaching hangry territory."

Reid drops his arms from around me and I immediately miss his warmth. "Liam's right. Food might help us think clearer."

"Exactly," Liam says. He sinks into the couch and opens a leather-bound binder containing the menu, rubbing his hands in anticipation.

In the time it takes for our food to arrive, I catch up my friends on everything Sheriff Jenny divulged. Under Liam's scrutiny, our cease-fire tenuous at best, I downplay my role in the investigation, focusing on arson instead of the suspects I may have provoked. I pet Madeline while I speak, grounding myself in the silkiness of her fur, the gentle vibrating of her purr. She seems happy in our room and, to be honest, I find her presence soothing, a reminder of Zin.

A hotel employee knocks on the door and wheels in a table loaded with covered plates and utensils. Madeline follows him as he leaves, no doubt hoping to be rewarded with scraps of food.

We settle around the small coffee table in our sitting room with our feast before us. In the center of the table are platters to share: kale chips coated in Parmesan and hand-cut garlic fries, which I suspect were on the house, thanks to Reid having placed our order.

As for the entrées, there's an impressive assortment. Three-bean chili for Sage, topped with cheddar cheese and avocado relish. Short rib tacos for Liam with shaved brussels sprouts and crispy fried onions. Chopped salad for Reid, chock-full of enough goodies to keep things interesting. And a bowl of comforting chicken soup for me, elevated with hearty root vegetables, fresh parsley, and buttery thyme dumplings that melt in my mouth.

With each spoonful of savory broth, tension leaves my body, and soon, the whirlwind in my mind calms to a dull buzz. Of course, that could also be thanks to the glass of pinot noir Reid poured for me, insisting I drink it, like smelling salts to a distressed damsel.

Damsel I am most certainly not. Distressed? Definitely.

"It'll be okay," Reid says. "We'll stick together and this will be over in no time."

"You sound like a sitcom," Liam says around a mouthful of taco.

"Doesn't make it less true," Reid says. "We just need to make sure someone is always with Parker."

I set my spoon down and dab at my mouth with a napkin. "Like I'm a child or something?"

"I call first shift," Sage says, throwing her hand in the air. At my pointed look she adds, "What? I want to hang out with my friend, preferably on ice skates."

Reid spears a bunch of frisée and smoked bacon with his fork. "Do you really think ice-skating is safe?"

"It's in a public place and we'll bundle up," Sage answers. "No one will recognize us with our scarves and hats. Besides, if they do, I dare them to take me on. No one messes with my girl and gets away with it."

Sage has a fierce streak, usually reserved for people who call her *cute* or go up against her in the courtroom. Her eyes sparkle with tenacity, a challenge to test her. She is not one to be underestimated.

I cock my head to the side, taking a sip of wine, subtle flavors of vanilla and berries dancing on my tongue. I'm not sure if it's thanks to my adrenaline calming down or the dose of liquid courage, but getting out of the hotel sounds appealing. "Sage does have a point."

"Guess we're on our own," Reid says to Liam. "Think there are any instruments in the rec room?"

Reid is the drummer for an alt-rock band called Spatula, which is how he and Liam first became friends. Liam subbed for their bassist for a show one weekend and the rest, as they say, is history.

"There's only one way to find out," Liam says, shoving the last bite of his taco into his mouth, licking each of his fingers in turn. "I'd also be down for a game of eight ball."

A cocky smirk appears on Reid's face. "If you want me to take your money, just say so."

"You forget, I've seen you play pool," Liam says. "So keep your money and, more aptly, I'll hold on to mine." His phone rings, a jovial whistling tune. He checks the screen before silencing it and tucking it back in his pocket.

"Aren't you going to answer that?" I ask.

"If it's important, they'll leave a message."

I narrow my eyes at him. "But it could be a client."

Since ringing in the New Year, Liam has been trying to get his fledgling freelance photography business off the ground, offering professional headshots, family portraits, and documenting special occasions. While I know the repetition of these jobs grates on him, he's proven to have a knack for making people feel at ease—getting them to loosen up in front of the camera. But that doesn't matter if he doesn't answer his freaking phone.

"Then I'll call them back Monday morning," Liam answers, wagging a fry at me before popping it into his mouth.

My eyes widen at all the things I want to say. I finally choose, "Take it from me, timeliness is huge for new businesses. If you don't respond soon, they'll just call another photographer. No skin off their back."

"Trust me, sis, I've got it covered." He rubs a hand over his messy raven hair, shifting under my scrutiny. "Don't you have enough to worry about?"

Message received. Truce over.

I drain the last of my wine and get to my feet. "You're right, I do. Now, if you'll excuse me, Sage and I have a date."

* * *

The storm may have wreaked havoc on travel plans, but it worked wonders on the village. Silver Creek is a winter wonderland with snow glittering on the sidewalk, blanketing pine trees, and landing on eyelashes.

With nowhere else to go, people have taken to the outdoors. The restaurants and shops along the cobblestone street, the mountain to take advantage of the fresh powder, or the ice-skating rink for more laid-back fun.

A feathered dusting of snow gathers on Sage and me if we're stationary too long. Bundled in thick jackets, gloves, hats, and with scarves wound around our necks and mouths, you'd be hard-pressed to tell us apart. Which is a huge gamble on Sage's part, and not one I'm likely to forget.

We traverse the frozen lake, gliding back and forth in our rented skates, losing ourselves in the anonymity of the crowd. The snow swirls around us, blowing across the ice in mesmerizing looping patterns. The rhythm and movements come back to me easier than they did for skiing, meaning I'm not the clumsiest one out here. That title is reserved for my friend, whom I eventually take pity on. I link my arm through hers and help her stay balanced.

"All right, spill the tea," Sage says. "How are you really doing?"

"Not great." I let out a long exhale, the back of my throat still singed from smoke. I know she's asking about my general well-being after the fire, but something else is bothering me. "How do you balance everything?"

"Everything, meaning . . . ?"

"Work, life, relationships, being a total badass."

"Well, the badass part comes naturally, obviously." She wobbles on her skates and digs her fingers into my arm. "The other stuff, I'm still figuring out."

My fight with Liam comes back to me, his words a wound that won't quite heal. About my being distracted and needlessly sticking my nose in other people's business, the closure he'd (accurately) guessed I craved. Leave it to family to know just what buttons to push. It doesn't help that Eli said something similar. "Do I seek out trouble?"

We bypass a mom pulling a young child on a sled, the woman skilled enough on skates to make the feat look easy, while Sage mulls over her answer like wine over spices. "You certainly get involved in a lot of investigations for a vintner."

I cast my gaze up to the cloudy sky. "What if there's something wrong with me? Like, why can't I just relax and leave detecting to the, well, detectives?"

She stops, or rather, slows to an ungraceful stop with both arms waving in the air. I spin around, scraping the edges of the blades outward against the ice in a snowplow stop before her.

"Listen up, missy, there's nothing wrong with you." Her blue eyes bore into me with a laser focus. "Trust me, on behalf of my many, *many* clients, I wish there were more people willing to step up and help their fellow humans."

Sage is too professional and idealistic to say so, but from what I've gleaned, the honeymoon phase of her new job as a public defender has come to a close. She has too many cases, not enough time, and is facing a system predisposed to punishing the disenfranchised. But she's learning and finding her way, and I have no doubt she'll do whatever she can to whip her office into shape.

"At least they have you." I link my arm through hers again and pat it as we continue skating.

"If only that were enough." She shakes her head, snowflakes tumbling free of her strawberry-blond curls. "But we're talking about you and your perpetual awesomeness."

"I don't feel awesome. Reid did something so sweet for me for Valentine's Day and you know what I got him?"

"Out of jail a few months ago?" she asks sarcastically. "Cuz I think that gives you a free pass on gifts."

And this is one of the many reasons I love my friend: perspective. For the first time this weekend, I don't feel like the worst girlfriend in history. Still, I'm determined to come up with something to do for Reid.

"Maybe, but I still feel terrible." I chew on my lower lip. "This holiday . . . it's not easy for me."

Sage went to a couple of Laura's celebrations with me, saw the extent to which my beloved aunt treated the women in her life to candies, empowering words of affirmation, and, above all else, love. Sage's own mother is a train wreck, only calling her daughter when she needs money or to feel better about herself. I remember the look of awe on Sage's face when she saw what matriarchal role models could be.

"I wondered," she says, cutting a worried glance at me. "Does Reid know about your aunt and Valentine's Day?"

"How am I supposed to dump all my sadness on him when he's being all romantic? I don't want to be a Debbie Downer."

"First, why can't those sayings use men's names—Dougy Downer or Negative Neil?" She huffs, rolling her eyes. "Second, and I say this as someone who cares about you, Reid would appreciate hearing how you feel. I know you, and I know you have this tendency to keep things bottled up. But he wouldn't view it as anything besides another part of you he's damn lucky to get to see."

I let the truth and wisdom of her words sink in, feeling feverish at the prospect. "You may be right."

"Oh, I'm definitely right." She continues, "Besides, there's too much pressure on Valentine's Day. What matters is all the days that come after."

"So, things are going well with you and Liam, then?"

"For the most part. I'm with you on him needing to take his freelancing more seriously, especially since even I've had to work a little this weekend. At the same time, I respect his work-life boundaries." She lowers her voice, a look of sheer horror entering her eyes. "Although, last night he said Matt Smith was the best Doctor."

"Blasphemy!" I exclaim, and then chuckle. "I have no idea who that is."

"All you need to know is that the best Doctor in *Doctor Who* is David Tennant."

"Got it." We skirt around a talented skater gracefully twirling on one leg. "I'm glad you have someone to have these extremely nerdy debates with."

She makes a sound alarmingly like a *pfft*. Then again, she could simply be blowing misguided scarf tassels from her mouth.

"You know I love your nerdiness. In fact, it saved my life."

"Good thing it happened when it did because my lightsaber hairpin is MIA," Sage grumbles. "After everything I went through to rescue it—and you, of course—it's poof, gone."

"Where did you see it last?"

"On the dresser in our room, next to my lightning-bolt earrings. I've looked everywhere—on the floor, under the bed, in every nook and cranny—and it's nowhere to be found."

I frown, steering us along the far bank, covered in steadily inclining pine trees that mark the beginning of the mountain. I recall the lady I overheard chastising Paisley for her missing sapphire necklace, and how Jenny mentioned she'd been called to the resort for the theft of a tennis bracelet. All the missing items along with, well, everything else makes my stomach churn.

"Was your pin valuable?"

"Mostly sentimental, but I suppose it could fetch a decent price tag online. Though why anyone would bother going to the trouble, I don't know."

"These things have a way of turning up."

"Yeah," she says glumly.

I make a mental note to check the lost and found when we return to the hotel, even though I'm acutely aware that there are plenty of things that *don't* turn up. Items and truths that are never uncovered because they've been purposely buried, secrets that remain hidden. Unless you go looking.

And just look where *looking* got me—the target of a murderer and none the wiser.

The Jacuzzi incident was dangerous enough, but the fire . . . that was downright deadly, and reeks of desperation. Had I stumbled onto something in talking with Paisley, Akira, or Hudson, gotten too close to some buried truth?

I flex my calf muscle, turning Sage and myself gently around the edge of the rink.

My gaze lingers on the tree line, and my thoughts wander to the missing arsonist. How did they manage to escape and, moreover, how have they evaded notice in the small interconnected world of mountain towns? Because if they were willing to endanger lives to protect open space, the land obviously meant a great deal to them. So much so that my bet is they didn't go far. That they're somewhere nearby, keeping an eye on things.

I shiver, and not from the cold.

Chapter Thirteen

"You know what I need now?" Sage asks, not even waiting a beat before continuing, "Hot chocolate."

We're strolling along the salt-covered sidewalk through the village, snow still falling at such a remarkable rate there's accumulation building up on the cobblestones, despite constant shoveling.

"Now *that* is a fabulous idea." I mean, really, when have I ever turned down chocolate?

We make our way to Chloe's, the cute café responsible for keeping me in caffeine this weekend. The windows are fogged from steam from espresso machines and milk frothers. Earthy aromas of coffee and fresh-baked bread greet us as we walk in.

There's a decent line leading to the counter with an old-school cash register, where the same bubbly barista dishes out equal helpings of espresso and small talk. I pull my gloves off, studying the handwritten menu pinned to an easel. The featured drinks and dishes are festive: cherry mocha, rose tea, and red-velvet cupcakes.

A display case full of delectable sweets, savory quiches, and an assortment of sandwiches makes my mouth water. An idea comes to me as I admire the chocolate-covered strawberries, drizzled with a glossy-white frosting. It takes shape in my mind, a tiny flake that snowballs, until I have it. What I'm going to do for Reid. If I can pull it off, that is.

After Sage and I order our hot chocolates from the barista, we scope out a table in the snug space. The café is crowded with people taking breaks from skiing, shopping, or ice-skating, watching the snow fall with a cup of something warm, or, evidently, wallowing in self-pity, as seems to be the case with Paisley Moore.

Paisley is at a table cramped in the corner. Her hair is in a limp ponytail and her blazer hangs from the back of her chair. Her collared shirt is as ill fitting and outdated as her pantsuit, blocky and beige. She's gazing unseeing into space. Her mug is full and her scone only has one tiny nibble taken out of it.

"Follow me," I tell Sage, and she falls in line behind me as we dodge and weave among tables and chairs. "Hey, Paisley."

Paisley's eyes refocus and she blinks. I wonder what she was thinking about that took her so far away.

"Hi." Her voice cracks and she clears her throat. "I'm on a break, but I'm sure someone else at the resort can help in the interim."

"It's nothing like that," I say. "The tables are all full, mind if we join you?"

Sage prods me in the back, probably trying to point me in the direction of an actual free table, but I hold my ground.

"I guess." Paisley moves her mug and plate as if they were as weighty and cumbersome as a bushel of grapes.

"Thanks," I say. We make ourselves comfortable, shedding our coats and scarves. "So, how is everything? Has the dust settled after the announcement about Boone and Silver Creek?"

Paisley reaches for her bag. "The table's all yours."

"No, wait," I say, hurriedly. "Don't go, please."

Sage must sense my urgency because she jumps in. "Ignore Parker. She means well, I promise."

"Thanks for the ringing endorsement," I respond.

"Anytime, friend." Sage clinks her mug with mine.

When I turn my attention back to Paisley, she's loosened her grip on the strap of her purse. She's frozen in place, glancing between Sage and me with a pained expression on her face.

Before I even realize what's happening, tears pool in her eyes and her lip quivers. Then Paisley Moore, the morose and seemingly apathetic manager of Silver Creek, completely breaks down.

There are different kinds of criers. The delicate criers who make you long to console them, the controlled criers who never allow more than a few tears to escape, and then there are the ugly criers, of which I am most certainly, as is Paisley.

Her face is pinched and red, her nose running, and a sob chokes out of her throat. Her tears humanize her, make her more beautifully flawed. It's as if her entire being softens and, despite her prior criticisms and lukewarm attitude, I feel a pang of pity for her.

"I'm sorry if something I said upset you." I pass her a napkin from the holder, leaning across the table. "Can I get you anything? Anyone?"

My questions result in louder sobs. Although, through her blubbering, she manages to shake her head. She dabs at her eyes and nose with the napkin and I can tell the worst has passed.

"You two are clearly good friends," she eventually says with a sniffle.

"We've had our ups and downs," I say. "Like the time I ate one of Sage's yogurts during finals week without asking."

Sage chimes in, "Or that time I dragged you to the theater for a *Lord of the Rings* marathon without warning."

"Extended editions," I add with a wince. "Despite all that, yeah, we're close."

I sip my hot chocolate. It's dark and bitter with a hint of sweetness. The undertones of cinnamon and chili pepper give it depth, and don't even get me started on the homemade whipped-cream topping.

"Don't take each other for granted," Paisley says, letting out a shuddering breath.

"Is that what happened with Akira?" I venture, recalling how Paisley ghosted her friend without any explanation. Maybe there's more to the story.

Stunned, Paisley slumps back in her chair with such force it squeaks against the floor. "I have a lot of regrets." With mascara smudged beneath her eyes, she looks exhausted and, from the way her shoulders droop, defeated. "Letting go of my friendship with Akira is one of them."

"Why did you, then?"

"It all started with a performance review last fall. I asked Annmarie what I needed to do to be promoted." Her voice takes on an edge like a sharpened knife, and it doesn't escape my notice that she crumples her napkin into a fist so tight her knuckles turn white. "She told me I needed to toughen up."

"That sounds like a lawsuit waiting to happen," Sage interjects, her whipped-cream mustache contrasting with the seriousness of her tone.

"I'm paraphrasing," Paisley says. "But the meaning was clear. I was too quiet, too much of a pushover."

That's not how I would describe the Paisley I've come to know. She clearly changed, and not necessarily for the better.

She continues, "After that, I quit skiing, quit talking to Akira—or anyone, really—to focus on my career."

Paisley's story isn't uncommon: a girl assumes she has to become someone else to get the job she wants. It's upsetting, nonetheless. And Annmarie, as a woman in a position of power, should have been more careful with the advice she was doling out.

I'd be jaded if I were in Paisley's pumps. But is it possible her animosity for her boss went past the point of jaded? Did her obsession with being promoted, her resentment at having to change so much, lead her to take matters into her own hands?

I grip my mug with both hands. "Why were you acting strange after getting off the gondola yesterday morning?"

Paisley gives a small shrug. "Because I was embarrassed."

I take another swallow of hot chocolate, waiting for

her to continue. Sage seems to understand my tactic—she would, from her experience at trial—and remains mum, her foot twitching beneath the table in time to the music playing over the speakers.

"I was hoping to meet Akira at the summit, okay?" Paisley squirms in her seat. "Even though she never responded to my text. I know. Karma, right?"

"You were trying to repair your friendship?" Sage presses.

"I thought she might appreciate a friend on this particular holiday. Last I checked, she was still hung up on Cash—God knows why—and since I'm the reason they're not together, I wanted to be there for her."

My eyes widen in shock. With all the hidden connections, Silver Creek is as much of a small town as Boulder. Who knows what other ties exist that I'm not privy to? "Cash was the guy you warned Akira off?"

"She told you about that?"

"Yeah," I say, my thoughts a jumbled knot of confusion. Cash seems like a decent guy; he's cute, funny, a talented chef. "Why don't you like Cash?"

"It's not that I don't like him, necessarily, it's that he has a track record with women." She drops her napkin onto her untouched scone, pushing the plate away from her. "Around here, he's earned a nickname: Breakfast-Lunch-Dinner Guy."

I glance at Sage. She shakes her head, just as flummoxed as I am. "What does that mean?"

"It's like this. If he's interested in a girl, he starts by asking her to breakfast, which, for those not in the know, seems like a fun and quirky way to kick off a relationship. If breakfast goes well, he moves on to a lunch date.

Then, if they pass whatever sort of test he seems to have, they go to—"

"Dinner," I supply.

"Exactly." She flashes me a wry smile. "And really, that's all fine—weird, for sure—but whatever. It's that no matter how far a girl makes it in his strange dating progression, he drops her without so much as a goodbye."

I decide not to point out the irony of this grating on Paisley. "So you warned Akira?"

"She was new in town, fresh chum for the sharks. I figured I'd want to know."

I reel through every interaction between Cash and Akira. Their familiarity with each other and charged interactions, Akira's intense distaste of Cash, and his innocuous banter. There's clearly still chemistry between them, track record or not.

"The dating world is tough," Sage says. "Yes, his method is untraditional, and verily offensive, but maybe there's a reason for his behavior."

The look Paisley shoots Sage is laced with apprehension and disgust.

I hurry to veer us back on course. "That's why Akira was so excited to play in his poker game."

Paisley turns her attention back to me. "I think it was payback but also suspect she still feels something for him."

It makes sense—the heart has a will of its own, even if your head is screaming at you to run in the opposite direction. I give Akira another silent cheer for winning the pot.

"So, that's it, then?" I ask.

Paisley tugs at the sleeves of her collared shirt,

smudged with a pale-pink shimmery eyeshadow I didn't even know she was wearing. "I guess."

I get the feeling there's more she isn't telling us. Questions rise in my mind like bubbles in champagne. Why the sudden about-face with her friendship? Was it really concern for Akira on this sensitive holiday, or was Paisley losing patience waiting for the prestigious job she desired, certain she'd be first in line with the boss lady out of the picture? And why meet at the summit? It placed her up there at the time of Annmarie's fall, which is quite the coincidence.

"What about all the snow that was on your boots? It was practically up to your knees."

Paisley dips her chin, her cheeks flushing such a deep red they rival the crepe paper Cupids dangling from the ceiling. "I fell in a snowbank."

"While you were waiting for Akira?" I ask.

"Yes. I looked around for her before giving up and returning to base and accidentally stepped in snow that was too deep."

I wonder if she's too deep in anything else.

Sage follows my lead as I get to my feet. "Keep reaching out to Akira," I say. "She'll come around."

Paisley just gives me a twisted smile, calling me out on my lie.

Because here's the thing about female friendships: They can be some of the most fulfilling relationships in your life, full of wisdom, laughter, and support. And chocolate and wine, naturally. But that trust, once broken, is hard to earn back.

With one hand pressed against the door, I glance over my shoulder at Paisley. She's retreated back into her private musings, staring unseeing out the window, perhaps wading through memories of a time when she didn't feel so alone. Or perhaps contemplating her next kill. You know, tomayto, tomahto.

Lost-and-found tubs are always full of an odd mishmash of belongings. Discarded shoes, which I have to question how someone failed to notice, single gloves, accidentally dropped and forgotten, and then there are the more cherished items. Jewelry, stuffed animals, books, some so worn you know there's someone missing it dearly.

We scour every inch of the forest-green plastic tub, but unfortunately for Sage, there's no lightsaber pin.

Nor is there a tennis bracelet or sapphire pendant. Not that I actually expected to stumble across them, but you never know. Once again, I can't help but speculate about the timing of the thefts and if they could be related to Annmarie. Was she a target, the owner of some precious gem? Was she wearing any jewelry the morning she died? I shake my head, flummoxed.

"Oh well," Sage says. "It was worth a shot."

"It may still turn up." I wrap my arm around her shoulders and steer her through the bustling hotel lobby, hoping a distraction will take her mind off her missing nerd-canon. "Come on, there's someone else we need to talk to."

We dodge and weave among groups of people, laughter ricocheting off the walls. It's only the afternoon and there's already a charged energy in the air, an unrestrained rowdiness as if anything could happen.

We find Akira at the hotel bar, a taster of red wine before her—something aged and jammy if the legs dripping down the crystal bowl are any indication. With a journal open before her, she alternates between sniffing, swirling, and holding the liquid to the light. She takes a dainty sip, breathing in and gurgling to help aerate the wine, and then finally swallows.

"And the verdict?" I ask.

"Needs to breathe, but it should pair well with the bison tonight." She makes a note in her journal and closes it. "Care for a glass?"

"Maybe later," I answer, eyeing the label with undisguised curiosity.

"I heard about the fire," Akira says, her voice laced with concern. "Are you all right?"

Of course, rumors of my brush with death would circulate the resort like CO_2 in fermenting must. I play for nonchalance, waving it off. "It succeeded in warming me up after a cold morning on the slopes." I shift on my feet, wrapping my arms across my chest. "Does stuff like that happen often around here?"

"Definitely not," Akira says. "This weekend is cursed."

"Can't disagree, there," I grumble. Seriously, I knew this weekend might be tough for me to swallow, but I never expected murder, theft, *and* multiple attacks on my person. This is as good a segue as any. "We bumped into Paisley a little bit ago."

"Oh?" Akira busies herself below the counter, emerging with another bottle of red. This one is a merlot with a simple cream label, the font a classic typeface.

Wine labels are like people. Intriguing artistry may convince a consumer to take a closer gander, but sometimes it's the basic designs that contain a truly special vintage. In other words, what you see isn't always what you get.

"She said she reached out to you about meeting at the summit yesterday morning," I say. "Is that true?"

She fumbles with the opener, accidentally pricking her finger. She sucks in a breath, pressing a rag to where blood pools on her thumb. "She sent me a text, but I never responded, barely even read it."

"You don't forgive her?" I ask.

"Would you?"

"Probably not," I acquiesce, although really, we can't have too many friends in this world.

"Not based on just a text," Sage says, removing her hat and teasing her locks of hair. "Ice cream should be involved and, at the very least, groveling."

Akira comes around the side of the bar, her hand wrapped in the towel. "The thing you have to understand about Paisley is that *she* doesn't even know who she is." Her eyes are locked on mine from behind her octagonal glasses, willing me to understand. "Before she started working here, Paisley was apparently super into art history, then, after she landed a job as Annmarie's administrative assistant, she took up skiing." The words pour out, an avalanche that's been building for ages. "When I met her, a few years after that, she was well on her way to becoming a ski bum. And now look at her, parading around in those ridiculous suits."

This view of Paisley is alarming, a chameleon who sheds her skin, morphing into different personalities to satisfy her whims.

"It makes it impossible to know what to trust," Sage says. She gives an ironic smile, the freckles across her nose extra prominent from snowboarding, the ultraviolet amplified by the reflective ice. "I'm familiar with the model."

Sage doesn't like discussing her mom, who, in addition to being a sorry excuse for a parent, essentially becomes an extension of everyone she dates. Honestly, I'm surprised Sage shared this much.

Sage's phone rings, the first few bars of the *Star Wars* theme song blaring from her pocket. She checks the screen, lines appearing on her brow. "I should take this." She points at me as she backs away. "I'll be right over there. Wait for me."

I give her a salute and then turn back to Akira. "Would Paisley have had any reason to harm Annmarie?"

"Of course." Akira says this as if it were entirely obvious. "Paisley blamed Annmarie for everything. Not giving her more responsibility—more money."

Passive. That's what Annmarie had called Paisley. Which meant the Olympian saw through her act.

"That fire you heard about, it wasn't an accident." I shudder, licking my lips. "It was intentional, meant for me. Any idea why I'd suddenly have a target on my back?"

Akira shakes her head, baffled. "You seem nice enough to me."

I smile gratefully; I've been called worse in my day. "Any idea where I might find Micah?"

"The liftie? What do you want with him?"

"To ask a few questions."

"You could try the kitchen," she offers. "He sometimes hangs out there begging for scraps of food from Cash when he's not working or boarding."

At Cash's name, there's the slightest inflection in her voice, just the opening I need. "So, you and Cash, huh?"

"It's that obvious?"

"Paisley may have mentioned something," I confess. "About you two, and his reputation."

"Breakfast-Lunch-Dinner Guy." She shakes her head, her entire face flushing a deep burgundy. "Can you imagine going out with a guy and then learning *that* was his nickname? It was mortifying."

"Did you guys hit it off?"

"Well, sure, but what does it matter? I was just one in a long line of conquests to him."

I can see why Akira feels that way, but I'm not so convinced. You see, I have a soft spot for guys who aren't as suave at navigating relationships as they are pickup lines. Heck, I'm dating one. Although, to be fair, Reid's proven far more apt at that than I have lately.

"What comes after dinner?" I ask, fiddling with my scarf. My grape necklace, the usual subject of my fidgeting, is tucked below too many layers of outerwear for me to reach.

"No one ever told me."

"Hmm." Perhaps no one made it that far, or perhaps the gossip mill has been too hard on Cash. Either way, I've badgered her enough with questions, and Sage has finished her call.

I flash Akira a wink, "Can't wait to see what wine you recommend at dinner."

Chapter Fourteen

The rec room is composed of two pool tables, a glass-enclosed music area complete with complimentary instruments, televisions mounted at each corner tuned to a local sports channel, and tucked along one side, a bouldering wall.

"If I'd known this was here, I would've checked it out sooner," I say, dancing my fingers along the slate-gray wall, routes designated by different-colored grips. Thin mats line the floor beneath, even though there's never far to fall with bouldering.

I suspect this climbing wall is more for decoration, that the hotel staff didn't actually expect guests to use it with the plethora of alfresco offerings. That's not about to stop me.

Sage's work call turned into a legal emergency—a

precedent to research, a subpoena or some such to file—so I met up with Reid and Liam.

They're finishing a game of pool, which Reid is handily winning. He points at the corner pocket with his cue and then confidently sends the eight ball rolling into it.

Liam lets out what almost sounds like a whimper. "Thank God that's over. What a bloodbath." From the number of striped balls left on the table, *bloodbath* is an accurate description.

"Let's see what you've got," Reid says with a nod at the wall.

"You don't need to tell me twice." I peel off my coat and boots, placing them carefully on a chair off to the side. I don't have chalk, climbing shoes, or flexible clothing, but that fits with what this sport is all about—getting from one point to the next with only what you have on your back.

I pull myself onto the royal purple route. My biceps flex and strain, and I have to press down harder with my sock-clad feet to make purchase. Endorphins course through my body at the mental and physical exercise, an internal sigh after the stress of the day.

The next maneuver will require balance and patience, toe first and then fingers, which will barely reach the grip, followed by the rest of my body. Before apprehension can settle in, I go for it. My toe nestles into the foothold no problem, but my fingers slip, barely managing to hang on. I steady myself and prep for the next maneuver.

Reid whistles and claps while Liam taunts, "You call that climbing?"

Even with an audience, I find myself able to escape into something akin to a runner's high. My body taut like the string of a perfectly tuned guitar, my subconscious meandering where it will, all sense of time suspended.

I think about knots. The figure eights when I go climbing, the cinnamon twists sold at the Laughing Rooster, and the gnarled shoots of grapevines.

When left to their own devices, grapevines will grow tangled along the ground, hindering the yield. However, when they're clipped and tied, neatly guided vertically, they produce more fruit.

If only I could figure out how to unravel the knots of Silver Creek—make sense of what happened to Annmarie, and why I'm now involved.

Faces flash in my mind: Paisley, Hudson, Akira, Cash, Boone, and a shadowed silhouette of the mysterious Micah.

That's when I slip.

My right foot dangles and my palms grow sweaty, making it impossible for my fingers to hang on. I fall backward, arms flailing, a shout of warning wrenched from my throat. And I bang smack into Reid, who tried to rush to my aid.

We both go down onto the mat in a mess of limbs. We try to pull ourselves together, but that results in me accidentally elbowing him and Reid nearly toppling me over with his long legs.

We descend into a fit of laughter at our awkwardness and lack of coordination. I'm still chuckling as Liam lends each of us a hand and pulls us to our feet.

"I thought we were trying to keep you safe," Liam scoffs, a patronizing edge to his voice.

"Right," I say, barely refraining from rolling my eyes as I dust myself off. "Speaking of, I need your help with something."

Liam lets out a sigh. "Guess it was too much to hope I'd get out of babysitting you."

"You should count yourself lucky." In a show of peak maturity, I stick my tongue out at him. "But seriously, I'd like some shots for my website and the mountains are a great backdrop." This is a blatant lie, the purpose being to get rid of Reid so I can get to work on my surprise.

"You got it, sis."

"In that case, I'll go get cleaned up for our evening," Reid says. He wraps his arms around my waist and lightly brushes his lips against mine.

The kiss leaves me craving more, which was exactly the point. I lean my forehead against his. "I'll catch up with you soon."

"Where would you like the shots?" Liam says, his camera bag slung over one shoulder. He follows me out of the elevator and down the hallway.

"Oh, that," I say with a wave. "Nowhere."

Liam comes to a full stop. "This better not be about the investigation."

I spin around, widening my eyes and holding a hand over my chest in mock offense. "It isn't," I say. "This is about a surprise for Reid, and your taking photos was a convenient excuse so I can actually pull it off."

Liam narrows his eyes at me, wary and full of suspicion "Where exactly are we going, then?"

"The kitchen."

He tips his head to the side. "Okay, I'm curious to see where this goes, and in support of you finally getting into the holiday spirit." He slips his hands in his pockets, momentarily mollified. "Who, pray tell, will be doing the cooking?"

"Yours truly."

"So, what'll it be? Toast, spaghetti, cereal?"

"Hey, I know how to make more than that." Even as I defend my culinary skills, a jolt of nerves slithers up my spine.

In the months Reid and I have been together, I've rarely cooked for him, and when I did, it was usually in the vein of the dishes Liam referenced. Comforting and tasty, yes, but simple; without much thought or planning. But that's why this gift might just be perfect. Or an utter disaster.

I change the topic. "Did you ever listen to that voice mail that could be—no probably definitely is—a potential client?"

"No," Liam says evenly. "Because it's the weekend, when normal people rest."

"Normal is boring," I say. We turn down another hallway, which leads to the kitchen, the resort becoming as easy to navigate as my tiny apartment in Boulder. "Can I listen?"

"If you promise to stop bugging me about it."

"Promise," I say, making a grabby-hand gesture.

Liam unlocks his phone and gives it to me. "Don't get your hopes up. It's probably spam, or a politician."

I press play and hold his cell up to my ear. Sure enough, it's a potential client in need of a photographer. But as I listen, my jaw drops until it's practically dragging across the floor. Because it's not just any client.

One thing not many people realize about Colorado is that we're a musical hub. Home of bands such as The

Fray, OneRepublic, and The Lumineers. And the rock legend seeking my brother's help is big. So big it would put Valentine Photos on the map for good.

Jimmy Mickelson became huge in the early 2000s as a member of a boy band and then broke out on his own. His soulful vocals, poetic lyrics, and catchy harmonies made him a bona fide virtuoso. These days, he sells out venues as large as Red Rocks in a matter of minutes.

"What is it?" Liam asks, concern etched in his features.

We come to a stop outside the resort restaurant, the glass-paned French doors closed to service, the vast space inside empty.

When I don't answer, just open and close my mouth again, flabbergasted, he continues, "Very cute, Parker. You've made your point."

Liam makes to take his phone back but I shake my head, finally finding my voice again. "No, you have to listen to this. It's incredible."

I hold his phone between us and put it on speaker, watching Liam's eyes grow wider as he listens.

"It can't be . . ." he trails off, stunned.

"It could, though."

"It must be a scam, some sort of weird joke." Liam blinks rapidly, holding one hand to his forehead. "Where would he even have found out about me?"

"Maybe from that local contest you placed in—the Colors of Colorado—or from your website."

He drops his hand to his side, entirely unconvinced. "So he was the one visitor."

"Jimmy Mickelson is notorious for spotlighting local artists," I argue. "But you'll never know if you don't call back." I dangle the carrot—er, phone—in front of him.

"Fine," he says. "Don't go anywhere without telling me. I'll meet you in the kitchen in a second."

It's the lull between lunch and dinner, but the kitchen is anything but quiet.

Sous chefs and line cooks are busy chopping vegetables, stirring sauces, and breaking down protein. Basically all of the little things that make dinner services go off without a hitch.

Steam wafts from saucepans and shouts echo through the space, snapped directions and exchanged witticisms. I stick to the perimeter of the stainless-steel haven, treading gingerly so as to stay out of the way.

I find Cash at the largest cutting board, carefully prepping a silver-scaled fish with opaque flesh and clear eyes.

"What's this going to be?"

His eyes flit to mine before returning to his task, and a very sharp chef's knife. "Peruvian ceviche. Lots of lime, chilies, and cilantro." He waggles both eyebrows, chin bowed, his hair curled into tiny corkscrews.

"I'll have to try it later."

"You should." He slices another perfect fillet and sets it aside and deftly flips the fish over. "But somehow I doubt you came here for a preview of the menu."

"I was hoping you could help me with something. A couple things, actually."

He sets his knife down, giving me his full attention, one eyebrow raised in undisguised curiosity. "Need another burner?"

"Yes, but not until tomorrow morning. And any chance I could borrow a few ingredients? I'll pay for them."

"How about you keep the ingredients—something tells me I won't want them back when you're done."

"Touché," I say with a chuckle, divulging the rest of my plan, finishing with, "It's for Reid."

"Consider it done."

"Thanks," I say, relieved. The ease with which he agreed to help me is further proof his dubious reputation as the Breakfast-Lunch-Dinner Guy isn't entirely justified. "Hey, have you seen Micah around?"

Cash snorts, going back to his precise incisions. "What do you want with him?"

"To ask a couple questions. Akira mentioned he might be back here."

I gauge his reaction to Akira's name. There is none. His features are unreadable, subdued, which from what I know of Cash, is telling enough.

A door on the far side of the kitchen island opens to the back alley, where there's a loading dock of deliveries and access to rubbish and recycling bins. Snow swirls around a figure I can only describe as a dude, with dirty-blond hair down to his ears, a knit beanie low over his forehead, and goggle tan lines stark across his face.

"You're in luck. Here he is now," Cash says. "No doubt scavenging for food instead of paying me what he owes from our game last night." He says this last bit animatedly and loud enough to get Micah's attention.

Micah hangs his coat on a hook inside the door and struts to my side. "You bellowed."

"The lady here wants a word with you," Cash says. "But take it outside my kitchen, please."

"Any chance of some fries first?"

"Do I look like a drive-through?" Cash shakes his

head with feigned annoyance. "There's flatbread by the soda fountain, wrong order from earlier."

"Aye, aye, Captain." Micah rubs his hands together and snags a slice of the flatbread—the same kind we tasted at happy hour yesterday, with root vegetables, chèvre, and hazelnuts. I'm tempted to take a slice myself but resist when Micah waves for me to follow him through the door and into the dining area.

The room seems more spacious when it's empty, noises echoing as they would in a cavern. The tables are strewn in clean cream linens, but the place settings haven't been laid out yet, nor the tea lights lit. The centerpiece roses perfume the air, not yet overcome by the cuisine.

I drum my fingers on the closest table, which also happens to be the one where I first presented my mulled wine to Akira and Annmarie. It was only two days ago, but it feels like a lifetime.

Micah leans against one of the pillars, looking completely at home, and flashes me a half smirk. "So what can I do for you?" He devours the sliver of flatbread in one bite, his eyes framed by long lashes.

"I was hoping you could answer a couple questions about the other morning. I, uh, heard you abandoned your post early."

He swallows too quickly, pounding at his chest. I worry I'll have to do the Heimlich—which wouldn't bode well for anyone—but thankfully he gets himself under control, pushing off the pillar and straightening to his full height.

Micah's eyes shift from lazy to sharp in an instant. "Hold up. That's not what happened." He pulls off his beanie and runs his fingers through his locks of hair. "Who are you, anyway? The rotation police?"

"Not even a little bit. I'm Parker." I flash him a benign smile, not giving any more explanation. "Boone mentioned he relieved you early."

"Yeah, I'm still new at this gig. Boone took pity on me, helped me out. I'd been chatting too much and the lift line got long."

"Why did he take pity on you? What were you struggling with?" Boone had only said that Micah was having a tough time and still figuring out how things work. Nightmarish images flash through my mind of a chairlift operator not knowing the whereabouts of the emergency stop.

Micah shrugs. "The line was getting long, restless, and trust me, a lot of the tourists are *not* used to being kept waiting."

My shoulders relax. "What did you do after Boone relieved you?"

"Hit the north bowl off of Petram with a few buddies. The snow was righteous."

Petram Peak is the neighboring mountain, still a part of Silver Creek Resort, and the bowl is supposedly one of the toughest in the state. It's also easy enough to verify, with witnesses to confirm his alibi, which means he probably isn't lying.

"What chairlift were you stationed at?"

"Oslo Outpost."

My fingertips tingle as recognition dawns on me. "That's the lift about halfway up the mountain, right?" Not adding that it's also the one closest to Lockdown Pass, where Annmarie was taken down.

He nods his head vigorously. "You've got a good lay of the land."

I give him a wry smile; as if I could forget where I'd watched Annmarie die. "Did you see or hear anything odd?"

"Odd, how?"

"Like, anything—or anyone—in the surrounding trees?" I refrain from suggesting an ambiguous shadow or shout.

"Nah." He lets out a chortle and continues, "Though I met a guy from New Zealand who was telling me about shredding on an active volcano. Sounded wild."

"While the chairlift was running?" I ask, my eyebrows rising into my bangs. No wonder the line got so long.

"I like to chat with people, so sue me."

The door to the dining room opens, the squeak of the hinge reverberating off the walls. Liam spots me and strides in my direction, hands in the pockets of his skinny jeans, a dazed expression on his face.

It's obvious I'm not going to learn more from Micah, and I'm dying to hear if Liam spoke to *the* Jimmy Mickelson.

"I'll let you get back before the rest of the flatbread is gone," I say to Micah, who rubs his hands together gleefully, disappearing into the kitchen like a child on Christmas morning.

"What's this about flatbread?" Liam asks.

"Not important," I say. "So, was the voice mail for real or an elaborate prank?"

"Real. Very real. I talked to Jimmy Mickelson's publicist, who's going to pass my message along. Jimmy needs shots for his upcoming tour—posters, flyers, social shares, the works." Liam runs a hand through his raven hair, blowing air from puffed-out cheeks. "I hope I didn't royally screw up."

Truth be told, my older brother doesn't have the best record in the screw-up department. But photography is something he cares about so deeply, even the monotony of portraits fulfilling his passion, that I go for encouragement. "I'm sure you did great."

"You were right. I should've called back earlier." Creases form on his forehead and around his mouth.

He's beating himself up plenty so I decide not to rub it in. "It was within a few hours, which is totally respectable."

He grunts, his blue-gray eyes searching mine. "Did you do what you needed for your surprise?"

"Sure did," I say. "Let's return to our Valentines, shall we?"

Chapter Fifteen

So here's the thing: despite all the people I've talked with about Annmarie, I don't know her any better than I did following our brief interaction.

Sure, everyone is familiar with her legend—Olympian, mega successful businesswoman, style guru. A fierce competitor in every aspect her life. But no one can tell me if she was funny, her political leanings, or if anything had been bothering her.

Which is why, before the door even shuts behind me when I return to our hotel room, I beg Reid to help me track down Boone.

He's relaxing on the couch, one arm sprawled behind him, his feet propped on the coffee table, a college football game on in the background. His sandy-blond hair is darker, with coppery undertones like port running through it, still damp from the shower and expertly mussed.

Every fiber of my being is aching to join him, to give in to the alluring gravitational pull that is Reid.

Instead, I position myself in front of him and flutter my eyelashes. "Come on, please."

He tugs on my hand, pulling me into his lap, enveloping me with his strong arms. Our faces are inches apart, so close I can see the flecks of gold in his eyes, like tiny yellow grapes dotting a vibrant-green vine. "Why is this so important to you?"

"Because I want to know who did this," I start, licking my lips. "Who killed Annmarie, who tried to freeze us on the rooftop and melt me into a puddle of Parker. I think Boone might know something."

"Why not leave it to the sheriff and enjoy this time together?" He folds me into the nook at his shoulder, tracing tiny circles on my lower back. "That was the point of this weekend, after all."

Oh, that nook. I lean in, turning my head into his chest and breathing in his aroma. Peppermint, citrus, and herbs, and a faint hint of fabric softener from his flannel shirt. I could stay here forever, basking in Reid's warmth, the chemistry coursing between us. I trail my fingers up and down his abs, palpable beneath his layers. If only . . .

Images assail my mind. Annmarie's crumpled, unmoving body. The complete darkness on the roof, the fear and chattering teeth. The smoke billowing around the hotel door and the taste of ash on my tongue.

"Trust me, I know. I wish things were different." I move off his lap and onto my own cushion, massaging my temples. "But whenever I sit still, I relive everything, and I'm terrified of what might happen next." My heart pounds and a cold sweat breaks out at the nape of my neck. Then I voice my deepest fear, the one I've barely acknowledged myself. "And I'm scared that even after we leave here, I won't be safe."

Reid sits forward, eyebrows furrowed in concern. "Why wouldn't you be?"

I shake my head, my hair brushing against the knitted pattern of my ivory sweater, focusing on cheers coming from the television screen. "Forget it, I'm being ridiculous."

"You're not getting off that easy." He tips my chin toward him so I can't escape his gaze—full of curiosity, impulsivity, and kindness. It completely demolishes me. "You can tell me anything."

"Because of what I know." A shiver rakes through my body, making me convulse. I wrap my fingers around the crystal beads of my necklace, willing it to give me strength. "The killer must have seen me talking to the sheriff, caught wind of my witness statement. Which means the shadow, the shout, however vague, were important."

Reid drops his feet to the carpeted floor and rubs the scruff on his chin. "And you think talking to Boone will help?"

"Everyone says he knew Annmarie best. She even left her estate to him. It can't hurt." I give him a tiny shrug. "I can't just do nothing."

"Well, we wouldn't be doing nothing." He flashes me a roguish wink, and that makes my cheeks burst into flames, the innuendo as subtle as an oaky California chardonnay. Which is to say, not subtle at all.

I nudge him with my shoulder. "You know what I mean."

"I do." He tugs on his boots and ties the laces. "Which is why I'll do it."

"Really?"

"Really." He snags his coat and hat, leaving me scrambling to catch up in layering for the heavy snow outside. "Did you convince Sage and Liam to join in your sleuthing?"

"Unintentionally." Although I'm sure Sage knew exactly why I was questioning Paisley and Akira. She's too smart not to pick up on my schemes. As for Liam, what he doesn't know won't hurt him.

I shrug on my coat and tie my scarf into a French knot. We're making to leave when Reid takes my hand. He zips up my coat and adjusts the collar with such tenderness my breath hitches. He brushes his lips over mine. "Let's go, Sherlock."

The flavors, colors, and textures of wine change during the aging process. Initial fruity or citrus notes fade, giving way to more subtle undertones like herbal, earthy, or honey. Oxidation can turn pale-gold liquid to amber, ruby, all the way to russet. And as tannins disappear over time, white wines become thicker, almost oily, while reds achieve a silky mouthfeel.

If people are the same way, what does that say about the aging gentleman before me?

The weathered lines in his tanned face, the scraggliness of his silver beard, the keen twinkle in his eyes. I wonder where Boone came from, which traits have been there all along and which have been brought out by experience.

Reid and I eventually tracked down the elusive new owner of Silver Creek. We'd started by tromping to the main chairlift, where the line was just as long, if not longer, as it was this morning, the crowd apparently undeterred by the howling wind and poor visibility. We'd dodged and weaved through skiers and snowboarders, their covered faces blurring together, until we found a harried resort employee who directed us here: to Annmarie's former office.

Located on the second floor, across from the conference room where I licked my wounds after the fire, it's every bit as posh as I imagined.

The centerpiece is a gorgeous desk made from refurbished wood. The surface is tidy with a sleek monitor, neat stack of papers, and fancy fountain pen. Elaborate floor-to-ceiling windows line one wall, and opposite those is a rack featuring very shiny and impressive skis. There's even a fireplace and stocked mini fridge for, I imagine, the long hours Annmarie used to put in.

I take a step farther inside, the wet soles of my boots squeaking against the pristine hardwood. On the mantel over the fireplace is a photograph of Annmarie at the ribbon-cutting ceremony outside of Silver Creek Lodge and, nestled against a merlot-red backdrop, shadowboxes holding her Olympic gold medals. They gleam, even in the muted lighting, and appear bulkier in real life.

If it were me, I'd have kept my medals at my humble abode. Somewhere I could gaze upon them adoringly, not so casually show them off to visitors. I find it telling that Annmarie kept hers at her place of work. Perhaps this space was more of a home to her than where she rested her head at night.

I mull this over while Reid makes up some excuse for our visit. Giving me a tour, by the sounds of it.

Boone leans back in Annmarie's office chair, giving the ergonomic number a run for its money. His unbuttoned flannel, waffled long-sleeve tee, and fraying vest scream *casual*, and are at odds with this place meant for silk and cashmere.

"Now, why don't you tell me why you're really here," Boone growls. He looks like he hasn't slept since the accident, deep bags under his eyes exaggerating his wrinkles.

"You caught us." Reid raises his hands in the air, a sheepish smirk on his face. "I came because of this one." He nods toward me.

"I wanted to—" I hesitate, trying to come up with a good excuse besides nosily digging for information. "To pitch you my mulled wine."

Boone's bushy eyebrows raise slightly, in either surprise or annoyance, the only reaction in his chiseled features.

I plunge forward, committed now. "I had a successful meeting with Annmarie when we first got here, and she voiced interest in purchasing a few cases for the lodge."

Boone doesn't respond right away, at least not with words. The corners of his mouth twitch downward and it's as if his entire person sags at Annmarie's name—the reminder of whom he's lost.

He works his jaw as though reining in his emotions and says with a huff, "I tried your stuff. Tasted like wine."

"Ah, what every vintner dreams of hearing." I hold a hand to my chest in jest, warding off the rising guilt at my prying questions. "Did you try it with Annmarie?" I ask, recalling the empty bottle I'd spied in the chairlift operator's station.

"Yeah, she stopped by and shared a taste before my shuttle home."

I can see it now: Annmarie bringing the hallowed beverage to share with Boone, giving him a taste of the new item soon to be added to the menu. Maybe catching up and chatting about their days like family. Maybe discussing a tidbit that could explain this mystery.

Or maybe I'm grasping at grapevines.

Reid snorts, adjusting his hat. "So everyone's still too scared to room with you?"

Boone twists his mouth into a strained version of a smile, tears glistening in his eyes. "No one was ever scared. Annmarie insisted I have my own accommodations. Had her heart in the right place, that one did."

Employee housing is available on a first-come, first-serve basis, and usually requires a roommate, which Cash and Reid were for a season. It speaks volumes that Boone has his own place, provided by a very generous Annmarie. I was right when I suspected I'd see a new side of her by talking with Boone.

I backtrack to something that's been bothering me. "Did she do that often?"

"Bring me wine? No." He runs his fingers along the wiry hairs of his beard. "That was a first."

"I think what Parker meant was come by your office. Your old office," Reid amends, glancing around the room in awe. "I don't remember her doing that when I worked here."

"You wouldn't've, would you?" Boone scoffs. "You were always in the kitchen or chasing after some snow bunny."

"So she did, then?" I prompt, half in an attempt to dispel images of my boyfriend with his prior amours.

"Everyone always wanted something from Annmarie—usually money, sometimes just a leg up. Except for me. I don't want or need anything in life, which I think she found refreshing."

That's a bold statement.

I cock my head to the side. "Everyone needs something."

"I'm a simple guy." He raises his hands, palms up in front of him. "I have everything I need here. A steady paycheck, roof over my head, the land beneath my feet."

"Safe to say, you have far more than that now with all of Silver Creek at your disposal," I say, testing the waters. Because, as unexpected as it was, Boone gained the most from Annmarie's death.

He drops his eyes to the desk. "I'd give it all up if I could."

"Really?"

"Of course, if I trusted any of the vultures scavenging around for an easy payday."

And the weird thing is, I believe him. The direct way he says it—the way he shrugs off the money, even views it with disdain.

"Speaking of vultures, did Annmarie ever mention the name Hudson Gray?"

"Might've." Boone levels me with a stare, cutting through my pretense for being here like a crisp sauvignon blanc through creamy burrata. "But you're going to have to tell me who you are and what you're really after."

* * *

I lay it all out on the metaphorical table. How I'm trying to figure out who killed Annmarie. How I'm afraid for my—and Reid's—safety. I withhold specifics, like a napkin tucked on my lap hidden from view, not wanting to give too much away.

Because, take it from me: In this world, you never really know whom you can trust. And even if you're convinced, people can surprise you. Like my ex-boyfriend who preferred his idea of me to the (IMHO, stellar) reality. Or my former assistant who proved to be a talented actress in place of a diligent mentee. Or Reid's family, whom I assumed I could trust based on extension.

So yeah, I keep a few choice nuggets to myself.

Still, the vulnerability leaves me feeling uncomfortable—exposed—but damn, is it effective.

"I still think my mulled wine would make an excellent addition to the menu here," I say as I finish explaining, forever the salesperson. "But that's not the real reason I wanted to see you."

Boone clasps his hands together on the desk. "Why didn't you just say so?"

My voice is cautious as I state the obvious. "Because I didn't think you would take me seriously."

Suddenly, the words he uttered in the bungalow that doubled as his old office float back to me: *If I ever find out who did this, there'll be hell to pay.* Perhaps he's been looking into Annmarie's murder, too. With how broken up he is, it's possible he's even more keen than Jenny or me to discover the culprit.

"Lucky for you, I do. But I don't got a lotta time, the suits have me in meetings all afternoon." Boone tenderly gets to his feet and moves to the window, his silhouette that of a gentle giant cast in an unwanted role. "I know about Hudson, their history, what he wanted from her. He's never been good with the word *no*."

The implication chills me more than my damp socks, slush having wormed its way into my boots during our jaunt outside. I cut a glance to Reid, whose uncharacteristic stillness portends his outrage. His thoughts must go in the same direction as mine.

Hudson almost hit us without realizing it, and he hounded Annmarie until her death. Who knows what else he's capable of?

"How long ago were they romantically involved?" I ask.

"Back when they were young pups; don't think it was ever serious, at least not on her side." He speaks facing the clouds and swirling snow outside, the mountain completely obstructed from view by the storm. "Hudson turns up every once in a while, sniffing around for favors. Annmarie usually sent him packing. But he was more determined this time and she never got the chance."

"I ran into him downstairs looking at old pictures of their club ski team." Just thinking of my conversation with Hudson makes me feel grimy and like I need a shower.

The glowing embers in the fireplace and dark backdrop imbue Boone's words with a heady importance. "Never did understand why Annmarie wanted that hanging for all to see."

I peel my tongue from the roof of my suddenly dry mouth. "Why not?"

Boone twists his neck, glancing first at me and then Reid. His tone turns conspiratorial. "Because of her coach. Did you notice him, the smug bastard at the end?" He dips his chin, his beard reaching his chest. "Pat did a number on her, was the reason she kept everyone at a distance."

"I figured that was because of her parents' early death," I admit with a frown. The media painted Annmarie as a talented yet tragic child, made to overcome loss too young, harnessing skills her parents were never able to appreciate.

"Well, that, too," he acknowledges. "I think that's what made it possible for that asshole to weasel his way in, get away with what he did."

"What's this about her ski coach?" Reid asks, tugging off his hat. His hair goes in every which direction, not unlike this conversation.

"He abused her."

This statement seems to suck all the sound from the room, leaving in its place a stillness, a numbness.

"What kind of abuse?" I ask as if from a distance, my own voice muffled.

"Only verbally, so far as I can tell. But that's enough, ain't it?"

With disgust, I recall the coach from the picture downstairs, the middle-aged man with the thinning hair and frown, an air of utter dissatisfaction about him. The coach, Hudson said, even had a hard time keeping up with Annmarie. Was it jealousy, spite, or some malignant evil that had driven him?

Reid takes my hand, lacing his fingers through mine in a gesture of support. His touch tethers me to the ground.

"I've never heard so much as a whisper about this," I say, forcing myself to swallow. "Her childhood coach?

You're sure?" Although if there's anyone who would know, it would be Boone. After all, Annmarie did name a run—Clymen—after his middle name, after all.

"Aye," he says morosely. "Took Annmarie years before she confided in me. It wasn't all the kids, either, just the talented ones like Annmarie."

He hangs his head. "It was a twisted relationship. She appreciated him for making her the best, but resented the things he used to say—what he used to call her."

"Poor Annmarie," I say, the statement hardly doing justice to what she'd endured.

No wonder Annmarie didn't let many people into her inner circle. Her entire life, she'd been contending with those who would use her for her success *and* a childhood that would leave anyone with scars. I can't even begin to imagine what that would be like—the level of pain that would result in.

Her advice to Paisley to *toughen up*, which at first seemed harsh and cruel, takes on a new meaning. Perhaps Annmarie was being genuine, showing a snippet of herself to her employee and sharing what helped her not just survive but thrive. Even if it wasn't the healthiest strategy.

Reid's voice, rough and full of emotion, draws me back to the present. "Is he still alive?"

I follow his train of thought like tracks left in the snow. What if he's *still* coaching? What if Annmarie decided to go to the press about the abuse she'd experienced? Had finally threatened to take her childhood coach down and make sure he never hurt anyone again?

"No," Boone says gruffly. "Pancreatic cancer. Took him too fast, if you ask me."

Okay, so no go on the coach motive.

I chew on my lower lip, stunned afresh by this intel. "I had no idea."

"No one did. Annmarie kept it quiet, like she did everything else." Boone's face is full of such poignant sadness, it practically drips from his features.

It's then that it dawns on me just how isolated Annmarie really was. During our brief wine-tasting meeting, she'd seemed so cool and confident, maybe a little stressed, but mostly happy. But for all her poise and success, she was alone.

I give Reid's hand an appreciative squeeze.

Chapter Sixteen

The revelations about Annmarie churn in my stomach like a too-rich meal and overly tannic wine: headache inducing and slightly nauseating.

In the sanctuary of our (feline-free) room, Reid and I talk in circles, cycling through potential suspects, who would have had it out for Annmarie, what her past might have to do with her present, and how hard it must have been to suffer all she had alone.

The conversation doesn't help the pounding at my temples, my headache no doubt a combination of dehydration from the altitude, the swift pressure change of the storm, and extreme stress.

There's ample room for pacing in our suite. I go back and forth in front of the window until I'm sure I'll wear down the plush carpet.

"Could have been another ski-resort owner trying to

eliminate the competition," Reid posits from the couch, nibbling on a handful of trail mix.

I pause, foot midair, and pivot toward him. "Would someone in that position really make that sort of gamble?"

"Ah, let me beguile you with the sordid history of Colorado ski resorts." He pats the cushion next to him.

Curiously, I take a seat, nuzzling back into the cushion. My poor feet practically let out a sigh of relief. Between the skiing, ice-skating, bouldering, and nonstop pacing, they're beyond sore. Too bad a soak in the Jacuzzi is out of the question. Possibly forever.

I snag my bottle of water from the end table and take a sip. It's weird how when you're thirsty enough, water has a flavor. Crisp, clean, and minerally. "What sort of sordid history?"

A spark enters Reid's eyes as he turns toward me. "Did you know there used to be a ski resort in the Springs?"

Reid is referring to Colorado Springs, the next major town south of Denver. Home of the breathtaking Garden of the Gods, lofty Pikes Peak, and impressive U.S. Air Force Academy, but to my knowledge, nothing resembling a ski resort.

"No," I say. "There aren't any now, are there?"

"That's because when the city sold it to Vrain Corp in the early nineties, they closed it so it wouldn't compete with their other resorts along I-70."

I've lived in Colorado my entire life and have never heard this story. "How do you know this?"

He shrugs nonchalantly. "Because I was curious. There are mountains and snow in Colorado Springs, why wouldn't there be one? Even Boulder has Eldora nearby."

Goes to show what a fresh perspective can teach you. Reid, being from Connecticut, wouldn't have the same bits of information ingrained in him so deeply they become unchallenged truth.

"Wouldn't that have broken antitrust laws or something?" No doubt Sage would be able to provide further insight if she were here.

He gives a full-bodied shrug.

If a company was willing to purchase an entire ski resort purely to shut it down, who's to say what else they're capable of? I mean, just the thought of investing that much money—tens of millions of dollars—to take down the competition is mind-boggling.

My cell phone rings, putting an end to that conversation. There's better service in our new room, which gives me a disproportionate amount of comfort.

"Eli," I say in greeting, "you have no idea how happy I am to hear from you."

"That doesn't bode well for your vacation." His voice is deep and smooth, the jibing almost undetectable unless you know him.

I chuckle nervously. "Let's just say there have been some developments."

His tone immediately turns guarded. "What sort of developments?"

Because I'm not sure how well arson will go over, I spare him the details. I have enough people worrying over me, one of whom is perched next to me on the couch.

"Nothing serious." I brush a stray strand of cat hair from my jeans, one of Madeline's, upon further inspection. "So, what've you got for me?"

He exhales and in the background, I can hear the

shuffle of paperwork and chatter. Eli must've gone into the station after I called earlier. You know, after my tumble on the slope but before the whole fire mishap, and hopefully after his lunch date came to a natural and satisfactory close. I mean, someone should enjoy their weekend.

"I dug up some dirt on Hudson Gray. Turns out, he recently acquired permits to develop the land neighboring Silver Creek."

I scoot forward to the edge of the cushion. This has to be related to the business dealings he was discussing with Annmarie. "What sort of permits?"

"Residential," he says. "Mr. Gray tried a few years ago after initially purchasing the land, but the city decided it would remain protected. Part of the national park."

So, Hudson had ambitions to build something neighboring Silver Creek, or expand the resort itself and cut himself in. Who knows if it was a play for money or a means to get closer to Annmarie again? Or both.

"Does he have a history of assault, restraining orders, anything of that nature?" I ask.

Eli inhales sharply. "Do I want to know why you're asking that?"

I cut a glance at Reid, whose jaw is clenched. "No, trust me, you don't."

"Well, he doesn't. Apart from a couple audits, which isn't surprising given the number of properties he owns, his record is squeaky clean."

"Suspiciously clean?"

"You know that's only a thing in the movies, right?" Eli asks, reminding me of my limited knowledge on the way the authorities actually operate. "Look, it's not my jurisdiction and I don't know what's going on up there, but I want to reiterate again that I think you should leave this to the sheriff."

"I appreciate your concern, and your help. Really." I shift, fiddling with the knit on the sleeve of my sweater. "How'd your date go?"

"Good, I think," he says. "We're going to see each other again tomorrow."

"Wow, so soon?" My voice takes on a weird encouraging pitch reminiscent of my mother. "That's a positive sign."

"Yeah . . ." Eli trails off.

There's an awkward silence, made even more awkward by the slight uptick to Reid's lips that tells me he's amused. I nudge his shoulder. Reid is too confident to feel anything as petty as jealousy over my friendship with Eli. That doesn't mean he won't revel in the fact I chose him over the detective last year.

Eli coughs to clear his throat, melting away any lingering discomfort. "You should get back to your weekend."

I lace my fingers through Reid's. "Wonderful idea."

"And try not to worry about this Hudson Gray. He's a real estate mogul after an easy payout, but he's harmless."

"Right," I say. "Thanks again."

I lean back, letting my phone fall into my lap. Why is it the more I'm reassured of something, the less inclined I am to believe it?

Eli referred to Hudson as a harmless mogul, but here's the thing about the word *mogul*: It has different meanings, depending on the context. On one hand, it could mean a powerhouse tycoon, an industry leader. And on the other, obstacles on a ski trail, bumps to be navigated. I wonder which Hudson really is.

Snow blankets sounds, even indoors, as if the entire world has donned a pair of noise-canceling headphones. Reid and I make our way to the third floor, our footsteps muffled. Outside the windows lining the hallway, snowflakes are large and dense and the ground is coated in a thick layer of white. At this rate, we'll be lucky to get out of here tomorrow.

I'm quite proud of the way I found out Hudson's room number. I called the front desk and pretended to be his executive assistant with a financial emergency, acting just snooty enough for it to be believable. The concierge lapped up my story, maybe because this happens often with the spotty reception, and doled out his residence: room number 303.

"Is there a way someone could get from Calgary to Clymen on skis, before Lockdown Pass?" I ask, referencing the run Hudson claimed to have been on when Annmarie fell.

Reid rubs his chin, his gaze unfocused as he pictures the map of Silver Creek stored in his mind. "It'd be tricky, and one helluva ride, but sure. Why? You wanna try it tomorrow?"

"Ha. Maybe next time."

We arrive at room 303. Reid and I stand side by side before the door, hands clasped. "Ready?"

Down the hallway, there's a housekeeping cart outside one of the rooms, and beside it, batting at an unraveling roll of toilet paper, is Madeline. She pounces, her ears twitching in consternation as her paws come up empty. That only propels her to try again and again, until she manages to upend the roll from the cart. The sheer innocence of the sight makes me smile, giving me the encouragement I need.

I nod in response to Reid and knock on the sturdy wooden door.

There's a commotion on the other side of the door and it opens, showing a disheveled Hudson. He's in the same sleek gray half-zip fleece and slacks from earlier, but his hair is in disarray and his eyes are rimmed with red, one still veined from a burst blood vessel.

He juts his pointy chin at us. "You," he utters as if he's discovered a bottle of wine has been subjected to taint. "What do you want?"

Reid's hand tenses in mine and I sense the anger radiating off him, his eyes gleaming with a challenge. He'd love an excuse to deck this guy.

"To continue our conversation from the lobby," I answer.

"I have nothing more to say to you." He's one step from slamming the door in our faces, and honestly, I can't blame him. Strangers showing up on his doorstep, demanding information, after I'd already insulted him earlier.

Only, we deserve to know if it was Hudson who locked us out on the rooftop in our swimsuits, Hudson who slid a piece of fiery cardboard into our hotel room.

"We know about the permits you had, your plans to develop the land neighboring Silver Creek."

"What of it?"

"That's what you were arguing with Annmarie about, isn't it?" I plant my feet on the ground, willing them to grow deep roots, somehow sensing matching Hudson toe-to-toe on stubbornness is the only way I'm going to get any information. "She didn't like what you were selling."

"You're way out of line."

"I wonder if the sheriff would think so . . ." I trail off.

His eyes dart from me to Reid, his thumb tapping the doorframe. Possibly trying to decide if I'm for real, which—spoiler alert—I absolutely am.

"Choose your words carefully," Reid says, his tone dangerously calm.

The housekeeper rescues the rogue roll of toilet paper and pushes her cart past, eyeing our strained stances curiously. Madeline follows close behind, eager for another stray bit of tissue to play with.

Hudson doesn't pay them any attention, doesn't see anything beyond us. Instead, he seems to deflate, any pretense of grandiose evaporating. He leans against the doorframe, arms crossed over his chest. If I were him, I'm not sure I'd want to air my dirty laundry where all can see—or, more important, hear—but he starts speaking, wholly unconcerned.

"Annmarie and I had been in talks to build luxe condos on the backside of the mountain, with the option of accessibility to a private chairlift."

I don't even want to know what those would go for. Millions, no doubt, for hardly any square footage. This is eerily similar to the expansion plans at H Basin that Sheriff Jenny mentioned to me. The ones that upset the local community and resulted in a fire that killed two people.

Hudson continues, "We were set to pull the trigger. I came here this weekend to get her signature on the final paperwork to execute, but for some reason, Annmarie backed out."

"Any idea why?"

"Wish I knew," he said. "I tried to ask her—"

"And to convince her otherwise," I add pointedly.

"Wouldn't you?" he challenges. "Everything was lined up, ready to go. Do you know how much time and money I've poured into this deal, and Annmarie, on one of her whims, decides at the last minute she wants to protect that precious sliver of the mountain." Sarcasm and animosity are dripping from his voice.

"Is that why you decided to seek revenge?" I ask.

Hudson's face flushes a deep red and he clamps his mouth shut, breathing rather loudly through his nose.

I sense rather than see Reid move his foot so it's positioned in the path of the door, ready to keep Hudson from shutting us out.

"Of course not," he says, his voice breaking. "I'd almost had her convinced to go through with it again. Leave the tree-saving for someone else." He grows emotional, his chest heaving and, shockingly, a tear slides down his cheek. "I would never."

"Why not?" Reid asks. "Make us believe you."

"I already told you, I was on a different run than Annmarie. I was nowhere near her."

"That's not enough," I say, shaking my head. "Just because you started on Calgary doesn't mean you couldn't have gotten to Annmarie at Lockdown Pass."

Hudson grimaces. He heaves a deep breath and answers, his tone sharp, "I would never because, despite all logic and reason, I loved Annmarie."

Here's the thing about love and hate: They're two sides of the same coin. Both such all-consuming emotions that can twist your thoughts and bend your will, and can turn from one to the other if pressure is applied in the right place. Like breaking an agreement and ending the only contact that remained between them.

Hudson turns his back on us, his hand trembling, and disappears into his hotel room.

I have definite misgivings about following a stranger into close quarters with a killer on the loose. But if we want to learn more, apparently it's a risk we'll have to take. .

I cock an eyebrow at Reid and he sighs and gives a shrug like *Why not?*

We venture inside. It's dark, the only light being what's naturally coming through the window, and so cold it feels as if the thermostat has all but given up.

Hudson's room is similar to ours, rustic log cabin meets modern luxury, decorated with wildlife photographs and an impressive pair of elk antlers. Although his is missing the view of the mountain, instead overlooking a parking lot and the rooftop of a neighboring building.

There's an overnight bag on the dresser, ski equipment piled in the corner, and on the nightstand, the wrapper to a Clif Bar. His meager belongings hint at a life as lonely as Annmarie's, especially given it's Valentine's weekend. Although maybe that's why he chose to visit now. To add a spark of romance to their business proceedings.

Hudson is sitting on the bed, his head in his hands, silver-streaked hair askew.

I lean against the mahogany dresser, blowing warmth into my hands, while Reid hovers near the door.

"This wasn't how it was supposed to go," he says.

"How what was supposed to go?" I ask.

"Anything."

"Preaching to the choir," Reid grumbles.

I shoot Reid an apologetic glance, tempted to hug him—to do whatever I can to turn this disaster of a vacation around. God knows, it certainly hasn't been the getaway we were anticipating.

I refocus on Hudson. "Let me guess, you were going to swoop in and dazzle Annmarie with your brilliant business plan, effectively sweeping her off her feet." I stop, worried I've overstepped. "Am I close?"

He pierces me with his gaze. "That's the gist, but it oversimplifies our relationship, neglects our history."

"What happened between you two?"

"Look, I know your impression of me and frankly, I can't blame you for jumping to the conclusions you did. But you should know Annmarie wasn't completely innocent, either." Hudson rubs his neck while we wait for him to continue, his shoulders hunching forward as if he were carrying a physical burden.

There's something he's dying to get off his chest. I can feel it, like a champagne cork ready to pop.

"She hurt you," I state.

He snorts, the sound loosely resembling a sob. "That's an understatement." His voice cracks. "She made my adolescence hell. Do you know how hard it is to drum up the courage to tell a girl you love her?"

"I've got some idea," Reid says quietly, a throwback to that hurdle in our relationship, one we're thankfully past. "It's harder than steel."

This comparison understandably seems to perplex Hudson, although I know it to be the material Reid's prized chef's knife is made of. "Sure," Hudson says, continuing, "Well, Annmarie was the first girl I ever told—the first one I felt that way about."

I suspect Annmarie is the *only* girl Hudson has ever felt that way about but remain silent, anxious to hear the rest of the story.

"You want to know how she repaid me? By joking about it with the entire girls' ski squad."

I furrow my brow in pity. "Ouch."

"She couldn't just let me down gently, in private. No, she had to use it as leverage to benefit her image." He hangs his head again, hands at his temples. "Despite all that, I continued to love her like a dog nipping at her heels. Love her still."

"No one deserves to be treated like that." *Not even an arrogant, fortune-chasing jerk like you*, I want to add.

"Truth is, her ruthlessness was something I always appreciated about Annmarie." He gets to his feet in one swift motion that puts both Reid and me on edge and strides to the dresser, where a bottle is perched at the far end. He takes a big swallow of who knows what, the plastic camouflaging the contents within. "I tried tapping into her empathy. I told her she owed me for what she put me through as a kid. But if she had any compassion, it was buried too deep."

That must have been what Hudson meant when he'd hissed *You owe me* during that first fight I overheard, right before my mulled wine tasting.

Annmarie had seemed suave and unaffected during our meeting. Then I remember the way her eye twitched, hinting at some underlying stress. Perhaps it was a remnant of her interaction with Hudson, a sign she wasn't as callous as she would have had everyone believe.

"Where do you think her ruthlessness came from?" I ask.

Hudson slouches into an armchair, his profile reflected in the darkening window behind him. "Our old coach was . . ." He trails off, searching for the right word. "Elite. Produced some of the best skiers in the world, but not without restitution."

"Meaning?" Reid asks. He leans against the wall, legs and arms crossed casually.

Hudson takes another swallow from his mystery bottle and winces, which convinces me it contains something far stronger than Gatorade. "Pat demanded perfection, was impossible to please. You developed thick skin or you would burn out." He looks at me, and I'm unsettled by his eyes, such an unusual shade of blue they gleam in the darkness.

"I take it Annmarie developed thick skin," Reid says.

Hudson nods solemnly. "Pat was especially hard on Annmarie. He was very vocal, used to taunt her by calling her *Hangmarie* for how she would hang on to the mountainside with her pole, failing to make a choice going into a turn."

"Hangmarie?" I ask, the nickname niggling in my mind.

"It could have broken her, that name constantly thrown at her—roared at her in front of her peers—when she had no one to console her at home. But it only made her stronger." He shakes his head, his lips twisted in an ironic grin. "No wonder she wouldn't take any crap from me."

"Hangmarie," I mumble again. I tap my lips with my fingers, willing my brain to churn faster, sifting through conversations and observations, even the most seemingly insignificant details.

That's when it hits me—what's bothering me about her coach's malicious nickname. The shout I heard before her accident was similar to Annmarie's name but wasn't quite a perfect fit.

It was Hangmarie, I realize with 100 percent certainty. Thrown into the wind right before the treacherous Lockdown Pass.

"Who would know that's what her coach used to call her?"

"What does it matter?"

I cock my head to the side. "Because unless you can tell us, you're the most likely suspect."

Hudson's skin turns ashen and he answers quickly, "Our coach, old teammates, maybe a very talented journalist." He pauses, the scent of hard liquor discernible on his breath, even from six feet away. "Annmarie hated being called it, resented it. She wouldn't have told many people. At least not willingly."

I push myself off the dresser, clicking my tongue, ready to be out of this dreary, cold room and away from this dreary, gray person.

"Thank you for talking with us," I say. "And I'm sorry for your loss." Although, even now, I can't tell—not really—whether Hudson is more broken up over his financial upset or the loss of Annmarie, the supposed love of his life.

Chapter Seventeen

In vino veritas is Latin for "in wine there is truth."

Now, there are a couple ways to interpret this. The most straightforward being that those under the influence of alcohol are more likely to be honest, sometimes brutally so. But I like to think there's a more romantic meaning as well. That when put through the fermentation process, the flavors of grapes are manipulated, exposing hidden nuances that would otherwise be undetectable.

What sort of truth is there in this case? Who am I to believe?

All I have is my intuition. And Reid, of course.

We're back in our hotel room with the heat cranked, both of us chilled. The snow outside falls relentlessly and the sun dips behind surrounding mountain peaks. Dusk is a tricky time, obscuring what was clear moments before while promising to shroud things further. Village shops glow warmly and the strands of lights twinkle above the cobblestone sidewalks. None of it is enough to cut through the impending darkness.

I throw myself onto our bed, my raven hair splayed behind me and my eyes fixed on the ceiling, not really seeing anything. Hudson's *burn out* comment rings in my ears, causing my chest to clench and my stomach to churn. If his intent was to rattle me, it worked.

I chew the inside of my cheek, focusing on what I *do* know. Certainties bubble to the surface.

Hangmarie. The nickname that haunted Annmarie since her childhood was what eventually killed her. I replay it in my mind, this time from the perspective of Annmarie.

She'd been skiing down the slope, basking in the notoriety of her former glory and masterfully navigating the moguls, nearing the difficult turn. She'd approached Lockdown Pass at breakneck speed, the turn infamous for its sharpness. There was a shout, her old nickname bellowed from the camouflaged thicket of trees. Precisely timed.

She hesitated, flooded with memories, emotions, and, above all, pain. Reminders of the hurt and abuse her childhood coach exacted on her. It would be enough to distract anyone.

The scare tactic worked, distracting Annmarie as she swayed near the trees. For just long enough that the murderer was able to surprise her, hitting her over the head with a hefty branch, hard enough to kill.

Was Annmarie alive when her killer moved her, repositioned her near the tree to make it appear like she had an unfortunate accident? Did her murderer watch her last breath leave her body? And who would—could—do such a thing?

I massage my temples; I'm missing something, I can feel it.

The mattress shifts as Reid sits next to me. He lays back and turns his head toward me, twirling locks of my hair through his fingers. "Want to talk about anything?"

I turn my head so we're nose to nose, relishing the closeness of him, the feeling of my hair being played with. "Did anything Hudson said stick out to you?"

Reid raises his eyebrows and exhales a deep breath. "Only that Annmarie had a harder life than I ever realized—ever would have guessed, given how she carried herself."

"In my experience, it's sometimes the happiest people who have the most tragic stories."

"It takes a lot of courage for someone to become something after all that."

We all carry fragments of our pasts with us, snapshots of the moments that have made us who we are. "If it doesn't kill you, it makes you stronger, right?"

Reid brushes his thumb over my forehead. "We're going to come out of this weekend a force to be reckoned with."

I grab his hand and press it to my lips. "You know I love you, right?"

"It's my good looks, isn't it? No, my skills on a board?" He tucks a hand behind his head, feigning a look of arduous indecision. "There are just so many things."

"Come now," I say, nudging him playfully. "You know it's that you keep me in truffles."

"Fair enough," he says through a laugh.

A sly grin spreads across my face. "I have a surprise for you, by the way. Tomorrow morning. Given we make it to tomorrow morning," I add, only half kidding.

"Parks, that's not necessary." Reid's eyes turn brooding and his forehead creases with worry. "I wasn't trying to put you on the spot with the night tubing, especially after we agreed not to exchange gifts." He winces and shakes his head. "I'm still new to all this."

"Hey, we're in this together, and if anyone messed up, it's me."

I swallow the bile pooling in my mouth. Somehow I know the time has arrived. The time I need to tell Reid why this holiday is so difficult for me, share this bit of myself—my history—with him. And trust that he'll take it for what it is: an offering by which to better understand me.

"Reid, there's something you should know."

He turns to me and waits patiently, his face open and accepting. So, I tell him.

I tell him about Aunt Laura and her Valentine's tradition of spoiling the women in her life, of the sheer adoration she would shower us with. But most of all, I tell Reid how much I miss her, about the ache in my heart when I'm faced with the memories. How I wish I could treasure the joy, if only the sorrow weren't so overwhelming.

When I finish, I can't bring myself to meet his eyes.

At some point, Reid propped himself up on his elbow, squarely facing me on the bed, the duvet pooling around us. He tilts my chin up with his free hand and finally I meet his gaze.

Far from the disaster when I shared this with my ex, Reid's eyes are full of empathy, understanding, and a spark of passion that tells me he doesn't think any less of me. Doesn't find me weak or overemotional.

"I wish I'd known sooner. I would've gotten you something different for Valentine's," he says.

"Like what?" My voice is rough with spent emotion.

"Something that involved booze, to start," he says with a smirk. Then his smile falters and his voice grows soft and unbelievably tender. "No, but really, I would've gotten you something to help keep your aunt close, maybe a bracelet to match that necklace you love so much, or a framed picture for you to put up in your tasting room."

I'm struck by his thoughtfulness, that he has such a firm grip on who I am. My chest clenches.

Reid continues, "At the very least, I would've known why you kept getting so quiet, so in your head."

"I thought I'd hidden it so well."

"Expert vintner? Definitely. Actress? Hmmm." He feigns indecision and shrugs. "I just figured you were upset about Annmarie."

"There was that, too." My hand finds his like opposite sides of two magnets, our fingers intertwining. "You know what I would like?"

"What's that?"

"To forget the hype of this holiday and find a way to do what's right for us."

"I'll toast to that."

While I'm not sure exactly how we're going to do it, at least we're on the same page. "To finding a way." I raise an imaginary glass in the air. He stares, bemused, until I jiggle his hand. "Come on, don't leave a girl hanging."

He pretends to clink his own imaginary glass with

mine and we both mimic taking a sip. "That might've been one of the nerdiest things you've done yet."

"Don't pretend you don't love it."

"I do. More than you know."

We lie side by side. The electricity that always courses between us is there, but I'm aware of an extra tether holding us together, an awareness that we're growing closer with each part of ourselves—our lives—we share. We gaze at each other as dusk turns to night.

While Reid busies himself ordering real glasses of wine to toast with, as well as dinner, to be sent to our room, I settle into the couch with my laptop on my lap and a fleece blanket draped around my shoulders.

With the miracle of the internet, the entire world—heck, the universe—is at my fingertips. If I can only figure out which question to ask.

To warm up, I open my email, where my eyes are immediately drawn to the first message. It's from the Colorado Wine Festival. Swallowing the lump in my throat, I force myself to click on it and read. And I let out an excited *squee*.

Because Vino Valentine has been approved as a vendor for the Colorado Wine Festival in Palisade. I fist-pump the air. Yours truly will officially have a spot among the top vintners in the state this July. This will give my business a welcome boost, especially now that Silver Creek is squarely out of the picture. Sure, an expansion won't be feasible anytime soon, but Zin and I will be kept in vittles this spring.

"Everything okay?" Reid asks from where he's perched at the desk, the phone cradled against his ear.

I shoot him a thumbs-up and he nods, returning to the very important task of getting us sustenance.

Buoyed by this bit of good news, I open a fresh tab and dance my fingers over the keyboard. Without realizing it, I've navigated to Twitter. Despite hashtags having notoriously short life spans, *#BauerPower* is somehow still trending. Then I see why.

Annmarie's obituary was published in the *Denver Post* earlier today. It features a picture of her from the Olympics, medals around her neck and an American flag flapping behind her like a cape, her eyes alight with victory.

I scour the text for clues. It recounts the glory she brought to our state, from her success in skiing to her business savvy. There are few details about her personal life, which I know to reflect her reality. The article finishes with a wish for her to rest in peace, and, per Annmarie's request, donations be made to a foundation that helps give disadvantaged and underprivileged kids the opportunity to learn to ski.

Sadness wells inside me as I continue scrolling through the hashtag. Soon, it becomes apparent that more news outlets have latched on to the story of Annmarie's accident being under investigation. Which means this place will be even more of a circus tomorrow, if that's possible, crawling with journalists and true-crime enthusiasts.

I gnaw on my bottom lip. Wine needs to be stabilized prior to bottling. If not, it can result in lactic problems, spritziness, and remnants of dead yeast. This can damage more than the flavor; it can cause a cork to blow. Silver Creek is a disaster waiting to happen—a proverbial cork ready to pop—unless equilibrium is restored.

My head spins with a sense of impending doom. I

have a bad feeling about the influx of people—what could happen with a killer at large. I focus on the lapping flames in our electric fireplace.

That's when I remember Hudson's *burn out* comment. With a renewed sense of purpose, I Google the Coalition to Save Earth. Articles from a couple years ago populate the screen. I choose one at random that basically sums up what Jenny already told me—after starting the fire in protest to development plans at H Basin, the group was disbanded and charged with arson and involuntary manslaughter. All, that is, except for the lone member who managed to escape.

I navigate back to the search results and scroll further into obscurity, even going so far as to click on the second page. And the one after that.

I'm not sure what I'm looking for but, like a good wine, I'll know it when I taste it—er, see it. I switch over to search images and, bingo, that's when I get lucky.

There's a photograph of the original members of the Coalition to Save Earth. It's grainy, but I'm able to enlarge it, zooming in on the eight men and women in the picture. Four kneel in front, with the others standing behind. They look eerily similar, much like how pets take on the appearance of their owners, with long scraggly hair, sustainably made clothing, and hemp. A rustic cabin is in the background and, from the tense expressions on their faces, they're serious about making a difference.

Now, trust me, I'm all about saving the planet (coming from Boulder, how could I not be?), but this group gives me the heebie-jeebies.

Like a shadow out of the corner of my eye, my attention snags on one of the members. I lean closer to the screen of my laptop, the tip of my nose grazing the monitor. Ice spreads through my core as realization seeps in.

I open the picture in a new window and zoom in again, and then zoom out, repeating the process as if I'm analyzing a tricky Magic Eye. Because I have to be sure.

But there's no doubt in my mind. I recognize one of the members. They're someone I've seen this weekend, chatted with on multiple occasions. And someone who could wreak serious havoc on Silver Creek.

That's when everything comes crashing into place—I know who murdered Annmarie, and why.

I have a plan. A plan to catch a murderer. Which sounds ludicrous, surreal, and very dangerous, hence the plan, which includes contingencies aplenty.

The first part is to loop in Reid, who's still on the phone placing our dinner order. With a nervous energy coursing through me, I wave to get his attention and instruct him to cancel our meal.

His face falls but he does as I say, perhaps sensing something major has shifted. His disappointment evaporates when I show him the photograph I discovered. Then shock settles in.

Reid goes through the same motions I did—zooming in and out to better study the picture. It doesn't take him nearly as long to reach the same conclusion.

"I can't even—" He shakes his head. "But yeah, you're right."

Reid sinks into a very chic yet uncomfortable armchair across the coffee table. He has a dazed expression on his face, his sun-kissed skin taking on a greenish hue, our dinner forgotten.

I close my laptop and lean forward. "Here's what I want to do." I lay it out for him, each and every step, which, if I play things right, will hopefully result in more than the culprit of two crimes behind bars.

Reid rubs both hands over his face, his shoulders tense and lightning flashing in his eyes. "I don't like this, but . . ."

"But?" I ask hopefully.

"You're in charge of your own person. If the sheriff agrees, you can count on me to have your back."

I attempt the equivalent of a wink-kiss emoji, which essentially ends up with me scrunching my face awkwardly. But he gets the gist.

I waste no time calling Sheriff Jenny. She answers her phone on the first ring with an abrupt, "Yeah."

"Hey, this is Parker Valentine from Silver Creek." I can't keep the agitation from creeping into my voice.

I hear a television on in the background, the cheers and chanted *De-fense* letting me know it's the same football game we were watching earlier. Jenny either mutes it or turns it off. "Has there been another fire?"

"Uh, no, actually, I'm calling because I know who's behind everything."

I sense the change in her tone immediately, the hunger and eagerness radiating through our connection. "Who is it?"

"You seem like the type who thinks outside the box, so hear me out."

"No promises." Her voice is no-nonsense, which is fair enough. There's a fine line between being helpful and obstruction of justice.

I spill all the facts. How I came to the conclusion I did, and even a theory as to how this person has managed to remain at large. I finish with, "They'll run again, just like they did before, only this time they might disappear altogether. Unless we approach with caution."

Jenny once mentioned the rules were different up here, that we were in the wilderness. I didn't believe her then, but I do now.

"You're using the word *we* an awful lot," Jenny says, but doesn't disagree with my analysis.

"Plant a vision of what you're selling, one of the keys of good business," I say. "Do I have your buy-in?"

"This isn't a poker game." She's waffling and I can tell she's right on the edge.

"Good thing, too. I don't have much to lose." *And my bluffing needs work*, though that certainly won't convince her.

"What do you have in mind?" Jenny exhales into the phone, her fervor to catch the culprit outweighing her apprehension.

I give her an abbreviated version, highlighting the points relevant to her and her team. "What do you think?"

"Smart. It might just work." From the little I know of Jenny, that's high praise. "But if I sense anything going awry, you need to stand down and me and my officers will take over."

"Absolutely."

My body is trembling when I hang up, a current coursing through my veins. There's no going back, which is as thrilling as it is terrifying.

I nod at Reid, who's been drumming on his knees

absently with his hands. A sign that he's even more nervous and tightly wound than I am.

I imagine what Liam will say when he finds out—the inevitable chiding and bickering—and promptly expel it from my mind. Sometimes the line between what's right and wrong is blurred and there is no easy answer. There's just doing what we can to make the world a better place than the way we found it. And this is my contribution. Achieving justice for Annmarie, setting things right before anyone else gets hurt.

The next thing I do is call the hotel bar.

A distressed bartender answers: "Alpine Bar at Silver Creek." There are shouts in the background and the sound of shattering glass. It must be busy, and the crowd rowdy, wired from the storm.

"Is Akira there?"

"Who?"

"Akira," I say louder.

"Hold on."

A second later, Akira comes to the phone. "Hello?"

"It's Parker. I need your help."

"Of course, whatever you need," she says, although she sounds exhausted and a touch skeptical. Probably from the mob at the bar.

"Before you agree, hear me out . . ." I give her a rundown of what I need and whom to invite. Leaving out the part about this being an elaborate scheme to unmask a murderer, naturally.

At the end, she's miraculously still on the line. "I'll make sure everyone is there."

"Really?"

"Any excuse to get out from behind the bar," she says

as there's another loud shout followed by the sound of shattering glass.

"Happy to help," I say with a nervous chuckle. I don't know how grateful she'll be when she finds out what I'm really up to.

Chapter Eighteen

Mulled wine has been around for a millennia. Initially created to salvage batches of subpar wine, the spices and honey leveraged to mask unpleasant flavors, these days it's a treat. A drink to spread warmth and good cheer. Or, you know, entrap a killer.

I stand at the stovetop in the kitchen, mixing a large stainless-steel pot full of burgundy wine, the last few extra bottles of my Snowy Day Syrah that I'd packed. Scents waft from the surface—cherries, vanilla, and smoke from the wine, citrus from the orange peel, a syrupy sweetness from the honey, and cinnamon and cloves from the spices.

Reid fiddles with utensils, a zester, peeler, and some sort of contraption to peel garlic, perhaps making mental notes of what doodads to purchase later, or perhaps curbing his mounting anxiety. "How much longer does it need?"

"A couple minutes. But we both know flavor isn't what's important."

He gives me a wry grin. "Maybe not, but we just can't help ourselves, can we?"

He's right, of course. No matter the circumstances, we'll both put our best foot forward when it comes to taste.

"You invited Liam and Sage?" I ask.

"Yes, I was vague, just like you asked. They'll be joining us shortly in the lobby." Reid holds my gaze, communicating the rest through his look. That while he wasn't keen on lying by omission, he did it for me, so we can all play our parts.

"Perfect," is all I say.

Sous chefs, line cooks, and servers bustle around us like a stream bypassing boulders. Cash shouts directions intermittently from where he's putting the finishing touches on crystal bowls of ceviche, the succulent fish from earlier paired with thinly sliced chilies, red onion, and cilantro.

Cash was nonplussed when I appeared in his kitchen and requested assistance, so soon after my last visit, when I begged him for a different sort of help. I suspect it's largely thanks to Akira that I was able to bum this burner at all with the dinner service now in full swing. But he acquiesced, giving Reid a pat on the shoulder and a warning not to steal any recipes. As if he would—or would need to.

And thus, each component of my plan has been put into action.

"You should come join us," I say to Cash as I assemble stemless glasses on a tray. "We're doing a Bauer

Power Happy Hour, as a way to commemorate Annmarie."

He glances up, his eyes soulful, a stray curl falling over his forehead. "I'll try to sneak out. Gotta try this wine I keep hearing so much about." His attention shifts so fast it practically gives me whiplash. "Order up," he shouts to a waiting server, adding one final squeeze of lime juice to each bowl.

"Always so loud," Reid says, tutting, holding a hand to his ear.

Steam rises from the surface of my mulled wine, the liquid at just the right temperature, warmed through but not boiling. Dubbing it complete, I go about scooping out the mesh spice packet.

As long as I keep moving, keep focused on the items to cross off my list, my doubts are kept at bay. The same can't be said for my nerves. Which accost me, making my mouth go dry and my hands shake, the wineglasses on the tray rattling against one another as I lift it up.

"Got it okay?" Reid asks, steadying my hands with his. They engulf mine, warm, strong, and capable.

"Sure." I swallow and say with more certainty, "Yes. Will you get the star of the show?" I nod toward the simmering pot.

"You got it, Parks."

Akira pokes her head into the kitchen. There's a sheen of sweat on her forehead, her flannel shirt is rolled to her elbows, and wisps of black hair have escaped her bun. She pushes her wire-rimmed glasses up her nose when she sees us, trying awfully hard not to look in Cash's direction.

She smiles warmly at me. "Ready whenever you are."

I let out one last exhale and hoist the tray, leading the way into the dining room. It's showtime.

The private dining room Akira secured for me is warm and inviting, giving off an intimate ambience. There's a single long table in the center of the room, lined with flickering tea lights and tiny vases of roses. The acoustics are muted, the chatter and commotion from the rest of the restaurant subdued. But the most important feature: a private entrance to the patio.

Through the glass doors, snowflakes continue falling, illuminated by streetlamps. The patio itself is cast in shades of black and white, almost grotesque with the piles of accumulated snow coating furniture such that you can't differentiate a bench from a wagon from a person.

I set the tray of glasses down on the cream-linen surface of the table and Reid carefully places the steaming pot of mulled wine on a heating pad next to it. Then I welcome my guests, those specifically invited tonight under the guise of toasting to Annmarie with my mulled wine.

I carefully ladle glasses of my prized concoction and pass them out to each individual, all sitting in chairs arranged on one side of the table, facing me and with their backs to the patio.

Hudson Gray is at the far end, his gaze fixed on the textured veins in the hardwood, none too happy to be here. Next to him is Paisley Moore, sitting primly in a seat, looking at her tablemates with apparent disapproval. After that are Boone and Micah, who are chatting animatedly about their recent poker game. On their other side are Liam and Sage, who are so perplexed and twitchy I'm afraid they're going to blow the whole charade. Akira takes a seat next to them, appearing relieved to be off her feet.

"Thank you all for coming," I say, resting my hand on Reid's shoulder, my other gripping my own cup of mulled wine. "We wanted to do something to honor—"

The door opens behind me, laughter from the main room spilling in. I twirl around to see who it is, so fast I make myself dizzy. A pit forms in my stomach and I barely manage to maintain my composure.

I sigh in relief. It's only Cash, which is ideal.

"Always have to make an entrance," Boone growls, shaking his head. "Now, get on with it. I've had a long day and would sooner be home."

Reid ladles Cash a cup of mulled wine and passes it to him as he claims the last free chair beside Akira, who stubbornly ignores him.

"As I was saying," I start, clearing my throat, willing strength into my voice. "We wanted to do something to honor Annmarie. I've prepared my mulled wine for your tasting pleasure, as a way to warm you up and help you weather the storm, both figurative and literal." I raise my glass in the air, and everyone follows suit. "I propose a toast. To the champion, the visionary, the legend. May the Bauer Power live on forever. Cheers."

"Hear, hear," Cash says.

I take an infinitesimal sip, wanting to stay sharp. Still, the flavors soothe me. Citrus, honey, and cinnamon; a comforting bouquet to my palate.

It doesn't escape my notice that everyone except for Paisley drinks, the manager studying me with narrowed eyes that make me squirm in my boots. I'd secretly hoped everyone would indulge enough to loosen their tongues and slow their reactions. But alas . . .

What follows is a heady silence, a poignant moment full of respect and, if I'm not mistaken, dismay. I'm almost disappointed I have to broach it.

"There is one other reason I called you all here. *In vino veritas*," I say, gripping my glass in the palm of my hand, mostly to keep from fidgeting with my necklace, an obvious tell for my nerves. "To share what really happened to Annmarie."

There's a general hubbub—gasps, puzzled looks, startled mumbling. Paisley wavers in her seat as if she might pass out. Hudson casts a look down the table, his jaw clenched, emphasizing his pointy chin. Boone may as well be a statue, his features hardly shifting as he treats himself to another swig of mulled wine, a twinkle of amusement in his sky-blue eyes.

Cash leans forward in his seat, elbows resting on his knees. He glances at Akira, who shakes her head, equally flabbergasted.

"Let's begin with Paisley." I pace the length of the table, stopping in front of her. She centers herself by adjusting the lapels of her blazer, her glare daring me to accuse her. "Even though you were upset over not being promoted and receiving some questionable advice, you went to the summit the morning Annmarie died to salvage your friendship with Akira. Not for revenge." I try for an encouraging smile but pretty sure it comes across more like a grimace with all the tension coiled in my belly. "Through all this, I hope you're able to figure out who you really are and not live someone else's life."

Paisley slumps forward, her lips pursed as if she'd bitten into a lemon. She fixes her eyes on me, an unreadable expression in them, before shifting her attention to Akira, who takes a pointed sip from her glass.

I pivot and turn to Hudson, who's as disheveled as before and clearly doesn't need more to drink, if his blotchy face is any indication. "You, Hudson, were genuinely in love with Annmarie, no matter how toxic that relationship may have been. And even though you were on the slope with her—were the last person seen talking with her—you didn't kill Annmarie."

The words come easier now, tumbling out of me like an avalanche, one everyone is keen to observe, no matter the detritus it will leave in its wake.

I continue, watching as Hudson bows his head, his eyes pooling with unshed tears. "Why would you? You'd almost had her convinced to go forward with your business proposal after she'd told you no all weekend." I hold a finger in the air, ready to drive home the clinching factor. "Besides, you didn't know the mountain well enough, having only visited a few times in the last couple months for business."

I pace back in the other direction, past Sage and Liam, whom I look to for encouragement. Sage winks at me despite her confusion and obvious discomfort, her face pale beneath her freckles. Liam shoots me a look of sheer desperation, pleading for me to finally heed his advice and stay safe.

I feel a pang of guilt at involving them, but this gathering had to be believable. Which meant my friends needed to be in attendance. I get a move on it, as much for them as for my own self-preservation.

"Cash," I say, coming to a stop before him.

He glances up sharply, his eyebrows furrowed defensively, his cross earring swinging from his earlobe.

"You're here because there were other truths uncovered this weekend." I soften my tone. "You should tell Akira how you feel. I have a hunch it might come out in your favor." I crinkle my nose and add with a wink, "Unlike your poker game."

He flashes me a cocky smile, somehow always at hand, even in the most tenuous of circumstances. "That obvious, huh?"

"Actually, no. That's the point." For all his bravado, I'd always sensed something between him and Akira. Hopefully this will give them the nudge they need to do something about it. Tomorrow is Valentine's Day, after all.

I turn to Akira. "Trust is hard to earn; so are second chances. Don't let your pride stand in your way of being happy." I want to add that it takes one to know one, that I understand the pain of deception, and that I hope she'll still consider me a friend once this is over. But there's no time, so I convey what I can with my eyes.

I straighten and continue my monologue, stepping forward until I'm in front of Boone, who sets his glass on the table before him and crosses his arms over his broad chest.

"There's one person here who was familiar enough with the mountain to know the most treacherous part and how to distract Annmarie, by shouting the nickname she was tormented with as a child, a nickname only someone close to her would know.

"But this individual made a mistake. Arson: their go-to. After nearly succumbing to flames myself, I researched the missing arsonist from the H Basin fire—something about that story stuck with me—and discovered the face of someone I recognized: Boone."

There are audible gasps as jaws drop along the table like dominoes. I sense Reid move to my side. His shock at seeing Boone in the picture had been like a gut punch. How could it be otherwise? This was a man he worked with, played poker with, proudly introduced me to.

"Granted, it was hard to tell, and was probably overlooked because who would suspect the chairlift operator from a neighboring resort?"

Boone is sitting stock-still, peering at me like a mountain lion would a deer. A very hungry mountain lion stalking a very pitiful deer. "Don't know what you're talking about," he says. His jaw is clamped so tight he barely opens his mouth to speak. "Or who you think you are. You're not the sheriff."

"You're right, I'm not, but it doesn't make what I'm saying any less true." I set my glass of wine on the table, gesturing toward Boone. "Annmarie brought a bottle of my wine to Boone's office the other day, often confiding in him and getting his take on business decisions. She told you about Hudson's development plan, didn't she? In fact, she'd already sought your advice."

There's no answer, but none is needed. "You managed to talk her out of it once, which was why she suddenly tried to call it off. But over my mulled wine, you sensed that Annmarie would eventually move forward with the plans and took measures into your own hands. You see, it occurred to me that the missing arsonist might not have gone far, that the land would have meant too much to them. While the Coalition to Protect Earth was disbanded, you took it upon yourself to continue fighting for their cause. To protect the unmarred wilderness bordering Silver Creek."

"This is ridiculous. I was working that morning."

Boone looks around at his fellow coworkers turned employees for support. "I couldn't have—would never have done that. I loved Annmarie like a daughter." He implores them with his voice and, convincing sod that he is, I can tell he's swaying some. Cash, Micah, and Akira appear sympathetic. Only Hudson and Paisley continue looking at him with suspicion.

"About that alibi." I slide to the right, placing myself directly in front of Micah. "Which chairlift did you say Boone relieved you from?"

It's obvious Micah would rather be anywhere in the world but in the hot seat. He squints, slouching deeper into his chair. His voice cracks as he answers, "Oslo Outpost."

I snap my fingers, swiveling back to Boone. "That's right! Helping out the newbie was a convenient excuse. But the thing about Oslo Outpost is that it's the lift closest to Lockdown Pass, where you realized Annmarie would be—you'd seen her pull enough promotional stunts to know it was her favored run.

"So you took a detour on your way there. You know the mountain better than anyone, knew which thicket of trees to hide in until you saw her approach. Then you shouted *Hangmarie*. But even distracted, she was an expert skier, which is why you came prepared. You pummeled her over the head with a tree branch, hard and swift enough to kill her, and then moved her body to make it look like an accident, wiping away your footprints and discarding the branch farther down the slope. The only thing you didn't count on was a witness: me."

It was Boone's shadow I'd seen moving between the tree trunks that morning, his deep voice I'd heard on the wind.

"None of you believe this load of bull, do ya?" Boone asks. He plants his palms on the table, glancing around him, his desperation tangible as everyone's skepticism grows. There's no one on his side now.

I swallow and force myself to continue, "Which is why, when you heard me telling Sheriff Jenny about what I saw and heard, you ducked out early away from the weekly poker game—claiming the pot was too rich for you—and locked me and Reid outside on the rooftop while we were in the Jacuzzi. You even cut the power to the building *and* the backup generator."

As instructed, Reid takes this as his cue to nonchalantly move to the doors that open into the main restaurant, knocking on the wooden panes as though he were overcome by emotion, which no doubt is partially true.

Boone doesn't even notice, doesn't have eyes for anyone but me.

I meet his gaze, feigning a confidence I wish I felt. "And when that attempt failed, you tried to smoke me out by setting fire to my room, didn't you?"

He doesn't respond, just rumbles his acknowledgment.

"What I don't understand is how you could do that to Annmarie, after everything she'd been through." I clench my hands into fists. "You were the one person she counted on. My God, she left you all of Silver Creek!"

"It was worth it," he spits, a strand of saliva clinging to his unkempt beard.

"To save a bit of land?"

"To preserve our planet for future generations."

"There are other ways." My hair brushes against my shoulders as I shake my head. My throat clenches and I have to force the next words out. "You could have protested, talked to Annmarie. She'd have given you anything."

"I tried to convince Annmarie not to go through with it, and she betrayed me," Boone hisses, sounding so alarmingly unlike himself. "She was prepared to go forward, no matter the cost. I didn't want to"—he breaks off, suddenly overcome with emotion—"she left me no choice."

I take a deep breath. "I think I'll let the sheriff take it from here."

That's when Boone chooses to act. He tips the entire table forward, sending the crystal glasses and stainless-steel pot of mulled wine cascading to the floor. Glass shatters and burgundy liquid gushes across the hardwood. My attention flies back to Boone, who yanks a pocketknife from his belt, leaps over the table as if it were nothing, and charges straight toward me.

Survival instincts take over.

Blood pounds in my ears and pulses in my vision as the world around me moves in slow motion.

My esteemed guests—Hudson, Paisley, Akira, Cash, Liam, and Sage—are safely on the other side of the table, the piece of upturned furniture working as a barricade to protect them. I hazard a glance at Reid, who's holding the door open for the undercover officers racing in from the main dining area. Jenny and even more officers pour in from the patio. But they're not fast enough.

Boone rushes me like a bull, deadly and full of rage but also singularly focused.

Which means he doesn't notice the wine he spilled

pooling on the floor by my feet, a moat between him and me. I back up slowly, hands raised in front of me. Fear floods my body and my stomach plummets straight to the ground. Still, I force myself to maintain eye contact.

It's ironic, really, that distraction—Boone's ultimate weapon against Annmarie—will be his downfall.

He continues charging at me, swinging his arm violently, not caring whom he injures with his knife. A guttural sound tears from his chest. With his towering frame, flared nostrils, and wild hair, he's more grizzly than human.

I wait as long as my wits will allow me, until he's almost upon me, and then, nimble as a cat, I jump to the side.

Unable to change direction, Boone hits the mulled wine, the liquid slippery on the smooth floor. He shuffles his feet back and forth as if he were on ice skates, waving his arms frantically to regain balance. One more large puddle sends him falling flat on his rump.

I'd laugh if the situation weren't so precarious.

If Boone was raging before, he's positively livid now. I know better than to underestimate him.

He gets to his feet faster than I'd have thought possible and lunges forward again, the sharp tip of his knife held in front of him.

But that bit of time was all the officers needed. They approach him from every angle, pistols drawn and at the ready.

"Hands where we can see them," Jenny shouts, taking up the rear.

Boone complies, placing his hands on the back of his head. But the second an officer tries to secure him in handcuffs, he wriggles free, making it two feet before he's intercepted. Two feet too many, in my opinion.

I scoot backward until I'm flat against the log siding. Reid sidles over to me, grasping my hand. I can see it in his eyes—the fear ebbing, giving way to relief.

It takes four officers, plus Sheriff Jenny, to eventually snap handcuffs around Boone's wrists. He fights the entire time, against his bounds and those confining him. No doubt he's already made himself believe he's in the right.

"We've been looking for you for a long time," Jenny says. She seems to take immense pleasure out of reciting Miranda rights. "Get him out of here."

The quartet of uniformed officers lead Boone from the room and into police cars waiting in the street beyond the patio, their sirens flashing blue and red.

When the door to the patrol car closes, I finally relax. I turn and throw my arms around Reid, holding him as close as he's holding me. We stay like that for a moment, basking in the simple pleasure of being able to hug a loved one, our immense good fortune of *having* a loved one to hug.

"We did it," I say, a giddiness spreading through my limbs.

Reid rests his forehead against mine. "I can't believe that worked."

"I can't believe I didn't suspect this was all a ruse," Liam says as he and Sage join us. "Or that you actually managed to pull it off." The adrenaline is slowly dissipating, leaving behind bewilderment and fatigue. We're going to need a vacation after this vacation.

"A little dramatic for my taste, but it did the trick,"

Jenny says, brushing her hands together. She sidesteps the mulled wine as she approaches us. "Nice job."

"Thanks," I say, facing her. "I couldn't have done it without help."

I nod at Reid, Liam, and Sage. At the remaining undercover officers. At the resort employees slowly pulling themselves together on the far side of the table.

Cash, Micah, and Akira huddle together while Paisley and Hudson cautiously check on each other. Through the doors to the restaurant, rubbernecking diners try to catch a glimpse of the action. I want to tell them they're better off not knowing—advise them to enjoy their meals, indulge in an extra glass of wine, order the ceviche.

Instead, I refocus on Jenny. Her forest-green sheriff's jacket is lined with snow from her time waiting on the patio for Reid's signal: moving to the door connecting to the restaurant and knocking, visible from the patio and audible from the restaurant.

"Was that confession enough?" I ask.

"Oh yeah." She rolls her shoulders back. "Boone'll be going away for a long time. Pity, too. I always liked that guy."

Reid dips his chin. "Me too."

"Not sure how we missed it," Jenny says. Her eyes are wide with self-admonishment, but she doesn't strike me as the type to be down for long.

I give a tiny shrug. "Sometimes it takes an outside perspective."

"At least we caught him in the end." Jenny shifts her weight, her fingers on her belt loop. "Well, I'll let you kids get back to your weekend." With a half smile directed at me she adds, "Try to stay out of trouble."

"No promises," I reply with a wink.

I've had enough of the murder kind of trouble to last a lifetime, but the fun kind of trouble, the type that leads to laughter and memories . . . that I could use some more of.

Chapter Nineteen

The next morning dawns with the promise of hope. A quick peek out the hotel window confirms the storm has passed. There's a thick layer of snow covering Silver Creek Village, at least two feet deep, that glitters in the unobstructed sunshine. The skies are a crisp blue and there's nary a cloud in sight.

Reid is still fast asleep, a mess of coppery hair barely visible over the duvet. We were up late the night before, basking in our newfound security, celebrating the justice we'd exacted, and commemorating Annmarie for real. And I can attest that Cash's ceviche tasted every bit as delectable as it looked.

I leave Reid a note instructing him to meet me downstairs when he wakes up. Then I slip out, as quiet as I can.

My surprise might be a complete disaster, but it's the

thought that counts, right? At least, that's what I'm banking on.

The lobby is bustling with skiers and snowboarders eager to take advantage of the fresh powder, groups of lodgers debating where they should go for breakfast, and guests checking out after a prolonged stay.

The older woman who complained about her missing jewelry is standing next to a pile of suitcases, tapping her French-manicured fingers impatiently—presumably waiting for her husband to bring the car around.

At the end of the repurposed-tree-trunk desk, an exhausted-looking mother and her young daughter sift through the lost-and-found tub.

"But I want my glove," the little girl whines, sinking to the floor like a limp noodle. She can't be more than four years old.

"I'll look again." The mom's voice takes on a desperate note as she turns back to the tub.

In the girl's hand is a single purple knit glove with a red pattern that I swear I've seen somewhere before. I cock my head to the side, trying to get a closer look without coming across as a creeper.

That's when it hits me: Madeline.

Madeline had been playing with a glove yesterday while I chatted with Akira. I'd assumed it was a cute winter-themed cat toy, but really the sneaky feline had pilfered it.

More pieces fall into place and realization dawns on me. Madeline didn't just steal the glove, she's been nicking items from other hotel rooms, too. I'd even caught her under the bed of Reid's and my suite, likely having snuck in with the cleaners.

She's a right little cat burglar. A klepto kitty.

Enlightened, I make my way to her cushy bed, where she's still fast asleep. I pet her silky gray fur, cooing in her ear gently to wake her up, "Good morning, sleepyhead."

Madeline yawns, giving me a view of her textured pink tongue and very impressive canines. Twitching her whiskers, she glares at me with her pale-gold eyes as if saying *Why did you wake me, peasant?*

"I know, you need your beauty rest," I say, scooping her into my arms. "This will just take a sec."

I plop her on the ground. She sits and progresses to lick her paw, watching from hooded eyes.

I perch in front of her bed, where I'd seen her deposit the glove after she was done playing with it. Located under a decorative table with a gilded picture frame overhead and roughly the size of a case of wine, her bed is plush velvet and a deep purple that bespeaks to her perceived royalty. I reach my hand around the edges of the cushion, stray cat hairs clinging to the Velcro of my jacket. Nothing yet.

I pull the bed out from under the table and, in better lighting, spot something glittering in the corner—a clasp of a silver chain. I tug it out, cradling the sapphire-blue pendant in my palm. I remove the entire pillow and, bingo, it's as if I've uncovered a hidden treasure trove. All the missing items are there: tennis bracelet, knit glove, Sage's lightsaber hairpin, along with a dozen other odds and ends.

Sensing a full-blown meltdown is imminent, I hurry to the mother and daughter, handing over the glove. "Is this what you're looking for?"

The mom offers me a profuse thank-you, her relief rivaling mine when Boone was finally apprehended.

"No problem," I say.

I make my way farther down the lobby desk, trying to get Paisley's attention. She's chatting with official-looking individuals in suits, one of whom I recognize as Annmarie's lawyer. Curious . . .

It doesn't escape my notice that Paisley appears different—lighter. Her hair is wavy and swept into a high ponytail that accentuates her cheekbones, and she's abandoned her boxy power suits for khakis and a floral blouse. She holds her head high with her shoulders thrown back. It's as if a weight has been lifted.

"Paisley is pretty busy this morning," Akira says, sneaking up behind me. Absently, I wonder if she ever leaves. Surely a wine director doesn't need to be present all hours of every day.

She's in funky layers, a long-sleeved shirt with a tee over it and skinny slacks tucked into ankle boots. Large hoops dangle in her ears, the same shape as her glasses, and her hair is piled into two knots on top of her head, a couple strands framing her face. Gotta hand it to her, she's got style.

Akira continues, answering my unasked question, "Paisley found out she'll be taking over the running of Silver Creek, at least until the courts finalize who will legally inherit Annmarie's estate."

"Good for her," I say, stunned by this turn of events. "No wonder she seems happy."

"She didn't look that way earlier," Akira confides. "She called a staff meeting first thing and told us, said she wanted to run things differently, with the help of her trusted friends. It was very unlike her—or the *her* she's been for the last six months. We all agreed, which I think made her feel better about the whole leadership thing." Akira clasps her hands together in front of her, her eyes alight. "So, all that being said, is there something I can do for you?"

I can't help but smile. Who knows if Paisley and Akira will ever be the close friends they once were—those sorts of fractures are hard to mend—but I'm happy to see them trying.

She's being so warm to me, I can't help but wince. "So, you forgive me for not letting you in on my scheme last night?"

"God, yes. I'm horrible at keeping secrets," Akira says. "Just look at all the gossip I've spilled to you this weekend."

I heave a sigh and ask, hesitantly, "And Cash?"

"We're going on a date tonight." She smiles broadly, her cheeks glowing, and then hurriedly clarifies, "A non-meal date. He's ready to let go of Breakfast-Lunch-Dinner Guy."

"Thank goodness," I say, and we both giggle like schoolgirls.

"Here, I found this." I pass Akira the tennis bracelet, pocketing the lightsaber pin to give back to Sage. "I think you have a thieving kitty."

I nod toward where Madeline is proudly sitting, her tail swishing across the floor, a steady purr emanating from her.

"No," Akira admonishes, studying the bejeweled bracelet.

"She's been nicking things from rooms and then stashing them in her bed."

"Madeline," Akira scolds. "Bad kitty."

The aforementioned trots up and rubs against Akira's leg, mewing through a purr, obviously more pleased with herself than ashamed.

"What are we going to do with you, little stinker?" Akira plucks her up and nuzzles into her sleek fur.

Madeline is clearly learning her lesson. And her lesson is that she can get away with just about anything. "At least she's cute."

"She's got that going for her."

I check the time and nearly jump out of my boots. "I've gotta go."

With one last pat on Madeline's head and a hasty goodbye to Akira, I dart out the door.

"Wine chick," Cash says in greeting when I stumble into the kitchen fifteen minutes later, paper bag in tow. "Or should I call you Detective now?"

"Parker will suffice." I shed my coat and scarf, hanging them on one of the hooks near the alleyway door.

It's not as busy this morning, guests antsy to enjoy the other dining options in the village after being cooped up in the hotel. There's a calm energy in the air, the sous chefs working at a leisurely pace that puts me at ease, despite the task ahead.

Cash waves me in, directing me to a cutting board next to the stovetop. There are two burners set aside for me, the one I've come to think of as my own and the one behind it. The cutting board is overflowing with colorful produce—onions, potatoes, peppers, avocado, and plump tomatoes. And in the center, the crown jewel: house-made chorizo.

"Your table is ready and all the ingredients are here,

as requested," Cash says, tossing a towel over his shoulder.

"Hopefully I can do everything justice," I say, swallowing nervously. "Thank you again. Really."

"It's the least I could do." Somehow I know he's referring to more than my help in solving Annmarie's murder.

"Glad things worked out," I reply with a wink, letting him know I picked up on his hint. I position the paper bag on the ledge behind the cutting board, safely out of the way.

"What's that?"

"Oh, um, dessert," I answer vaguely. No need to alarm him with the fact that this is also backup in case my meal goes up in flames.

Cash sees through my bluff; must be all that poker. He rubs a hand over his curly head. "You need any help?"

I'm tempted by his offer, more than I care to admit, but I shake my head. It's important that I do this solo. "I've got it."

"Okay," he says, not quite buying my reassurance. "I'll be over there if you need me."

I pour all of myself into the food. Reid has made me so many delicious meals over the last few months, it's my turn to surprise him with something delectable and homemade. Something from the heart.

Only, it doesn't quite go according to plan.

The chorizo, which was meant to be browned, quickly goes up in smoke. I barely salvage it, scraping away the charred bits from the pan, with more than a few concerned glances cast my way from Cash and the sous chefs.

My head buzzes with recipe steps and sweat beads on my forehead as I chop, mix, and sauté.

The potatoes are the next part of the dish to go awry,

somehow both glomming to the roasting pan and failing to get crispy.

I push my bangs off my forehead, fanning myself. Seriously, how do chefs make this look so easy?

Miraculously, I reach the assembling stage. I add scrambled eggs, cheddar cheese, chorizo, and potatoes to a large flour tortilla and roll it up. The tortilla is stubborn and immediately unfurls, sending ingredients scattering across the plate. Grinding my teeth, I try again, and again, until it loosely resembles a burrito. Then on top, I add slices of avocado and homemade pico.

I stand back to admire my handiwork.

Sure, my knife cuts aren't as picture-perfect as Reid's, juice from the salsa is smattering the rim of the plate, and the tortilla is broken in spots from my manhandling. But I did it.

"Not bad, wine chick," Cash says, peeking over my shoulder.

"Think Reid will like it?"

"Oh yeah, totally," he answers, a little too quickly, before striding away.

A jolt of worry courses through me at serving one of the best chefs in Boulder—correction, in all of Colorado—my fare. I tamp down my uncertainty.

I recall how Aunt Laura would spend hours crafting extravagant sweets for her Valentine's Day parties—cakes, chocolates, and expertly molded marzipan. And the thing was, as delicious as they were, we'd spend more time marveling at them than eating them. They became the centerpiece for conversation, part of the macro experience.

It's the thought that counts.

So, I pour glasses of bubbly, adding a squeeze of

grapefruit juice. The sweet-and-floral notes of the champagne along with the citrus will cut through the spice. Or numb our palate if my food is terrible. So, win-win.

I arrange everything on a tray, shrug back into my coat, and, with the paper bag tucked snug under one arm, schlep it to where I told Reid to meet me.

The patio looks different this morning. The grotesque shapes that had been obscured by shadows are illuminated in sunshine. Piles of snow cover surrounding planters, tables, and chairs, already melting from the warming temperature. Icicles dangle from the resort rooftop, water dripping from the tips and onto the ground, nature's decoration.

There's a walkway shoveled for us, the two feet of snow along the edges heaped up to my waist. Our table is modest but dry and bookended by heat lamps that will keep us cozy.

The centerpiece is a vase with a single rose whose petals are beginning to curl, reminding me of something out of a gothic fairy tale. Our plates are covered so the food stays warm, and our cutlery is rolled into napkins. Ice waters and cocktail flutes finish the place settings, the rest of the bottle of champagne chilling in the snow.

The door to the resort opens and I stand up quickly, bumping into the table. I curse under my breath, catching the vase before it tumbles over.

"What is all this?" Reid asks, his lips twitching into a half smile. He takes in the setup, his green eyes twinkling with amusement.

"Just whipped a little something up." I lift the silver covers off our plates with a flourish. "Voilà!"

Reid steps down the salted path, momentarily speechless. I take his hand and guide him to his seat, planting a lingering kiss on his cheek. He turns and kisses me full on, taking my face in his hands. It's a study in exquisite contrasts—the softness of his lips and the roughness of his scruff, the chill in the air and the heat between us.

I nuzzle his nose with mine as I pull away, not wanting the food to get, well, any worse than it already is.

Reid unrolls his napkin and considers the cuisine before him. "This looks . . ." he trails off.

"God-awful, I know," I say with a laugh, scooting in my own chair.

"I was going to say creative." Reid picks up his fork and takes a hesitant bite.

I await his critique, sipping on my champagne to calm my nerves.

He chews slowly, looking out of the corner of his eyes as he's apt to do while the cogs in his brain churn through flavors and cooking techniques.

And this has to be the longest it has ever taken anyone in the history of mankind (and womankind, Sage would be quick to correct) to consume a bite of food.

"And?" I prod.

"It's delicious."

"Really?" I spear a forkful of burrito, making sure to get a little bit of everything, and almost spit it into my napkin. "Liar."

It's not inedible, which is the best that can be said for my attempt. The potatoes are still slightly raw, the chorizo is bitter and overdone, and the pico is way too spicy. Guess I shouldn't have added that second jalapeño.

Reid's face is red as he reaches for his drink. He takes a large swallow, swishing the cocktail around in his mouth.

We both start laughing at the same time. I raise my glass in the air and he does the same. "Happy Valentine's Day. Here's to many more."

"Here's to us," he adds.

"Cheers." Our eyes meet over our flutes as we clink and sip. The bubbles of the champagne tickle my nose, but my gaze remains fixed on Reid.

We each take another sip to fortify ourselves for another bite. Reid holds his fork over his plate, uncertain which element to brave next.

"You don't have to eat it," I say. "Maybe my real gift to you is *not* forcing you to eat my cooking."

To Reid's credit, he shovels more into his mouth. "Not a chance. I'm going to savor this."

He must have gotten a giant chunk of pepper because his face turns a deeper shade of red, his eyes swimming with tears, and he downs half of his water. I take pity on him. "Make sure you save room for dessert."

I procure the paper bag sporting Chloe's logo from beneath the table and pull out two lavish red-velvet cupcakes. "I saw these with Sage yesterday and they looked too delicious not to try."

"Cupcakes for breakfast?" Reid asks.

"What's the fun of being an adult if you don't indulge in dessert sporadically?"

He needs no further encouragement. "Good point."

We peel the lining of our cupcakes and take giant mouthfuls, much happier with this baked good than my attempt at a meal. It's decadent; moist and chocolatey, and the frosting is criminal. Creamy, flaked with vanilla, and swirled into a peak rivaling the surrounding mountains.

Leaning back, I take a dainty sip of champagne, swishing the wine around in my mouth with my eyes closed. Tropical fruit, hints of floral notes, and refreshing pops of acidity and effervescence. Not exactly what I would have selected to pair with red velvet, but it's spectacular in its own right.

When I open my eyes, I find Reid watching me. "I've always enjoyed watching you taste wine."

"It's the gurgling, isn't it?"

"While that is invariably attractive, I was referring to how relaxed you look," he says. "You seem to go somewhere else."

A warmth spreads through my chest. "I could say the same thing about watching you taste food," I say, although quickly amend, "Not necessarily this food, but in general."

"So, would your aunt Laura have liked this?" Reid asks quietly.

"Absolutely." As much of a disaster as my cooking turned out to be, I have no doubt she'd be proud.

He takes my hand beneath the table, lacing his fingers through mine. "Then she lives on."

"Yes, I suppose she does."

"I wish I'd gotten to meet her."

"She would have loved you."

He practically preens. "Really?"

I nod silently, giving his fingers an extra squeeze.

How I wish Aunt Laura could see me now. See the business she invested in flourishing, the love and community I've found, the traditions I'm building for myself.

But Reid's right, her memories are living on. And far from the sadness and grief I've been consumed with all weekend, in this moment, I feel a surge of hope and joy. A way to move forward.

I smile at Reid across the way and he flashes me a mischievous grin, a gleam in his eyes I can't quite place.

Chapter Twenty

We shove the last suitcase into the back of Reid's jeep and position our skis and snowboards on top—well, all but mine, which were a casualty of the fire. Clumps of ice cling to Sage's and Liam's gear from their final runs this morning, which they took while Reid and I enjoyed our cupcake breakfast.

I cross my fingers as Reid rests his hands on the trunk, which he barely manages to click shut. Our belongings seem to have multiplied, as if each suitcase accrued interest while we were here.

The roads are clear, the chemicals in the salt and the warmth of sunshine effectively melting the snow into slushy puddles. Steam rises from the asphalt and rooftops, and overhead, the sky is crystal clear. It should make for a pleasant travel day.

"Let's get a move on it," Liam says, rubbing his hands together.

"What's the rush?" I ask.

Sage beams, practically bouncing in her boots beside Liam. Her strawberry-blond hair is clasped with her recovered lightsaber hairpin, matching her R2-D2 scarf.

"Did we miss something?" Reid asks, looking from their excited faces to me. I shrug in response.

Liam scratches at the back of his neck. "I have a, uh, meeting to get back to in Boulder."

My eyebrows shoot straight up and into my bangs. "On a Sunday? What happened to weekends being purely for fun?"

Liam nudges me with his shoulder, his way of communicating I might have been right about a few things this weekend. I nudge him back; he made some good points, too.

"When you've got a side hustle, turns out you've gotta, you know, hustle." He kicks at a chunk of ice at his feet, sending it skidding across the parking lot. "And when Jimmy Mickelson suggests a time to grab coffee, you don't say no."

Holy Viognier, the rock legend himself might commission photographs from *my* brother. I bark out a laugh, clapping my hands together gleefully. "Congratulations."

"It's too early to celebrate yet. He's taking pitches from multiple photographers." Liam shrugs like this is no big deal, but his cheeks redden as he meets my gaze. "If it hadn't been for you sticking your nose in my business, I would've missed out entirely."

I take this to mean our tiff is officially over and smile in relief. "Happy to oblige."

"Just don't go making a habit of it."

"Of course not," I say, my tone entirely unconvincing.

Liam doesn't pick up on my pretense, instead shuddering an exhale, already riddled with nerves for his meeting.

"It's going to go great," Sage says. Her encouragement carries the weight of déjà vu, being so similar to what she told me before my big meeting. Hopefully Liam's has a better outcome. "You'll get the gig for sure."

"Okay, I definitely missed something," Reid says.

"Don't worry," I say. "We'll fill you in on the way home."

With extra incentive now, Reid hops into the driver's side while Sage and Liam pile into the back.

I shove my hands into the pockets of my puffy vest and take one last look at Silver Creek. This weekend went nothing like I'd planned. Mayhem, murder, an actual cat burglar, *and* a near Valentine's disaster. Not to mention, no wine contract to speak of.

But the resort takes on a sparkle, with the elegant lines of the lodge and the majestic mountainous backdrop. It's still standing, as are we.

I'm just reaching for the door handle when there's a shout behind me. "Parker, hold up."

I turn to find Akira jogging toward me. "I'm glad I caught you," she says, slightly out of breath, her glasses fogging.

"You're just in time," I say, patting the top of Reid's jeep. Inside, Liam, Sage, and Reid watch us curiously. I hold one finger up to them, signaling that I need a minute. "What's up?"

A coy grin spreads across Akira's face. "Well, I spoke with Paisley and told her about how delicious your wine is, and how perfect mulled wine would be on the menu at the lodge, and she agreed to purchase a few cases and see how it sells." Her smile broadens and her shoulders rise up to her chin in excitement. "The Bauer Power Happy Hour might turn into a real thing."

Shock and elation flood through me. Here I thought I'd ruined any chance of securing a contract with Silver Creek. I blink rapidly, bringing a palm to my forehead. My daydreams of expanding Vino Valentine cautiously resurface in my mind.

"That's amazing," I say when I finally find the words. "Thank you so much."

"I'll be in touch," Akira says. "Also, I should mention I've made a lot of contacts over the years—sommeliers and fellow wine directors around the world—I'd love to give them your information."

I'm stunned speechless, because this goes beyond anything I'd ever allowed myself to imagine. To even begin to imagine. "That would be incredible," I stammer. "But why?"

"The wine I tasted the other day was exceptional. I'd love to try more varietals next time I'm in town. And," she continues with a shrug, "I like to advocate for good people."

I'm touched. I hold a hand over my heart, trying to stave off tears. "Would it be weird if I give you a hug?"

"After this weekend? Definitely not."

I give Akira a tight squeeze, grateful to have made another friend in addition to a business contact.

With one last profuse thank-you and a promise to talk soon, I finally get into Reid's car, my face glowing with the events of the last few hours.

"Good news?" Reid asks, eyebrow cocked.

"Very," I say, nestling into my seat. "Vino Valentine has the potential to become a major label."

"That's all fine and good, but do you have a *celebrity* interested in your handiwork?" Liam boasts nonchalantly from the backseat.

"Okay, someone has got to catch me up," Reid says, putting his jeep into gear.

"Good day for the Valentines," Sage muses, tugging off her fingerless gloves. "It figures, it is Valentine's Day, after all."

I twist in my seat to look at her. "I'd say it's a good day for all of us."

Reid turns onto the interstate that will take us back to Boulder. We get a final view from the frontage road of the cascading mountains dotted with pine trees, skiers and snowboarders flying down the slopes, and the quaint village with the wide blue sky overhead.

One of the perks of mulled wine is that the components don't have to be perfect. The wine might be lackluster, the cinnamon stick cracked, the orange peel containing varying amounts of citrus oils, the honey crystallized. But when given time to simmer together, the flavors mesh and elevate one another. Maybe that's the key to life, friendship, and love. If so, I can't wait to see what happens next.

Recipes and Wine Pairings

Rosemary Roasted Nuts

(Serves 4 to 6)

3 cups whole roasted unsalted cashews
2 cups pecans halves
1 cup whole almonds
Vegetable oil
1 teaspoon salt
2 tablespoons minced fresh rosemary leaves, divided

Preheat oven to 350 degrees F. On a sheet pan, coat nuts liberally with vegetable oil. Add salt and half the rosemary and toss to combine. Roast for 20 minutes, stirring halfway. Add remaining rosemary and salt, to taste, and stir well. Serve warm or at room temperature.

Pair with mulled wine, recipe following

1 bottle red wine*
2 tablespoons honey
1 cinnamon stick
3 whole cloves
The peel from half of an orange

Add ingredients to saucepan and warm over low heat (making sure mixture doesn't come to a boil) for 30 minutes. Pour and enjoy!

***I prefer a full-bodied red that can stand up to the spices, such as a Syrah, merlot, or cabernet sauvignon.**

Cozy Chicken Soup with Thyme Dumplings

(Serves 4 to 6)

1 whole (2 split) chicken breast, bone in and skin on
Olive oil
Fresh-ground pepper and salt, to taste
1 yellow onion, diced
4 carrots, peeled and medium-diced
4 stalks celery, medium-diced
2 leeks, chopped
2 garlic cloves, crushed
6 cups chicken stock
¼ cup fresh parsley, finely chopped
1 cup all-purpose flour
2 teaspoons baking powder
1 tablespoon dried thyme
2 tablespoons butter
½ cup milk

Preheat oven to 350 degrees F.

Coat chicken breast with olive oil and place on a sheet pan. Sprinkle with fresh-ground black pepper and salt and bake for 45 minutes. Once chicken is cool enough to handle, remove the meat from the bone, discarding the skin. Dice meat into 1-inch pieces.

In a large pot, add 2 tablespoons of olive oil, the onion, carrots, celery, leeks, and ½ teaspoon of pepper and a pinch of salt. Sauté together, stirring occasionally, for 6 to 8 minutes, or until onions are translucent. Add garlic and cook for 1 minute. Add chicken stock, chicken, and parsley, and simmer for 30 minutes.

In a bowl, combine flour, baking powder, thyme, and a pinch of salt. Cut in butter until mixture resembles fine crumbs the size of peas. Stir in milk. Drop teaspoon-sized spoonfuls (the dumplings expand a surprising amount!) into the soup. Cover and cook for 10 minutes.

To serve, ladle broth, chicken, veggies, and dumplings into bowls and enjoy!

Suggested wine pairing: a crisp Sancerre with nutty and citrus flavors and a buttery, herbaceous aroma.

Red Velvet Valentine Cupcakes

(Yields 20)

1 stick butter
1½ cups sugar
2 eggs
2 tablespoons red food coloring
2 tablespoons cocoa powder
1 cup buttermilk
2¼ cups flour
1 teaspoon salt
1 teaspoon vanilla
1 teaspoon baking soda
1 tablespoon vinegar

Frosting

3 tablespoons flour
1 cup milk
2 sticks butter
1 cup sugar
1 teaspoon vanilla

Preheat oven to 350 degrees F.

Cream butter and sugar together. Mix in eggs, food coloring, and cocoa powder. Add buttermilk alternately with flour. Mix in salt, vanilla, baking soda, and vinegar.

Scoop into lined muffin pan so that batter is roughly halfway up each cup, and bake for 15 minutes.

For the frosting, in a saucepan, combine flour and milk and cook over medium-low heat until it thickens (~10 minutes), stirring constantly with a whisk. Set aside and let cool. In a separate bowl, cream butter, sugar, and vanilla until fluffy, and then stir in flour-and-milk mixture.

When cupcakes are cool enough to work with, top with frosting and enjoy!

Suggested wine pairing: a medium-bodied pinot noir with fruity and floral notes on the tongue and aromas of vanilla and smoke.

Acknowledgments

I wrote the entirety of this book during the pandemic, and there were times when I worried I wouldn't be able to do the story justice, let alone finish it. And I wouldn't have if it weren't for the following people.

Thank you to my entire team at Berkley. I really couldn't have asked for a better home for my books, and I continue to be immensely grateful for and impressed by everyone I've had the pleasure of working with.

A special shout-out to my editor, Miranda Hill, whose brilliant feedback not only elevated the characters, relationships, and mystery but also made me smile.

Thank you to Pamela Harty and The Knight Agency for your constant support and wisdom. We really do make a great team.

Thanks to Samantha Dion Baker for illustrating such eye-catching cover art for my books, and to Brooke Hoover for bringing Parker to life in the audiobooks.

Thank you to my longtime friend Jill Hovey, who offered names for my fictional resort as well as fascinating insights into Colorado's history that provided delicious fodder for this story.

Thank you to my parents, who have supported me nonstop in the writing of this project—and all others. Your generosity, work ethic, and optimism continue to be an inspiration to me.

Thanks to my husband, John, to whom this book is very appropriately dedicated. I'm not exaggerating when I say I couldn't have done this without you. Thank you for all the child-wrangling, cheerleading, love, and support. I'm so lucky to have you as my partner in life.

Thank you to my sweet and feisty daughter, Sophie. Even when the world seemed dark, you filled our house with light and joy.

And last but certainly not least, thank you, readers. I appreciate you more than words can say.